To Ro

ABOUT THE AUTHOR

I served with the Metropolitan Police in London for thirty years. I worked at Carter Street Police Station (radio callsign: Mike Sierra) and from the Elephant and Castle, down the Old Kent Road, round Camberwell, skirting Kennington (not to be confused with Kensington) and back up the Elephant, was my old stomping ground. In the late eighties, Carter Street closed to be replaced by the brand spanking new Walworth Police Station (radio callsign: Mike Sierra). I now have Mike Sierra.

My police expertise was emergency response and communications. Having retired, I live on a narrowboat cruising the UK's inland waterways and cursing the Faraday Cage effect of the steel hull. Cruising and cursing – that's me – catch me if you can.

www.pauldurston.com

Published in Great Britain in 2023
By Diamond Crime

ISBN No: 978-1-915649-34-8

Diamond Crime is an imprint of Diamond Books Ltd.

DIAMOND
BOOKS

Thanks to...

Dr Robin Lawrence MRCPsych for his insight and, particularly, his patient explanations around amnesia – many of which he had to repeat. Phil Murray (ex-tecco) whose wealth of investigative experience is invaluable for me (being a lid). Vicki Bradley, Vicki Jones, Fraser Massey and Jane Phillips (my writing group) for reading, re-reading and re-re-reading my work and commenting, re-commenting and re-re-commenting on my work. Jeff Dowson, Phil Rowlands and Steve Timmins of Diamond Crime who show faith in my work. Hazel Durston – my daughter and social media guru. Rebecca Ferguson of Fergie Design Limited – my website designer and guru. Caroline, my partner, who tolerates my absence when present – or is it my presence when absent? And you – my readers.

Cover and book design: jacksonbone.co.uk

Cover photograph: iStockphoto

For information about Diamond Crime authors
and their books, visit:

www.diamondcrime.uk

For my brother, Kevin.

IF

WE

WERE

ONE

PAUL DURSTON

News Report 6th September 2019

Dissociative Identity Disorder:
The woman who created 2,500 personalities to survive

There was only one woman in the witness stand that day but out of her came six people prepared to testify about the extreme abuse she had suffered.

"I walked into court, I sat down, I made the oath, and then a few hours later I got back into my body and walked out," Jeni Haynes told the BBC.

As a child, Jeni was repeatedly raped and tortured by her father, Richard Haynes, in what Australian police say is one of the worst child abuse cases in the country.

To cope with the horror, her mind used an extraordinary tactic – creating new identities [or alters] for her to detach from the pain.

And in the landmark trial in March, Jeni confronted her father to present evidence against him through her personalities, including a four-year-old girl named Symphony.

It's believed to be the first case in Australia, and perhaps the world, where a victim with diagnosed Multiple Personality Disorder (MPD) – or Dissociative Identity Disorder (DID) – has testified in their other personalities and secured a conviction.

"We weren't scared. We had waited such a long time to tell everyone exactly what he did to us and now he couldn't shut us up," she said.

On 6 September Richard Haynes, now 74, was sentenced to 45 years in jail by a Sydney court.

CHAPTER ONE

CHARLIE

Lavender – who I'm partnered with today, complete with garlic breath and flowery language – gets back into the car and hands me a latte.

"Thanks." We watch the radio as we take our first sip. And…

"Mike-Three. Mike-Three. Peckham Road junction Shenley Road. Fight. Three persons involved. Driver altercation. Mike-Three."

Oh god. Driver altercation… Come on, I can do this.

This new car has superb cup holders. As Lavender acknowledges the call, I flick on the neenaws, swing out from the queue of traffic and onto the wrong side of the road. Oncoming motorists squeeze over.

"The blue van – hasn't seen you." Lavender's backseat driving.

Wrong side of a keep-left bollard.

"The woman with the pram." More advice from Lavender.

The Wyndham Road traffic lights are red – treat as give-way.

"Mind that friggin' truck."

I screech to a halt on the far side of the Wyndham Road junction, neenaws still going, lean over and poke

Lavender in the chest. "Me driver. You operator. Either shut the fuck up or get out."

Lavender sneers. "Just keeping us a-friggin'-live."

I'm off again. Shouldn't have done that. Not to Lavender.

He's poking at the mobile data terminal. I don't expect there to be any intel relating to this call, but at least it's keeping him quiet.

I kill the sirens as I pull up on scene. I'm out but... I'm out but... A boy... I'm out but... A girl in a red coat... I'm out but... Strong hands... Lavender... Lavender...

For god's sake – it's nothing more than a minor damage-only. I hold myself – hug myself – push and squeeze the roaring away. The drivers are squaring up to one another but they soon calm down when confronted with Lavender and his deft use of the word *friggin'*.

Driving away, Lavender's looking at me. I check my mirrors – burning vehicles. It's coming back.

"Charlie."

Pounding flames. Oh god. More than just looking at me. Screeching tyres.

"Charlie. Stop the car. We must talk."

No. Not talking about it. Dripping skin.

"Charlie. You froze. Stop the car."

Even Lottie, my alter who I only met following the tanker incident back before Christmas, has come up onto the *stage*. She's pushing.

I pull over, front nearside wheel bouncing onto the kerb, and let Lottie take the *spot*.

Lottie's talking to Lavender but I can't make out what's being said. All I hear is crushed thunder. Thank god for my Dissociative Identity Disorder. All I feel is searing heat. All I see is falling bodies and rising flames. Thank god for dissociated me. All I smell is burning flesh. Will I ever get that burning petrol tanker out of my memory? Thank god for Lottie.

* * *

LOTTIE
Must deal with Lavender. Must talk like Charlie.

"I'm okay." I lift my coffee from the cup holder.

"Was that a flashback?"

"Flashback?" I sip my coffee.

"To the tanker incident."

"No. I'm tired. I'm driving the fast car and we're sent to bloody silly calls like that."

Lavender leans towards me and I push back against my door.

"Do I need to call Sergeant Cantrell?"

"That won't be necessary." I take another sip.

"Charlie. I can't carry you. This isn't the first time you've frozen."

"I didn't freeze."

Maintaining this is impossible. There's movement outside the car – someone walking past. Charlie says when Lavender stops swearing, he must be taken seriously.

* * *

CHARLIE

The thunder and flames are subsiding. I'm coming back. That guy walking past the car – I know him. Almost back. Must deal with Lavender. He's seeing through Lottie.

I'm back. I push, Lottie moves aside and I resume the *spot*.

I point at the guy walking past the car. "Stop him."

Lavender sits back, grabs his coffee and slurps.

"I said stop him."

Lavender sniffs. Then he's out the car. "Oi. Chummy. Wanna word."

The timing's perfect. Has Lavender seen through us? Right. Distraction. Must create a distraction.

I extract my phone, I'm out the car and, with elbows on the roof, snap off a picture.

Lavender's all, "Where you going, chummy? Is that herbal I can smell on your breath? What's in your friggin' pockets, chummy?"

I walk over and put a hand on Lavender's shoulder.

He backs off.

I face the lad. "You were in the Half Nelson that time. Back around New Year. Soon after the tanker incident. You came over and said 'respect'. I appreciated that. So, you can keep whatever you've got in your pockets – this time. And that makes us even. Next time, you're fair game."

I return to the car and jump in behind the wheel.

Lavender slumps into the passenger seat. "Friggin' 'ell, Charlie. What was all that about?"

The lad nods at me and continues along the pavement.

"Reciprocity, Albert. Reciprocity."

"Sounds like a word Wade friggin' Oliver, that boyfriend of yours, would use."

Lavender might be back swearing again but this episode won't have been forgotten. "Yes, a Wade word."

"How's he getting on? Special Branch?"

"Well, SO15."

"It was Special Branch in my day. Whatever. Makes friggin' sense." Lavender's moved on. He's slurping his coffee. Everything's okay – for now. "A place he'd fit in, Special Branch. Posted there before he finished his friggin' probation."

"He's just done his detective training."

"Not much call for that in Special Branch."

"SO15 investigate terrorism for god's sake."

"Not the Special Branch half."

"Now, now, Albert."

"My name's Lavender."

Must get more distance from that episode. "Here, got something for you." I show him my mobile and the picture I'd taken. "I've circulated it round our Team."

"You haven't. Charlie, tell me you friggin' haven't." He checks his phone. "You friggin' have."

"Looks like you're offering chummy a cup of coffee."

"That friggin' cyclist's a wide-berth job. Those lights are green. That pedestrian's unsteady on his feet. There might be a kid behind that tree. Steer into the skid. Check your mirrors. Only straight-line braking. Mind that friggin' truck."

He's like that for the rest of the shift. Worth it though.

* * *

LOTTIE

Charlie has settled so, while she patrols the streets of Walworth and Camberwell, I go on my own patrol – the *dressing rooms* of our inner world.

Gillian. How are you?

Oh no. Lottie. I can't. Don't make me. Please don't make me. I can't. I can't.

Nothing like that. You may relax.

You promise?

I promise. All that has ended.

Gillian relaxes but is still uncomfortable.

I look around Gillian's *dressing room*. Why we attributed these names escapes me. I must, however, apprise Charlie. She has her *dressing room*, I have mine. Only one *spot*, obviously, but a number of *dressing rooms*. These names serve a purpose, I suppose, but are barely an approximation. Controlling how these spaces look and feel is like controlling dreams. Presently, all is red and, standing on a mound that leans upwards, I can see a bridge in a desert. For Gillian, it would be whatever her imagination has conjured up. I understand her anxiety. The last time she saw me, I sent her out to take the paedophile's abuse. For me, that was fifteen years ago. For Gillian it was yesterday evening.

I am not here to send you out there, Gillian. Over. All finished. Never again will you have to face that.

Okay, but why are you here?

To tell you that I want you to meet someone.

Will he hurt me?

Gillian is suspicious, understandably.

No. Not at all. You will like her.

Her? Who is it?

Charlie.

Charlie! You told me she ran away and I had to do horrible things.

I have to keep reminding myself that Gillian is not a person but the image of a person – my image. Never quite the same, but her appearance always has common features. A ribbon in her sandy hair. Turned up nose. Freckly. She always wears a dress, now blue. Last time I saw her, her dress was green. White socks. Sandals.

Charlie is unaware of you. It will be a shock for her.

Why doesn't she know about me?

Because of a barrier – Charlie on one side, you on the other. I learned how to cross that barrier.

You said Charlie ran away and that was why I had to do horrible things.

I did say that and it was not just Gillian. Because Charlie ran away, I also had to do horrible things – as Gillian puts it.

She did but back then, she was a little girl like you. She knew nothing about it – nothing about us. You, me, Jemima and Floella. We did all those horrible things so Charlie could carry on. Now, as a big lady, a police officer indeed, she can look after us. She did not know she was running away.

How was making me do horrible things protecting us?

That was then. Things have changed. We will find those people who did horrible things to us and we will teach them a lesson.

I don't want to see them ever again.

Gillian is calming down.

You will not see them again. Charlie will because she will find them and teach them a lesson.

Why must I see Charlie? I don't want to. She ran away and I had to do horrible things.

Meeting you will help Charlie deal with the horrible people.

Will she kill them?

At-a-girl, Gillian.

Yes.

Good.

Now. Gillian. When you meet Charlie, you must be nice. Do you promise?

Okay.

I mean it, Gillian. You must be nice.

Okay.

Really nice.

Okay.

I love you, Gillian.

Love you, Lottie.

* * *

CHARLIE

Wade and I have agreed – no outward show of affection when we're with workmates. The intimacy everybody thinks we share isn't there. We've tried. I can't. Lottie absents herself. If she knows, she hasn't said anything. I don't see how she can't know considering the emotions that must be raining down from on high. Wade is great.

Says he understands and time will heal. But how much time? How much healing? How long before he buggers off?

We've all come round the Half Nelson for an after-work sesh and Wade's there, waiting.

"It's mid-afternoon. You're out of work early."

"I've a load of reading to do." He taps his case.

"I'm surprised you can bring stuff out of the office."

"It's not sensitive."

I know that look – he's up to something. "Good day?"

"Interesting."

Asking Wade what was so interesting is a question I've learnt not to ask as it means in two-and-three-quarter hours I'll wish I hadn't.

"How was your day?" he asks.

"Lavender," I say.

Wade, too, knows not to ask.

Cantrell comes in and does her party-trick of buying everybody a drink. She's standing next to me and looks up. "Kathy will be your operator tomorrow. Lavender has a surprise coming his way. Hi, Wade. Glad to see you're not forgetting us poor schmucks at the coalface."

And she's gone, diving straight into a conversation with some of the others.

Kathy would be here if she could but she's got a prisoner and the circumstances demand she stays – something to do with domestic violence, there are kids involved and it's all a bit heavy.

Lottie's come out onto the *stage*. What's caught her attention?

Mary Cantrell. I believe her behaviour can be described as mischievous.

She's always got an alternate agenda.

This non-vocalising is great. We're in a crowded pub and Lottie and I can talk without anyone knowing. Well, almost. If I'm on the *spot*, I look as though I'm talking to myself. I raise my glass of wine to my lips.

She has no surprise for Albert Lavender. Her surprise is for Katherine Bond.

When Lottie has the *spot*, she gives nothing away.

I've learnt so much about myself since meeting Lottie. Yes, okay, the abused childhood, the Dissociative Identity Disorder, my alter Lottie. I'm probably an alter myself... No, what I mean is, I've learnt more about the difference between Lottie and me. Everything she does and everything she says is considered. I'm much more fire-from-the-hip. Lottie would call me impulsive.

Kathy? Lottie thinks this is to do with Kathy?

So what d'you think Cantrell's up to?

Katherine's reaction to that domestic violence incident is, how shall I say, uncharacteristic. She has withdrawn into herself. Mary Cantrell has noticed and is posting you together as she thinks you will find out the cause of Katherine's upset.

Lottie does have a funny way of talking.

I'd probably have done better if I hadn't known that.

You have always lauded the advantages of intel.

Gossip isn't intel. Hang on, our Inspector's coming in. This must be a first. Oh shit, he's heading our way. Tell you what Lottie, you can deal with this.

Thank you – so much.

"Hello Inspector Brady. Surprised to see you mixing with the hoi polloi."

"Charlie, you don't have to be all posh in front of me."

Lottie, speak like me.

"Sorry Guv'nor. Wade was just telling me what it's like in Special Branch and I got a bit infected like. Know what I mean?"

It's SO15 and I don't speak like that.

"Enough, Charlie. Wade, good you're here. Any help you can offer in respect of this would be welcome." He turns back to me, well, Lottie. "Kathy Bond has reacted out of character to something. She's being posted with you tomorrow. Try and find out what's bugging her. Report direct to me or Sergeant Cantrell. Everybody here will want to know what I've been saying. Tell them I was giving you more feedback on your recent NCA board that you failed."

Ouch.

* * *

CHARLIE

The guv'nor got you there.

Was the National Crime Agency really just being polite giving us an interview? Humouring us?

Lottie's embarrassed about failing that interview.

They'd never have taken us.

We need access to their facial recognition systems. The National Crime Agency must have the best.

Leave that to Eileen. In MI5, off-the-grid checks are easier.

To short-cut social media, we need to be in investigations.

She still can't believe she failed that interview.

What investigative experience have we got?

You make more direct crime arrests than anyone. In fact more than the rest of the Team put together.

Nicking's not the same as investigating.

I know. We have some investigating to do now – Katherine Bond.

Thank god she's moved on.

You're right. I wonder what that's all about.

It's been six weeks since we got the result of that board and Lottie still hasn't got over it. Actually, I'm pleased. Lottie needed a knock-back. She feels she's let the side down.

Even with all the others in our little gang from the children's home, where we suffered sexual abuse, now in useful positions – Eileen in MI5 and Zach, Rob and Ursula in Revenue and Customs, Serious Fraud Office and the Benefit's Agency, in that order – all our results have come from social media.

Results?

Can murder be called a result?

Still no sign of detectives coming knocking about Frank Amos – the one murder I've been involved in. Yes, I did join in. Yes, I did minimise the forensics we left behind. Yes, I thought Frank Amos deserved it – filthy pervert – but it doesn't make it right.

I say Frank Amos is the only one I've had anything to do with. Lottie instigated the Peter Daventry and Vincent Pope killings but, if things go tits-up in respect of those two, can I point the finger at Lottie and say it was nothing to do with me?

Provocation.

There's been case-law about provocation. Doesn't really work fifteen years after the provocative act – or acts.

One of Lottie's favourite comments is the therapeutic effect of killing one's abuser. Won't stand but I've seen it. Compare Zach and Ursula with Rob and Eileen. Zach killed Peter Daventry and Ursula killed Vincent Pope but I'd never seen the before and after. Then came Frank Amos, Eileen's abuser. No question of mistaken identity – it was him. And look at Eileen now. Wow. To be honest though, I do sense reservations from Eileen.

Still wrong though. If we're caught, we're going down. DS John French of Homicide and DI Steve Reeve of DPS have locked onto us. They don't know about our condition but that wouldn't deter them. In fact they'd turn it to their advantage. Lottie calls them Humpty and Dumpty but they're not daft. They know it's us and they're just one small piece of evidence away from making a murder charge stick. If they get it, we're stuffed.

I've had this conversation with Lottie many times. Can I turn her? Not a chance.

CHAPTER TWO

LOTTIE

Eileen places her drink on the table, shrugs off her bright yellow jacket, places her helmet next to her drink, spins her chair around and sits on it – backwards.

She folds her arms onto the back of the chair, rests her chin on them and looks at me. "Nice wig. Red hair suits you."

"We're not here to discuss wigs? And speak up. There's a hell of a din in here."

"The main reason I chose this pub is because it's noisy." She looks around but no one is paying attention to us. She looks back at me and leans forward. "Hell of a din? Why are you talking like Charlie?"

"I'm practising."

"What for? Why not be yourself."

I wish she would move on.

"Why talk like Charlie? I prefer you sounding yourself – you know, like Lady Catherine de Bourgh."

I look away.

"You know. That posh lady from Pride and Prejudice."

I sit back, arms folded.

"Lottie. Are you listening to me?"

I suppose I ought to humour her. "How else would we be able to converse?"

Eileen laughs. "That's better…"

Having locked my bike to some railings down a side street, I have been awaiting Eileen at the Duck in Pimlico. She has news of Robert's abuser. This pub is horrible and Charlie would agree, but Eileen chose it. My spectacles and wig are irritating but they ward off unwanted attention. That YouTube clip of Charlie dragging the boy from the burning car five months ago is still being viewed.

Eileen killed Frank Amos, the paedophile who abused her when she was eight, but I do not believe she has felt the release Zachery and Ush felt when they killed theirs. Robert's abuser is still to be identified. And mine. And, of course, Travis Hendry – the warden of our children's home who facilitated access for a paedophile ring.

"…right. Rob's abuser. Zach gave me three names. Two are non-starters. The third is worth an approach. Frederick Traube."

"Frederick Traube?"

Eileen sips her drink. "Mid-forties. Family. Lives in Kingston. No previous. No markers. He's on social media but is essentially inactive. Haven't figured out his profession. Zach spotted him in the background of a photo taken at some kind of social function. He's a good likeness for Rob's abuser but we know how unreliable that is. What's raised my interest is the social function he's at. It doesn't seem to fit with him."

"Social function?"

"That's the funny thing. Most of the people there have declined their tags, but he hasn't. Either he doesn't get the tag thing or he's unaware of it. If he is aware and comfortable with it then we can eliminate him. As for what the social function was, seems like some sort of award ceremony. Zach, Rob and Ush are checking what they can but I don't expect much from them. You happy for me to bring Wade in on this?"

"Involving Wade would be good... and Charlie."

Eileen sits quiet for a few moments. She purses her lips and looks away. When she turns back towards me, she is all smiles. "How've you been getting on? Had much time out and about?"

"Some. Not much."

"Been able to spend time with Ush?"

"Not really."

Eileen leans forward and puts her hand on mine. "Make time – Charlie will understand. Speaking of whom," she sits back, "how are you getting on with Charlie?"

Talking about this is something I avoid. However, talking about it with Eileen might be beneficial. "Charlie and I can now communicate, without talking."

Eileen's eyes open wide. "Non-vocalised communication. That's great. Must make life so much easier."

"It has. It was difficult and there is still some way to go. When Charlie has the *spot*, she looks like she is talking to herself."

"That's such good news. I've heard Charlie's an advanced driver now, emergency vehicles with blue lights, sirens and everything."

"Yes."

"That must be exciting."

"I disappear for that."

Again, Eileen pauses. She looks down at her drink and swirls it.

Our conversation lacks something. I think I know what it is. Better take it slowly. "You are looking good."

She closes her eyes. When she opens them again, she looks tired. Drained. Not even that. Flat.

Since despatching Frank Amos two months ago, she has shown little progress. "Ush and Zachery's reactions to despatching their abusers were different. I suppose all our reactions will be different."

"Lottie. I don't know. I just don't know."

"Have you considered a relationship?"

She swirls her drink again, her lips tight.

"Maybe a bit early for that."

Eileen looks down and rests her forehead on the back of the chair. All I can see is the top of her head. Dyed blonde hair, tied into a ponytail hanging down her back. Dark roots show her hair's true colour.

I place my hand on her shoulder and squeeze. "Give it time."

She looks up. "You know what, Lottie…"

A pause. I do believe that I will find whatever she has to say uncomfortable. Eileen is different from Ush and Zachery – she thinks about things on many different levels. Maybe explains her success as an analyst in MI5. Well, here it comes.

"...you were right, there is a release. I felt free. I felt as though I'd pushed it behind some impregnable wall, far away, where it couldn't hurt me. What happened to Frank Amos was right. Charlie would say it's wrong but she's talking about the law. But if it was so right, if it was so just, why am I racked with guilt? And why, if I'm feeling so guilty, am I pushing so hard on Frederick Traube? I don't know, Lottie. I don't know what's fair or right anymore. I pushed hard for this. You know I did. I helped Rob, Zach and Ush overcome their qualms but... I don't know, Lottie. I just don't know."

I look around. No one in the pub is paying attention to us. The general noise is louder than when I came in.

Eileen sits back. "I'd better go. I'll find out what I can about Frederick Traube." She passes me a sheet of paper. "For Wade. It will give him a start. See where he gets with it." She's up and swinging her yellow jacket round her shoulders. "I'll be in touch." She squeezes on her helmet and slips out of the pub.

Oh my. That was very unexpected. I close my eyes and think over what she said. No doubt she spoke from the heart, but whether killing Frank Amos was a good thing or not is a struggle for her. I better start heading home. Maybe involving Wade in identifying and locating our abusers can help Eileen resolve her churning emotions. Anyway, I still have this wine to finish off. Best not to, really, considering I have to cycle home. I sit forward and open my eyes. A man has taken the chair Eileen was sitting on although he has turned it around and is sitting normally. He is, perhaps, a little older than me. There are three others standing behind him, looking at me too. "Oh. I am sorry. Miles away. I am just about to leave freeing up this seat for you and your friends."

"Actually, I'd rather like you to stay. I'll get you another glass of wine?"

"That is awfully kind of you but I must be heading off."

He turns and looks at his friends. "Apparently I'm orfully kind and she must be heading orff." They laugh. He looks back at me. "I'm sorry, but I insist."

One of his friends heads to the bar whilst another grabs a vacant chair from a nearby table. He sits, puts his arm around my shoulders and leans in and kisses my ear. I push away, no good. Then I feel his tongue in my ear.

"Get off me." I push away, harder. He will not let go.

What the hell's going on?

Thank goodness. Charlie has come up onto the *stage*.

Charlie. Help me?

Where are we?

A pub, Pimlico.

Disguise?

How can she be so calm? The man is getting more aggressive.

Red wig, spectacles.

How'd we get here?

Bicycle.

Have we got a mobile?

I was meeting Eileen. So, no.

* * *

CHARLIE

How did Lottie let this guy get so close? Thank god we've perfected our non-vocalised way of communicating.

The bloke sitting opposite must be the king pin. The pub's clientele are all male. Most are sneering and jeering. A few don't approve – not enough to intervene.

Where's my warrant card?

At home too.

Oh, for god's sake. Move over.

Gladly.

The bloke next to me is still excavating my ear with his tongue. A glass of wine is placed in front of me. I pick it up and smash it on the table ensuring the glass shards and the wine fall into his lap. The pub goes quiet. Everyone is looking. The bloke jumps up, the glass falling from his lap. There's a damp patch. "You bitch," he shouts.

I walk over to the bar and set down the broken glass. Ignoring the bar staff, I turn back and face the man whose tongue is now back in his own head. He's between me and the cycling gear. "You look like you've pissed yourself."

The mood in the pub hasn't changed – spectators, every one of them.

"You bitch."

That, I think, is the best he can manage. "Do I deserve a slap?"

"You deserve more than that."

The bloke who I'd labelled the king pin has stood up. "Hey, mate. She's not worth it."

I change my stance. "If you're gonna slap me, you better be quick. Get it done before I kick your bollocks up your arse."

"It'll be more than a slapping, you skinny bitch." He raises his hand.

Right foot, front kick – BANG.

He's on the floor.

I step over him and pick up my jacket and helmet.

"Good night, gentlemen. It's been an absolute pleasure."

I leave the pub. One of them even opens the door for me.

Lottie. Where's the fucking bike?

* * *

CHARLIE
You okay?

Charlie, I am so sorry.

That's a first – Lottie sounding contrite.

What happened?

I met with Eileen. Then, after she left, those men came over.

How did they get that close?

Not sure. It all happened so fast...

She's rattled.

Lottie, don't worry about it. The advantages of being a multiple.

What might have happened if I were on my own?

Gang rape.

Lottie goes quiet. I've over-egged it but Lottie must learn to keep her antennae up.

Look, Lottie. I reckon they were just four blokes having a laugh. One of them was taking photos for Christ's sake. Who suggested that pub?

Eileen.

Oh, right. She'd have chosen it because it doesn't have CCTV. Trouble is, because of that, it's a dive. Did you see the table where the blokes were gambling? No big deal but at the table next to them, the older guy was taking stolen goods and the two younger guys were burglars. Drugs were being dealt on the table near the bogs. Did you arrive before Eileen?

Yes, by about twenty minutes.

And you didn't see any of that?

How can something so obvious be so missed? To be fair, I know coppers who would be blind to all that. Wade's one.

Apologies, Charlie. I let my concentration slip.

No harm done. At least none that a shower and ear-cleanser can't resolve. There was so much criminal activity in that pub, the local CID must be aware of it. There could have been a surveillance team in there. Possibly even undercover cops.

So you could have kicked an undercover officer in the testicles.

Ah, good. Lottie's recovering.

Possibly. Good test of his dedication to duty. D'you think we were recognised?

No. But we may be. There was that guy taking photographs with his mobile phone.

What? This mobile phone?

Charlie!

Shall we have a look! Oh. I'm sorry, Lottie, I wasn't quick enough. It's locked itself.

I slide off the back, remove the battery and drop both phone and battery down a drain.

There is one other thing, Lottie. This bike's worth over a thousand quid. If you have to leave it outside a pub, leave it in full view. Don't lock it up to railings down some dingy side-street. Better still, run. It's only a few miles.

Like I say, Charlie. Apologies.

I unlock the bike and take us home.

* * *

LOTTIE

When we get in, I wait, patiently, as Charlie and Wade kiss and cuddle. Although they have been an item since the Frank Amos killing, things are not working out for them.

Charlie is on duty tomorrow morning so she soon disappears down to her *dressing room*, leaving me with Wade. I hand him the sheet of paper Eileen gave me and head for the shower.

Wade needs to see the identification and locating processes. If I had won that post with the National Crime Agency, I may have been able to assist Eileen. However, for whatever reason, I did not. Wade, being in Special Branch, or whatever they call it now, is better placed to support Eileen.

I expected Charlie to rip into me over that incident at the Duck but her enquiry about where I had left the bike was as bad as it got.

I do believe she is enjoying being a multiple.

Wade looks up from Eileen's sheet of paper as I come back into the living room, rubbing my hair with a towel.

"So, Wade. Your thoughts?"

He folds the paper up and slips it into his jacket pocket. I have not told him about the incident in which Charlie relocated that gentleman's testicles. Gosh, that looked painful – the expression on that man's face as he lay on the floor, knees pulled up to his chest, arms straight down between his legs... The interesting thing was that, judging by the expressions on the faces of all the men there, it was a shared experience.

"Frederick Traube." Wade shrugs. "How do you think that's pronounced?"

"Eileen said Trow-buh."

"I'll see what I can do but I'm still very much the new boy. I need to get my feet under the table."

"It seems that Zachery and Eileen are the ones doing most of the work. Robert and Ush's contribution is minimal and I have so little time. In fact, I feel left out."

"Lottie, you know full well that none of this would be happening without you."

I check the *stage* and *wings* – no sign of Charlie. "Wade, may I ask you a question?"

"Fire away."

"This is murder. No getting away from it. Murder. Why are you involving yourself?"

"You've asked me before and I've explained – because I'm Charlie's friend. That also makes me your friend. I also think our judicial system is incapable of delivering justice in these circumstances."

Despite having this conversation before, I remain unconvinced. "But, as a police officer, you have sworn an oath to uphold the law."

"And it's frequently said, the law can be an ass."

"So, at what point do you go from flouting the law to upholding it."

I know Wade has thought this through and his explanation will be consistent. I just want to understand how he thinks, how he rationalises all this. Maybe this time he will give a little more.

Wade sits back and looks at me. "Like I've said on a number of occasions, I will only change direction if I think it will benefit Charlie – and, therefore, of course, you."

His patience with me is second to none. He has said that before. "I want more."

"You want to know whether I'd take this approach across the board." Wade knows my thoughts better than I do.

"Exactly. Why only paedophilia?"

"Because it helps Charlie – and, therefore, of course, you."

"So, committing murder is acceptable to you."

"No. I don't find committing murder acceptable." A little show of exasperation but he carries on, his voice even. "I will, however, commit murder if I think it will help Charlie – and, therefore, of course, you."

"You keep saying that."

"Because it's true. I don't think Charlie deserves to go to prison. Prison is where she'd end up if you'd continued your rampaging vengeance thing without changing the MO. There have been no arrests because Charlie and I instigated a change in the way you confront your suspects. The Frank Amos killing has not been linked with the Peter Daventry and Vincent Pope killings. Had they been, you wouldn't have stood a chance. As it stands, you have two very competent and confident detectives who know that Charlie is involved in the Daventry and Pope killings. They simply don't have the evidence and are unlikely to get it as resource is not being channelled into the 'Charlie' line of enquiry."

He is talking about DS John French of Homicide and DI Steve Reeve of DPS. "Humpty and Dumpty."

"Deride them all you want, Lottie, but they are two fine detectives. They don't have a hunch that Charlie's involved in these murders. They know she's involved. They will not stop. I believe that when, not if, they find that piece of evidence, your house of cards will come tumbling down."

His irritation with me is becoming clear. If I push a bit harder, he might give me a bit more. "Would you kill Humpty and Dumpty?"

"No."

"Why not? You as good as killed Frank Amos."

"Killing Frank Amos, protected Charlie. Killing John French and or Steve Reeve would not protect Charlie."

"Protect her from whom?"

"From you, Lottie. From you."

Ouch.

* * *

CHARLIE

Lottie's upset. She's vacated the *spot*.

I'm getting the hang of this. When in the *dressing room*, I don't know what's going on but, if Lottie's on the *spot*, I become aware that something's upsetting her. Like earlier this evening, when her space was invaded by those four men – it wasn't sirens or klaxons sounding, like in a submarine, but there was the same effect. Actually, a submarine describes this well. Lottie panicked, I became aware and up-periscoped. Same thing now but I'm naked in bed, tucked up under the duvet.

"Definitely weird." Wade's padded in and hung his dressing gown on the back of the door. He's wearing nothing but his boxers.

"Join the club."

"Lottie's been prying, trying to elicit my motivations. I think I've reinforce what she doesn't want to hear."

"That she's the threat?"

"Essentially."

That would have been what upset her and alerted me. She's buggered off to the *dressing room* leaving the *spot* available.

Despite the half-light, Wade knows it's me and not Lottie. How he knows, beats me. He slips his hand under the duvet and caresses my tummy.

"That's nice," I say but I've tensed up.

Wade moves his hand up to my breast. He's watching me.

I take his hand and move it away. "I'm sorry."

I shuffle across the bed and he slides under the duvet somehow removing his boxers all in one movement.

I want to be intimate, I want sex, it may even be what I need, but it sickens me. Oh, god. All I want is for these feelings to go away. "I'm sorry."

"Don't be. Early days. When you're ready."

We lie together, arms and legs entwined. I hear his breath. I feel his heart. I kiss his forehead. "I'm sorry."

Lottie's been behaving differently. How could she have let those guys get so close? Something's distracting her.

Wade lifts his head and looks at me. "You're distracted."

"Hey. I'm sorry. Lottie's up to something."

Wade rolls onto his back. In the darkness I feel his irritation. No, not irritation. Frustration.

"Wade. Why do you put up with me? Apart from some awkward fumbling, we haven't been intimate. We haven't made love. We haven't…"

Wade has put his finger on my lips. "I'll tell you why. It's because I want to be with you."

"I fascinate you."

He heaves himself up and rests on his elbow looking down at me. "You do fascinate me but that's not the reason I want to be with you. I want to be with you because…" He looks away. Strange for him to be unable to find the words. He looks back at me, "...because I want to be with you."

"Do you love me?" I can't believe I asked that. Oh, god, what will he say?

"I don't know what the word *love* means. What I do know is that I want to be with you."

I think that's why I love him. Yes, I do know what the word *love* means. I love him because he tolerates me. I love him because he's there for me. I love him because he takes considerable risks for me. Yet I shy away. "Wade, I'm sorry."

"Sleep now."

"I mean it. I'm sorry."

"And I mean it. Sleep now."

CHAPTER THREE

CHARLIE

"Sargie's posted me with you." I'm checking the car as Kathy bounces into the front passenger seat.

"What's up with Lavender?"

Lottie's come up onto the *stage*.

"The CID have a search warrant and he's familiar with the premises."

"Oh, right. He'll love working with the... friggin' teccos."

"Not so sure the teccos will love working with... friggin' him."

I drive out onto the main drag. Kathy seems her normal self. See how things go.

All that training, all those hours at high speed, all those hours in the skidpan and I still can't get this car to move in the way Lavender can. When Lavender's behind the wheel, it's like the car drives itself. One day I'll have this car gliding.

"Thompson Avenue. There's a disqual I want to check out."

"Sure." I take us round there.

"There. That Toyota."

I stop.

Kathy's out and walking round it.

She gets back in. "Hasn't moved."

I carry on.

"You and Wade getting on okay?"

"I enjoy his company. He seems to enjoy mine."

"You wouldn't have said that six months ago."

I laugh. "You're right there."

"How's Joel?"

This is straightforward catching up. Because of my driving course, we haven't seen each other for a while. "I've moved on. Joel's still an important person in my life but I've stopped meeting up with him on top of Kevan House."

"I'm pleased about that, Charlie. Your infatuation with his memory was causing concern."

Oi. This is supposed to be you finding out about Katherine. Not *vice versa*.

I know. I'm baffled.

"You know, Kathy, I'm pleased I've moved on from Joel. It couldn't have been healthy chasing a ghost. The more I..."

"*Mike-Three. Mike-Three. Freeman Games, 107 East Street, Central Station Alarm. Mike-Three.*"

Kathy grabs the handset. "Received by Mike-Three."

I flick on the neenaws and we're off.

"The owner's set it off opening up. Doesn't know or forgotten the process for cancelling." Kathy always has the answers.

"Maybe. We don't often get false alarms from this address."

We're there. The alarm's blaring away. Kathy's out and heading towards the man inside. There's a shop opening up opposite. I beckon the guy over. "Do you recognise him?"

"Yeah, that's Jim. Never set his alarm off before. Must be having a bad day."

"Thanks." I call Kathy and let her know but she's already on her way out.

We're back in the car.

"Mike-Sierra from Mike-Three. Result."

"Mike-Three. Go ahead."

"Freeman Games. Alarm set off in error. Owner on premises. Central Station informed."

"Received by Mike-Sierra."

"Mike-Three out."

I drive away having failed to coax the car to do it itself.

Out onto the main drag again. This is strange. There's a good-looking guy at the bus stop, early thirties, well built, neat and tidy… and Kathy's said nothing.

Did Katherine see him?

Lottie is paying close attention.

Yes.

Ummm.

Ummm indeed.

"That cyclist," I say. "The bike's not his."

I flash him, but he doesn't stop. Again. He still doesn't stop. I move up alongside him.

Kathy winds her window down. "Could you stop a minute? Quick word."

He stops and I stop. "Jeez. I thought that was going to be slowest pursuit in Met history."

"Me too." Kathy opens her door but looks back at me. "What makes you think it's not his?"

"His legs are too long."

"Oh, right. Gotcha."

"But don't worry."

"What?"

"If the bike's nicked, he'd have had it on his toes by now."

I shake my head as Kathy goes and speaks to the guy. **She does seem quiet and maybe a little distracted.**

Something's up. She's not herself. She's always a laugh a minute.

Kathy gets back in. "He's borrowed it. Belongs to his brother. Nice bloke. Offered to give me a ride on his handlebars."

That's more like the Kathy we all know and love. But she's stopped.

"What sort of ride?" I ask.

She doesn't smile or even register what I said.

Strange.

Yeah, and this'll be one very long shift.

* * *

CHARLIE

We don't return to the Nick for breakfast but stop at a Greggs. Kathy does the honours and I find a secluded spot where we can enjoy some peace and quiet as we devour our bacon baps and coffee.

The radio comes to life. *"Mike-Four. Mike-Four…"* The rest is only of interest to Peckham's fast car.

Kathy carries on eating her bap.

I break the silence growing between us. "We haven't been out clubbing for ages. Fancy something like that?"

"But you're accounted for."

"Wade won't mind."

"Nah. Wouldn't be right."

This isn't Kathy.

Lottie and I shouldn't communicate like this in front of others. I can't do it without looking as though I'm talking to myself. It's okay, though, as Kathy's engrossed with her phone.

Not right for who? You or her?

You might have something there. Christ, how the hell do I broach that subject?

Allow me.

No switching. It freaks people out.

I carry on. "If not a club, just a drink or something. Maybe a bite to eat. Spend some time together. It's been ages, what with my suspension and then the driving course. How about this afternoon?"

"Love to, Charlie, but I've plans."

"Anything special?"

"There's this guy I've been seeing. I've been thinking of giving him the ol' heave-ho, but then he does something and I change my mind. I've been stuck in this kind of loop for a while. I need to ditch him."

"Anyone I know?"

"No. Not at all. He works…"

"*Mike-Three. Mike-Three. De Laune Street near Kennington Park Place. Theft from motor vehicle. Suspects on scene. Mike-Three.*"

Kathy acknowledges the call.

We're there minutes later but all we find is a car with a smashed window and a sarcastic informant.

Kathy manages to trace and contact the owner. She's walking around the vehicle, talking away into her phone.

I wait in the car staring at the smashed window of the stricken vehicle.

What do we know about this guy?

The car's the same model and colour... the one that roared out of the flames backwards... across the pavement... shopfront... driver on fire...

Charlie. What do we know about this guy?

Lottie's saying something.

Charlie. Calm down.

I'm good. I'm good.

I catch my breath. In for four. Out for six.

Another flashback?

I lean forward and push my forehead against the steering wheel.

Something like that. It's over now. What were you saying about Kathy?

What do we know about the guy?

Kathy doesn't have problems with guys...

My breathing's coming more easily.

...guys have problems with her.

She can be forthright. There have been a few times when her mouth has got her into trouble and you have had to bail her out.

Forthright? You mean gobby. She gets brave when I'm there.

My mind's still on the car but I'm calming down. **Ummm. I wonder. There is a lot to wonder about.**

* * *

CHARLIE

It perked up later in the shift. A few calls that didn't amount to much but we did make one arrest – suspicion of theft. There turned out to be evidence of handling so CID took it over.

We're round the Half Nelson now. After losing it with that car, I'm not in the mood but I want to spend time with Kathy. No one else from the Team has turned up.

"Soda and lime."

Kathy? Soda and lime?

"I'll be talking to Michael this afternoon. I'll need a clear head."

"Michael?"

"Yeah, this guy I've been seeing."

"Kathy. You seem in two minds."

"Maybe. Look. Don't bother with a drink for me. I don't like to leave you on your own but I want to concentrate on Michael. See you tomorrow." She heads out.

"Hey. Wait."

She turns.

I throw my arms round her and hug her tight. "You take care."

Instead of hugging me back, she pushes me back. She smiles – more grimace than smile – and she's out the door.

"Kathy alright?" the barman asks, placing my glass of wine on the bar.

"She's fine. Difficult day."

He moves away to serve another customer.

Michael is the cause of this.

You don't know that.

Obvious to me.

Hey. Me hunch. You evidence. Stick to the script.

"Hey, Charlie. You friggin' talking to yourself now?"

Ah, shit. "Hi, Lavender." He's turned up with half the CID. I acknowledge the detectives. I know them all. Problem is, they make an audience and Lavender plus audience, of course, means… story time.

"A friggin' tecco sidled up to me once, handed me a completed information and said, 'Here, Lavs, we're spinnin' a drum tomorrow, TSG and everything, but we've forgotten to get the search warrant. We're a bit tucked up doin' all the prep so would you nip along, see the Stipe and swear this information for us?' The tecco concerned was told by his DCI, 'This one's a bit dodgy, get a lid to do it.' I knows it can't be too dodgy or he'd have approached one of the skippers. The dodgier the information the higher rankin' lid the teccos approach. Very dodgy, Inspector. Quite dodgy, skipper. Bit dodgy, PC. No problem, tecco. Pointless, crime squad. And they all think the Stipe doesn't get it. So I'm in the witness box swearing this friggin' information when the Stipe holds up his hand. I stops. 'Officer,' says the Stipe, 'tell me about the source of the information.' 'Your Worship,' says yours truly, 'as it says on the information, it's a source who's proved reliable in the past.' He grants the warrant, passes it to his clerk who passes it to the usher who hands it back to me. As I'm leaving the court room, the Stipe says, 'Officer,' I stops and turns round, 'the next time you swear an information for a search warrant, I would like to see the source who has proved reliable in the past. It would be so nice to meet him after all these years.' I nodded and got out of there a bit friggin' sharpish."

Would Lavender really speak that way to a Magistrate?

Lottie, everybody's laughing because they know it's complete and utter bollocks. If Lavender had spoken to a Magistrate like that he'd have been leaving the court room through a different friggin' door.

I should hope so too. Changing the subject slightly, it was interesting how, when he came in, he thought you were talking to yourself.

I lift my glass of wine to cover my lips.

Unlike Kathy, Lavender can be sharp.

Something to work at.

Lottie moves on quickly.

Katherine. Out of sorts. Distracted. Not her normal mischievous self. Something has changed in her life. This change coincides with the arrival of Michael.

Lottie thinks she has it all sewn up. I just wish she'd shut up and talk about it when we're on our own.

Alright. Alright. It's Michael.

Thank you. So now we can tell Sergeant Cantrell and get back to killing paedophiles.

The temptation to throw this glass of wine in Lottie's face is strong… but I resist.

* * *

CHARLIE

It doesn't take long to finish the wine and I return to the Nick. Cantrell's already gone. Inspector Brady's free. I appraise him. He's thankful. Weird. I change into running gear and head home. Running clears my head, helps me look at things from a different perspective. Kathy's got mixed up with someone she wishes she hadn't. The thing that's weird is that it's attracted so much attention. Kathy's well capable of looking after herself. As I cross Camberwell Green, I move onto my own problems. It's well after four when I'm battling my way through my front door locks. I don't expect Wade home until after six. Punchbag session. Quick shower. Lottie emerges. Not such a quick shower. Housework, Lottie disappears. That done, I sit at my desk and open an old book I've found called Roadcraft. I remember the instructor – "Don't drive fast. Drive quick."

My mobile pings – it's a message from Wade. He's going to be late. Shame, I wanted to grill him on why he was out early from work yesterday. He's up to something. He didn't even take his case to work today. I resist the temptation to rifle it.

Come on. Roadcraft. If Lavender can make the car drive itself then I bloody well can.

* * *

LOTTIE

Sebastian?

Lottie. What brings you to the aaaabbbbyyyyyssssssss?

Where else would I find you?
Who's not stepping up to the plate?
No one.
What d'you want to chat about?
Charlie.
What about her?

I loathe this place. Bright darkness. Groaning silence. Flat mountains. Sebastian has made it his home. How he imagines this place is unknown to me. He has never said.

You must meet.
Ridiculous.
Two things – Charlie needs to understand and her flashbacks are persisting.
While we're dissociated like this, flashbacks are hers and hers alone. As for wanting her to know about our inner world, tell her.
Telling will not suffice. She needs to see.
No.
Sebastian. She must.

Gillian looks like a little girl. She is a little girl. Sebastian looks different every time I see him. Sometimes tall and elegant with a white scarf and hat. Other times a bruising boxer with arms as big as his legs and covered in tattoos. At this moment, he is matt black, unreflecting.

I will come up and meet her.
No. She must come down.

A hand emerges from the unreflection. Then an arm. A shoulder. A head.

Why?

Sebastian now stands before me. Suit. Waistcoat. Silk scarf. Hat.

I want her to understand how our mind has been fractured and broken.

CHAPTER FOUR

CHARLIE

Another day. Another Early Turn.

I have the new guy, Iffy Ibbotson, as my operator. Don't know much about him other than he's old, well, in his thirties, and has spent all fifteen years of his service in uniform, on the streets, wrestling with scrotes in the gutter – though his previous gutters were Bexley's – not many scrotes lounging around in Bexley's gutters.

He's not talkative which is good, although the silence between us is getting heavy.

I try not to think about freezing. Maybe I need to stop thinking about freezing. I need to stop thinking about not thinking about freezing. Oh god.

We've been on duty for over an hour and I've taken him on a tour of the ground starting with the borders. Elephant & Castle, New Kent Road, Old Kent Road, skirting Peckham and Dulwich and round the back of Camberwell, where I live...

"If you live on the ground, I'm surprised you've been posted here." He does speak.

"I must be the exception that proves the rule."

The quiet descends again.

...along the border with Brixton, Kennington and back up to the Elephant & Castle.

Locations – grotty estates, seedy estates, hot spots, tasty pubs, where the druggies hang out...

It's been a quiet morning. Other units have taken the dawn chorus of opening-up alarms and scrotes don't tend to be early-risers.

I can't stand this silence anymore. "What brought on your transfer to Walworth?"

"If I'm honest, I'm not really sure. Bit of me, bit of them. I was bored with Bexley and Bexley was bored with me. So, win win."

"Were you Bexley all your service?"

"If you're talking elapsed time, just feels like it. If you're talking real time, I was Stoke Newington, Brixton, Croydon, Peckham, Rotherhithe..."

"What? Brixton? Peckham? Rotherhithe? You'll know this ground as well as me."

"If you'd asked, I'd have said."

"So I must do twenty questions. Have you been in any specialist units?"

"If, by specialist units, you include Traffic, Dogs, Mounted, CID, Diplomatic Protection, Royalty Protection..."

"Stop, before you recite the entire Met Police Menu..."

"...no."

"You know what, Sergeant Cantrell's gonna love you."

"If, by love, you mean something carnal then, sorry, not my type. If, by love, you mean someone who will help bolster her Team's figures, then you may well be right."

"You a thief taker?"

"If you stop that car in front of us, I'll show you."

* * *

CHARLIE

Lavender's now driving the fast car because Iffy and I are in with the driver of a ringer.

Experts from Central came and dived under the bonnet exposing tampered engine and chassis numbers. It wasn't just the bonnet – they gave the car the equivalent of an intimate search revealing orifices I never knew cars had. They interviewed the poor driver, who's turned out to be an innocent victim with no idea he'd just bought a stolen vehicle.

"If the prints they've lifted give any matches, we could be in for interesting interviews with some top-end vehicle thieves."

"How did you know?"

"If you mean what made that car stand out, not sure. It just didn't look right."

I know what he means by 'just didn't look right' but... "That's easy with people. How do you spot it with cars?"

"If you mean, recognising what makes a car look embarrassed, I suppose it comes with spending a few years with the Dodgy Motor Boys."

Lavender's been caught up in an incident on Rotherhithe's ground and Iffy and I have taken over the van as its crew's in with an arrest.

"So, come on, you haven't really explained. What makes a ringer stand out?"

"If the number plate looks weird, worth a stop. If it looks like it's had a recent paint job, worth a stop. If it's a Toyota with a Mazda badge on the back, worth a stop. Cars like that are probably hot. You've got experience of diving into hot cars."

He's looking at me. My breath's catching... no... I'm alright.

I like Iffy. On the face of it, he's an irritating prick but, I don't know, there's a lot more to him below the surface. Of course, I have sympathy for people with hidden depths.

* * *

CHARLIE

"How are things with Kathy?" It's gone six when Wade gets in. He's been at work since six this morning and he's dog-tired but there's something about his work that exhilarates him.

I don't want to talk about Kathy. Though I'm tired too, I want to talk about what's in his case. Lottie's even come up.

What's woken you?
Same thing as you.
Wade's up to something. This could be funny.
Your humour has always baffled me.

I pour two glasses of wine, sit down with him and ask the question. "What's in your case? You left it at home today."

"Captured." Wade smiles. "Can't get anything past you."

"No. You can't. What's in the case."

He gets his case, opens it and takes out a folder. "Papers by eminent people in psychiatry and psychology about – well, two things really – how seriously DID is taken by the psychiatric community and communication between alters in a DID system."

Aw. How sweet.

Lottie. Don't distract me.

Wade continues. "First. Supporters versus sceptics. About half and half. Half support and half are sceptical. I'd say that, on meeting you, the half that are sceptical would change their stance."

"If we meet them, we'll be convincing them there's no DID here."

"I get that."

"At least until after we've dealt with Travis Hendry."

"I get that too. Second. Other papers indicate that alters can communicate with one another – not just voices in the head but actual conversations. I wondered if you could, perhaps, communicate with Lottie in such a way."

"Wade. We already are."

That brings down his fop of hair. He leans forward, sips from his glass of wine and recovers his composure. "Well. Maybe that explains why you look as though you're talking to yourself sometimes."

Something to think about, Charlie.

Shhh.

I'm dead beat but need to get away from this. "Anything interesting happen today?"

Wade settles back, looking smug. "Not really. Well, one thing. My skipper sent me to brief a group of seniors on a situation that's developing in Eastern Europe. It's that story that's been in the papers but the detail has eluded the commentators. However, one of the commentators has shown remarkable insight so there's a question mark over the source of information..."

Charlie, falling asleep whilst engaged in conversation is rude.

I open my eyes. Wade hasn't noticed.

Engaged in conversation? He wasn't talking to me. He was talking. Lottie, would you deal with this?

No way. You asked the question. You pay attention.

Jeez. It's gone six-fifty. I'm Early Turn tomorrow.

"...and the question that needs addressing is which of our informants should be approached, as that could influence understanding of third parties which in turn influences the message they return to their clients. A fascinating discussion ensued which achieved nothing, but demonstrated which senior officers understood and which didn't. The funny thing there was that those who understood the least spoke the most. Some of them hadn't even read the file. I couldn't believe..."

Lottie, this is boring me stupid. I've been up since five this morning.

Alright, alright. Leave it with me.

* * *

LOTTIE

Wade looks at me. I have no idea how he does it, but he recognises the difference. "Charlie has retired to..." must be careful, if I say 'her *dressing room*' Wade will pick up on it immediately, "…the *dressing room*."

"But this is such fascinating stuff."

"Wade, I have read all the media so anything you say I already know and that which interests me you will avoid telling me because of its classification."

Wade retrieves his fop of hair and sits forward. "I know this isn't everyone's cup-of-tea. Maybe we should head for bed."

"Wade. I am not Charlie. I am Lottie."

He recovers his fop of hair, again. "Sorry. I'm tired. I didn't mean… You know what I didn't mean."

I change the subject. "Any progress with Frederick Traube?"

He shakes his head.

"You go to bed. I have the *spot* and no intention of wasting it."

Wade gathers himself, he too will be getting up early, and heads through to the bedroom where he will sleep alone.

* * *

LOTTIE
Actually, I have no intention of staying on the *spot*.

I head down.

Jemima. We must talk.

Is that all?

Yes. I spoke with Gillian and Sebastian earlier. Charlie must meet us all.

Charlie should be left in blissful ignorance.

Of all of them, Jemima is the easiest to get along with.

Charlie is now aware.

Why's that my problem?

Not your problem. Our problem.

No. It's Gillian's, Floella's and my problem.

With such little experience of the outside world, I understand their limited perspectives.

Charlie and I live day-to-day with the consequences. You think we don't?

Day-to-day means something different for us all. We can help each other.

How? How can we help? Gillian's a little girl. I'm a moody teenager and Floella's... well, Floella's Floella...

Moody teenager? Never heard that from Jemima. Accurate though. Jemima is a little older than Gillian but tracking ages is difficult in our inner world. I see her as a ten year old with big hair, baggy dungarees and orange plimsoles. The image I have of Gillian keeps changing, but Jemima's is always the same – for me, that is. Of the three of them, Jemima was the easiest to send out to face the abusers. Never had to call Sebastian when Jemima's turn came round. Gillian would cry, Floella would kick up a terrible stink but Jemima would say, *Okay, Lottie,* and head up to the *spot*. Resisting the temptation to send Jemima every time was hard.

...You've always dealt with Charlie. What's happened that we need to be involved?

We are killing the abusers.

You're what?

You heard me. Killing them.

Awesome.

Jemima's mood has shifted one-hundred-and-eighty degrees.

And we need Charlie fully committed.

How can I help?

Show Charlie what the abuse has done to us.

Tell me where and when.

Thank you, Jemima.

I am leaving as Jemima calls.

Have you spoken with Floella yet?

No.

Good luck with that.

* * *

LOTTIE

Floella. Hi.

Get away from me. I don't want to see you. I don't want to hear you. I don't want to know you.

Floella is ten years old, dressed like a fairy holding a magic wand with a star at the end.

Floella, we need to talk.

You need to talk. I don't need to talk.

You are very angry with me.

You tricked me.

I have never tricked you. I have been nothing but open with you.

I have been honest and open with her but I understand how Floella feels and why.

You said I would be alright. I hurt. I ache. I bleed.

True. I did say that. You are with friends.

You are not my friend. You send me out there to take that pain, that agony. And Sebastian.

Does Sebastian hurt you.

Well, no. But he takes things away.

What does he take away?

I am not even sure of the extent of Sebastian's influence.

He once took away my colours. Another time he made everything flat. Another time he made everything cold.

I will speak with Sebastian.

Too late.

That will never happen again.

I don't believe you.

Floella, what you are scared of is all over. We must break this. There is someone you must meet.

He'll stick his thing in me. It'll hurt.

One of us.

Us?

Yes.

Charlie?

Yes.

If I see Charlie, I'll kill her.

Killing Charlie is impossible for Floella.

Charlie will kill the men who hurt you. When she does, we can move on. We can move on as a family.

With Gillian and Jemima?

Yes.

But Gillian's a little girl. Jemima's covered in pimples.

That is only how you imagine them. If you take the *spot* now, you will find that things have changed. We are all grown up.

You're tricking me into going out there. I'm not going. Bring on Sebastian. I don't care. I'm not going.

I understand where Floella is coming from. From her perspective, she was abused yesterday.

You do not have to go anywhere. I will bring Charlie to see you.

I don't want to see her. I don't want to see anyone.

This is important.

I don't care.

It is not just important for me. It is important for all of us.

I don't care, I don't care.

She is starting to annoy me. There is a darkening.

See what you've done. You've brought Sebastian. You said you wouldn't and you have. You're a liar.

Sebastian is the size of a mountain and I stand next to one of his brown brogues. When he speaks, his voice is soft.

If Lottie's suggesting you should meet Charlie, it's for the best. Accommodate the meeting, Floella.

How Floella perceives Sebastian is unknown to me but she is scared, holding her arms up before her face and stepping back.

Floella. The meeting with Charlie – accommodate.

Sebastian's attitude is harsh.

Was that really necessary?

Another shift. I pull on the oars of a rowing boat. Sebastian trails his hand through inky water. Willow tree fronds brush my shoulders. Sebastian lounges back.

Charlie's obstinate. Floella's like her. My influence over the children is waning.

His voice is soft.

I shake my head.

I will not abandon the children.

You are like a big sister to them. The example you set is important.

Explains why I need Charlie in on this.

I pull the oars in. The boat moves on its own. Sebastian seems to be weighing things up. I wait.

Sebastian lifts his hand from the water. It is dry.

What you have done for Zach, Ush and Eileen was done at the expense of Gillian, Jemima and Floella. You understand that and, despite not liking it, you know it's true. Introduce the children to Charlie and you could well find yourself out on a limb. It's the right thing to do and, as you know, all too often, the right thing to do is the most uncomfortable.

CHAPTER FIVE

CHARLIE

Cantrell has posted Kathy as my operator again – as if I haven't enough to be thinking about. We've been out for an hour, dealt with two calls and, with the exception of what we need to say to get the job done, we haven't spoken. One of those incidents was a minor damage-only and I didn't freeze – not even slightly. Maybe things are getting better... in that respect.

I hardly slept last night. Wade was up with me – wanting an early start.

Kathy, always so talkative, always expressing an opinion, always so cheeky, has been behaving so out-of-character. Finding out what's up with her will be hard. Lottie would be better at this than me but handing over the *spot* means handing over the car as well. Beats me why Cantrell isn't dealing with this.

Sod it. I stop at a quiet spot and switch off the engine. I release my seatbelt and turn so I'm facing her.

"How's Michael?"

"Don't you start. Has Sargie put you up to this?"

"Last time we spoke, you said that you were thinking of giving Michael the ol' heave-ho. Are you still together or no?"

Kathy looks at me for the first time this morning. "You can tell Sargie that Michael and I are just dandy. Could we get coffee? Then maybe the radio will come to life and put an end to this torture."

"What do you mean? Torture?"

"Oh. What's the use?"

"Kathy. For over seven years, we've been best mates. Through good or bad. Okay, so this is a bit of bad. Why are you being like this?"

"Being like what?"

"Mike-Three. Mike-Three. Peckham Road near junction with Southampton Way. Personal Injury RTC. Ambulance on way. Mike-Three. Over."

Kathy grabs the radio. "Received by Mike-Three."

Another bloody car crash. I start the engine and pull my seatbelt across. The relief in Kathy is clear.

Katherine has a problem with you.

Not now. I'm driving. And you know exactly what I'm driving towards.

Sorry.

We arrive on scene. Two cars are blocking the road. One's rear-ended the other. Kathy's out and heading towards the drivers who are talking to each other. It all seems calm. Injuries are minor. Kathy cancels the ambulance. I take a deep breath and muck in with Kathy to sort it out.

Doesn't take long. Traffic's moving freely again and I hide the overwhelming relief that I didn't freeze. I felt the nervousness but I could push it away – force it down – control it. I don't know.

Time for grub and I drive us back to the Nick. I make a point of sitting in the rest room and not moving. I don't want Kathy thinking I'm all squealy-squealy back to Cantrell.

Charlie, may I speak with you now?

Lottie's popped up.

Of course.

I think Katherine might be upset with *you*.

Whatever for?

Identifying that is the challenge.

Lottie's so good at these blinding glimpses of the bloody obvious.

I asked her about Michael – she bit my head off.

You must be subtle.

Something for you then. Lavender's driving the car while we're on refs. You've got half an hour. Kathy's just coming back from the loo. Remember, talk like me.

Okay. Okay. Oh, and Charlie, well done at that incident.

I know. I didn't freeze but it's still scaring the shit out of me.

* * *

CHARLIE

Lottie leans across and smiles at Kathy. "Back on Tuesday, it seemed you were in two minds about Michael. Often helps to talk such things through. I'm here for you."

Call that subtle?

At least Lottie's doing a pretty good job of talking like me.

66

Shhh.

Kathy closes her phone. "I like Michael. He's thoughtful and considerate. He's good in bed. I enjoy his company. But I'm not sure he's the one for me and the longer I let it go on, the more difficult it will be to break up with him."

Worked.

Lottie does seem to have prompted Kathy to open up.

"I've never met him. Will you tell me about him?"

"He's about my age. Bit taller. Works in finance. I once told someone he's an accountant – he was very quick to put me straight. He's a little overweight but then, so am I. Is that enough?"

"What d'you mean? Enough?"

"Enough for you to report back to Sargie that I'm not heading for some kind of meltdown. You could do me a favour and tell her what she needs to hear to get her off my back."

"I'll do that."

"I'd appreciate it." Kathy opens her phone again. "Now, I'm trying to read something about inflation and stagnation. It's boring as hell but I'd like to sound not quite such a dork when Michael's talking about it." She puts her head down and we're forgotten.

Charlie. Your thoughts?

Lottie thinks she's done such a great job. She's useless.

I'd like to meet Michael.

A financier. That would be a scintillating evening.

I said that wrong. I *need* to meet him.

Why?

Verify what Kathy's said.

Do you not trust her?

We can chat like this when Lottie has the *spot* – she doesn't look like she's talking to herself. Something I need to work at. Then there's something Lottie needs to work at – she needs to sharpen up.

Regarding this, no. She could be spinning any ol' yarn. Like you said, it's me she's upset with. Okay, so we get Cantrell off her back, which means we have to be ready to answer Cantrell not asking how we verified what Kathy said. That means we need to meet Michael. If that goes well, it will ease things a bit and then we find out why Kathy's upset with me.

Katherine is not being accommodating. How will you arrange to meet Michael?

We've got a long weekend coming up. Call in the gang.

Zachery, Ush, Robert and Eileen?

Yes.

Who else would I mean for god's sake?

What makes you think you can order them around?

Call it reciprocity.

* * *

CHARLIE

Lottie did it. She got the gang to come to my flat that Thursday evening. Wade was there too.

I briefed them. Some surveillance. Catch him on his own. We decided Rob and Ursula, pretending to be lovers, would make the best approach. The only adverse observation was from Eileen saying that taking days off at short notice required feigning sickness and feigning sickness on a Friday is never a good idea. We all agreed and I carried on with the briefing which amounted to no more than teaching them some rudimentary surveillance tactics. Between Wade and me, we kitted them out with changes of clothing. The difficulty would be communication as the only digital things we'll carry are the awkward-to-use burners. We decided on a few hand-signals.

Went like a dream.

By 6am we were plotted up outside Kathy's address – terraced house in Catford. A white male, mid-forties, slightly overweight, came out about 6.45am. Then Kathy appeared in the doorway calling him back. She gave him what looked like a pack-lunch. They kissed. Identification – tick. This was Michael. He walked to the train station. Caught a train up to Victoria. Tube to Farringdon. Walked to a block of offices.

As luck would have it, a Starbucks was opposite. We took it in turns, hour about, to keep watch on the office block.

At 5.30pm he emerged with three colleagues and walked to a pub. The pub wasn't crowded. Zach and I took the table one side of them. Wade and Eileen got the table on the other. Rob and Ursula stood at the bar waiting for a suitable opportunity. Then the pub started filling as local offices emptied and there was standing room only. Michael was talking business with his three mates and then they started talking cars and, unbelievable luck again, one of the mates asked Michael how he was getting on with that police officer friend of his. Michael looked all sheepish as he said he might have landed on his feet there, but it was early days and see how things go and, hey, guess what, Kathy's best friends with that Charlie Quinlan who dragged the boy from the burning car. Remember her? They remembered. If only real surveillance ops would go this well.

Then, to cap it all, the three others left while Michael still had a beer to finish. He opened up his phone, maybe messaging Kathy, and Ursula and Rob asked if he minded them sitting at his table. He didn't mind. Rob's superb at this sort of thing and Ursula's wavy blonde hair and fluttering brown eyes certainly help. They soon had him engrossed in conversation. Not only is he a financier but he's good company – attentive, witty.

After giving the signal to abandon the surveillance, Wade and I left while they were chatting and went to Kathy's place – she was in. Couldn't believe it. Wade and I have changed our appearance, returning to normal. If Michael turns up while we're there it's unlikely he'll recognise us as from his neighbouring tables back in the pub.

"Charlie. What an unpleasant surprise."

We'd decided Lottie would handle this.

Don't forget, Lottie. Talk like me.

I feel I need to remind her.

Shhhh!

"I feel as though I'm losing a friend. Not just any old friend. My best friend."

"And you brought Wade. Backup?"

"Wade's tried persuading me not to do this. He failed and here I am. Whatever I've said, whatever I've done, I'm losing my best friend. I've gotta know. And I ain't gonna find out while chasing around in a fast car."

Ain't gonna find out?
Shhhh!

"You should have taken Wade's advice. I suppose as you're here, you better come in."

Kathy doesn't offer drinks or anything. Lottie and Wade wouldn't have accepted.

We sit in her sitting room. I hope Lottie doesn't prevaricate and goes straight in.

"Kathy. What's wrong?"

Don't beat about the bush.
Shhhh!

"Okay. Fair play. You're being up front. I'll be up front. You got all the attention after the tanker incident. All the rest of us got was 'keep calm and carry on'. Have you any idea how much that hurt?"

"Lavender said as much. I felt like shit. But Kathy, what exactly could I have done about it?"

"You were handed an interview for the NCA on a plate. Who, with no experience of investigations with the department, let alone any specialist squads, would even be considered? You should have been paper-sifted. But no, the hero cop, the national treasure... What did they do when you fucked that up? Oh, an advanced driving course. Must give the hero cop an advanced driving course."

"I still do not understand. What exactly could I have done about that?"

Kathy's eyes narrow. "What could you have done about it? I'll tell you what you could have done about it." She's now shouting. Not just shouting, screaming. "You could have turned it down."

"I tried."

"Not hard enough, Charlie. You know full well, those advanced driving courses come round once in a blue moon. It was my turn. It was my fucking turn."

"I did turn it down. The superintendent would not listen. He told me he was keeping me, particularly my hands, out of harm's way. I had no option but to take the course."

Kathy has gone quiet.

Contrition?

"Look. Katherine. Kathy. I don't see any reason why this should upset our friendship. I'll leave now. But I want a hug."

Kathy returns the hug but not really.

There's a sound of a key in the lock.

"That'll be Michael. You may as well say hello."

"It'll be lovely to meet him but we won't stay."

Sure enough, Lottie extricates us a few minutes later with promises we'll meet up soon. Michael makes no mention of the tanker incident and, for the few minutes we're there, he behaves like a perfectly decent, likeable, friendly sort of bloke and he even goes some way to acknowledge that Kathy and I have fallen out a bit and we could arrange an evening out. He knows a nice restaurant up in town. We say that would be nice and we're soon out of there.

* * *

CHARLIE

So. It is the driving course.

I don't answer Lottie's conclusion. Wade, too, is quiet. It's like that till we get home.

We need to talk. Wade's good at distinguishing between us but when we do the quick switching he can get lost. To help him, I get a blue tea-towel and a green tea-towel. Wade sits on the sofa and I sit on a dining chair opposite him.

Lottie takes the *spot* and waves the green tea-towel. "It is the driving course."

Wade sits forward. "I agree. The concern was that Kathy had got involved with someone who was mistreating her. We can exclude that, and Kathy's anger over driving course allocations is justified. Bit extreme, but understandable considering everything going on round the hero-cop status Charlie has."

Lottie waves the green tea-towel again. "Yes. Obvious, when you think about it. It seems that surveillance operation we mounted was taking a hammer to crack a nut."

"Worked though." Wade shakes his head. "Convincing Cantrell will be an uphill struggle. We can't tell her about our little surveillance op."

Lottie waves the green tea-towel. "We can start at where we went round to see Katherine and, as luck would have it, Michael came in shortly afterwards."

Wade nods. "Yes. That would work."

Lottie waves the green tea-towel. "Charlie. Have you anything to contribute?"

I think this will upset them. I take the *spot* and wave the blue tea-towel. "Everything Kathy said was complete and utter bollocks."

I let them stew.

After a moment or two, I relent. "Wade, you said Kathy's reaction was a bit extreme. More than a bit extreme – it was way OTT. There'll be another course within six months and if she doesn't get that one she'll definitely get the following one. She'll be an advanced driver within the year and it doesn't warrant that reaction of hers."

Lottie waves the green towel. "What did you see, Charlie?"

I wave the blue towel. "You had to talk like me. It was inevitable that you would slip up a couple of times. Kathy wasn't looking at us. The only time she did look at us was when you slipped up. Then, when you called her Katherine, not only did she look at us but there was a reaction she couldn't control. She covered it up very quickly but it was there, plain as day."

"I didn't pick up on that." Wade's intrigued.

"Nor me." Lottie waves a retrospective green towel. She continues. "So you think everything she said was covering up how she feels. If correct, we are the problem – well, you Charlie, she is not aware of us – and not because of the post tanker incident attention or the seemingly unfair allocation of driving courses."

I wave the blue towel. "We can do something constructive. If we put Cantrell's mind at rest, that will ease things for Kathy."

Wade comes in. "She'll be thankful and she may feel more like talking with you."

Lottie waves the green towel. "We can try it and, if it works, we might get to the bottom of this."

I wave the blue towel. "Sounds like a plan. I'm tired. I know it's early but I'm going to sleep. I'll leave you two to figure out what we're going to say to Cantrell. I'll be in the *dressing room*. Lottie, you have the *spot*."

CHAPTER SIX

LOTTIE

Charlie, I have an admission.

What do you mean?

I only took a share of the abuse.

There is a long pause – long even for the elastic time frames of our inner world. I intended delaying this, wait until things settled, but, with what Katherine has been saying, at least Charlie's interpretation thereof, time, I think, is running short.

Explain.

There are others.

What?

I think it right that you meet them.

I don't understand.

Charlie's far from stupid. She understands. This is her way of dealing with another shocking revelation.

When Travis Hendry ushered in the paedophiles, it became too much for me. Others formed to share the load. It became my role to choose who would take the *spot*.

You chose?

There are three. Floella, Jemima and Gillian. I think you should meet them.

Not just you and me?

No.

Charlie's reaction to this is very calm. I expected her to fly off the handle at me. I know Charlie has amazing control over her emotions or, at least, how she shows her emotions.

Why didn't you tell me?

I am telling you. It was only four months ago that you learned about our DID. I was going to leave it longer but the developments with Katherine has made it more important than awaiting the right moment.

I'm not happy.

Not happy? It hardly shows.

I understand.

Who's on the *spot*?

The *spot* is vacant. We are in bed with Wade. Asleep – sort of.

So, you're going to introduce me. Lead the way.

Unbelievable. How can she be so calm on receiving this information? Makes me wonder whether she already knows. What is more, can Charlie even do this? I am banking on the fact that when I caught Charlie descending into the *abyss* soon after she tried to throw us off Kevan House, I took her hand and guided her back. So she has at least been there. I have been navigating these regions of our mind for more than fifteen years. All I can do, is my best.

* * *

LOTTIE
Charlie, Gillian. Gillian, Charlie.

Hello, Charlie.

Gillian. This is all new to Charlie. Explain who you are, what you look like and what you do.

Okay. Lottie said you'd be coming. She told me that I won't have to do horrible things. Are you going to make me do horrible things?

No, I'm not. But I'm very confused. Will you help me?

Okay. I'm ten. I'm wearing a green check dress. I have white socks and sandals. My hair is yellow. Lottie says it's sandy.

Your hair is lovely. You've put in a lot of effort getting ready for me.

Charlie is coming across as confident – a good thing.

Not really. Some.

Would you tell me what you do?

Okay. Last night, Lottie came and said I needed to meet you. The night before that I had to meet a big man. He was horrible. He stuck his thing in me. He made me...

Gillian, you don't need to explain any more. Can I say what I see when I look at you?

Oh dear. What will Charlie say?

Okay.

I see a brave little girl who will do anything for those she loves. I want to help you. Tell me what I can do for you.

Goodness. That was unexpected.

Lottie says that you're a policewoman and you can look after me. Not just me, there's Jemima and Floella too. You can look after us all.

Gillian. Can I ask you a question?

Okay.

When you look at me, what do you see?

A policewoman. You have a skirt and a tunic and you have shiny black shoes and black tights and a funny hat and you have a scarf with black and white squares.

That's because I am a policewoman and I'm going to keep you safe. This is all new to me but Lottie will help me and, together, we will keep you safe and you will never have to do horrible things again.

Okay. I like you, Charlie. You're nice.

That's a lovely thing to hear you say. I'm sorry that when I was a little girl, I wasn't as brave as you and ran away. I'm going to make up for that. You never need to worry about doing horrible things ever again.

Okay.

I'm going now, but I will see you again. It's been lovely meeting you, Gillian.

Wow. Charlie was brilliant. She made Gillian feel so comfortable and secure. I wish I could do that.

* * *

LOTTIE

Lottie, before we meet the others, tell me...

Charlie pauses – this is a difficult place to understand and find words for.

...what just happened? Sorry, not what happened but what was I seeing? If I was looking at myself, why was I seeing a ten-year-old girl who looks nothing like me. Doesn't even look like me when I was ten.

I, too, must choose my words carefully.

You were not seeing a real person. You were seeing an image that our mind presented to you. The best analogy I

can give is dreams but, in dreams, you have no control. Here, you have some control. You can communicate with your alters and you have learnt to do that without vocalising. But you have little control over how they appear.

You appear like me.

Yes. And in here, our inner world, you appear the same to me. The inner world, though, is made up of regions of our mind. Some of those regions have been blocked off from one another and we are now breaking down those barriers. The medical world call them amnesic barriers.

Isn't this what Doctor Slattery, what are the letters after his name? MRCPsych? Isn't this what he'd have done?

Trust Charlie to raise Doctor Slattery.

Yes, but he would not have taken you by the hand and led you through the maze which has become our mind. He would have given you a bulldozer.

I think I understand what you mean and that you need to reveal all this gradually. But I want you to understand that this situation we have, this inner world I think you call it, depends on trust. I'm past surprises. I'm past second guessing everything. I need to see it all. I need to understand it all. And, at the end of it, I need to trust you.

I both understand and agree. Let us visit Jemima.

* * *

LOTTIE
Interesting image Gillian had of you.

She described the sort of uniform a policewoman would have worn fifteen years ago. Maybe she saw one. Maybe she met one.

I am leading Charlie to Jemima's *dressing room.*

I had not thought of it like that. If we had met a police officer back then, around 2005, 2006, I doubt I would have missed it. Charlie, this is Jemima.

Hello, Jemima. I like your orange trainers.

It seems Jemima appears the same to Charlie as she does to me.

I like my trainers too.

Would you tell me how I look to you?

You look like Lottie.

Would you describe Lottie?

Tall.

What does she wear?

A grey jacket and skirt. She has high heels. Her hair is done up in a bun.

Does she always look like that?

This is what Charlie is so good at – asking question after question without being threatening. I have seen her do this so many times, though with different people and in somewhat different surroundings.

No. Sometimes she has her hair down.

What colour is her hair?

Brown. Same as yours.

What am I wearing?

Running gear.

Sums me up, I suppose.

Jemima is looking away. I will not interrupt Charlie but losing Jemima would be bad.

Are you upset with me?

Jemima looks back.

What for?

For running away and leaving you to face the horrible men.

No. That's what I do.

When was the last time?

The day before yesterday.

How does that...

Charlie has stopped. She was going to ask Jemima about how something that happened fifteen years ago could only seem like yesterday. Realisation of the enormity of what has happened to us is dawning on her.

The children have lost time in exactly the same way Charlie has. Whereas Charlie lost days, Gillian, Jemima and Floella have lost years.

Charlie has gathered herself.

...I'm sorry, Jemima. I've only recently learnt about all this. I find it quite confusing. Lottie's helped me. Will you help me too?

I suppose so.

That would be great. You rest now. We'll talk again. Soon.

* * *

CHARLIE

Floella, this is Charlie.

Why would I ever want to speak to you?

I haven't even said anything. Floella is brash and rude. Probably explains why Lottie left her to last. Not a problem. I've dealt with a lot of stroppy people.

Because you and I are the same person.

We are not the same.

You can be as bitchy as you want but it still doesn't alter the fact that you exist to protect me.

And what choice did I have?

None. Just like me.

Just like you? I told Lottie I'd kill you. She still brought you here. What does that tell you about her?

She won't get one up on me like that.

I once tried to kill Lottie.

I don't believe you.

I did, I tried to throw her off a tall building.

That's stupid. If you'd done that you'd have killed yourself. And you'd have killed all of us. You chickened out.

Lottie stopped me.

Typical Lottie. Saved her own skin.

Saved your skin too.

Floella's gone quiet. She looks like a ten-year-old girl dressed in pyjamas with a blanket wrapped around her shoulders. I'm getting used to this. It doesn't matter what she looks like. I'm not seeing her. I'm seeing an image of her that I've created for myself. It also doesn't matter what she thinks she looks like – or what she thinks I look like. In this weird inner world, experiences are whatever this compartmentalised brain of ours presents.

I tell you what, Floella, it's been good meeting you. But you don't want to help me. I get that. You're done with helping me. But things have changed. Now, I can help you. Call it, reciprocity.

What's that?

I'll tell you next time I come and see you. And I suggest,
young lady, you change your attitude. There was a time
when I would run away and leave you on the *spot*. Yeah,
you had to take some sh...

I must be careful – I'm talking to a ten year old.

...take some shocking stuff but, at that time in our life,
you were calling the shots.

I wasn't calling the shots. Lottie was calling the shots.

Yeah, and you got the *spot*. And you could have killed
me. Why didn't you?

Because of Sebastian.

I close my eyes. So much for the trust. Floella – I must
concentrate on her. I feel like I'm being mean with a ten
year old girl. I've got to get out of here.

Floella, we will talk again. When we do, you will listen.
I'll be back before you know it.

Lottie and I leave Floella. We surface. I'm in bed.
Wade's asleep. Should I wake him? Tell him what I've
discovered – well, what Lottie has shown me? No, I have
to think about all this. Wade can help me get my
thoughts in order but, to do that, I must have some
thoughts in the first place.

Lottie is hanging around on the *stage*. I'm not
surprised. She's probably wondering whether I noticed.
I'll let her know that I have.

Lottie, who the fuck's Sebastian?

* * *

LOTTIE

Charlie noticed. Not the sort of thing Charlie would miss.

In fact, is there anything Charlie misses?

Sebastian enforced my decisions.

So, when I ran away, you decided who would take the abuse and Sebastian ensured they did.

Correct.

How?

He can persuade. Basically, the children are more frightened of Sebastian than they are of the abuse.

In truth, I do not know.

I must meet Sebastian.

Follow me.

I lead Charlie down deep and deeper still. Past oil rigs and submarines. A shoal of fish becomes one big fish but clouds darken and wind ruffles a field of corn.

Charlie, what do you see?

Not much. I'm falling. Windows are flashing past. I feel I'm being watched.

You are being watched. What do you hear, Charlie?

I hear a voice. Booming. Echoing.

Meet Sebastian.

A field. Blue sky with clouds of people I think I know. Burning grass. Swirling smoke. I wonder what Sebastian has for Charlie.

Charlie floats on her back, arms out, eyes wide but she seems relaxed.

I may have resided here for years but I have never grown accustomed to it. These images and sensations are created for me by my mind, but a part of my mind that is not me. This is Sebastian's domain. No wonder he can scare the children.

We are in a plane. No, not a plane – no engines, no sound – a glider. I can see out along the wings. In the seat in front of me is Charlie. To Charlie's left is Sebastian in his tweed suit, white silk scarf and hat. It pleases me that Charlie is meeting this changing, incomprehensible world the children face.

Sebastian turns to speak.

As a singleton, these imaginations you are experiencing would make sense as they would be your imaginations. As a multiple, you must become accustomed to shared imaginations. There are no barriers down here. Go now. There is nothing here for you but confusion. You are in a living dream.

I take Charlie and leave. The glider spirals away, upwards. Heading up to the *spot*, we both stop on the *stage*. Wade is sleeping. I can feel the warmth and comfort of the bed and I know Charlie can feel it too. She has a lot to digest. I leave her to it.

CHAPTER SEVEN

LOTTIE

We have gathered at Zachery's apartment. Eileen is taking charge, Ush is feigning interest, Robert is being the great ameliorator and Zachery is being the perfect host. All I want is that they come to the right conclusions.

The odd ones out are Wade and Charlie. Wade is standing to one side, tapping his mobile phone, or telephone as he calls it. Although he seems aloof, I know he is alert to and picking up on every word, every nuance. Charlie is on the *stage*. She has been very quiet since I introduced her to our inner world. She woke up with Wade that Saturday morning and, although Wade tried to engage with her, she did not utter a single word.

I spoke with Charlie and she agreed I should bring Wade up to speed.

He, too, has been very quiet.

Wade went to work on Monday and Charlie insisted on visiting the children again. I was against the idea but Charlie, as is her wont, proved me wrong. They loved it. I think they loved the attention. The biggest change has been Floella's attitude. Incredible – I have never known her be so polite. Sebastian too, coming forward with helpful explanations.

Charlie suggested they come up and take the *stage* occasionally to experience the outside world. Floella was keen. Jemima was suspicious but wanted to try it. Gillian was scared and would only come up if Jemima and Floella came with her.

Sebastian said no. The children do what Sebastian says.

"Lottie, are you okay with that?"

That was Eileen. I have no clue what they were talking about. "Sorry. I drifted."

I thought Charlie was distracted but she is actually pushing – wow – she has barged me off the *spot*.

"Don't worry, I was paying attention. And no, I'm not okay with that. There must be more of a difference. The Daventry and Pope killings were so similar we now have two experienced detectives breathing down our necks. The Amos killing has not been linked to those but we are only one tiny piece of evidence away from a murder charge that'll stick."

"So you're going to say we should stop." Ush is scornful. "How do you think Rob feels about that? And what about Lottie? This isn't just about you."

"Ush, that's not fair..." Rob tries to reduce the tension that Ush has introduced but Charlie talks over him.

"It's alright, Rob. Ursula, I'll answer you but my answer is not just for you. It's for everyone. Over the past few days, Lottie has introduced me to our inner world. There's more than just Lottie and me – a lot more. In here," Charlie taps the side of our head, "is a team geared up and ready to take the abuse. Between us are barriers so we don't know or don't really know what's happening. I think these barriers are the walls of our *dressing rooms* – we've all got one but I don't really understand. Lottie's shown me how to jump these barriers but there are so many unanswered questions. For example, of the five of us, why was I the only one to develop this defence… this DID? And then it came to me. Average. Eileen used the word *average*. Back at Ursula's when you were all first telling me about the abuse. Remember? She used the word *average*. She said, 'We were visited, on average, once a month.' Average. Think about it."

Charlie has stopped – not because she has nothing more to say. She has stopped for effect. I can see the others are uncomfortable. I am uncomfortable.

Wait. Charlie has stood up.

"I've always thought of Lottie as a different person. An alien who's gate-crashed my body. But she's not. She's me. And I'm her. And the same goes for the others. Three small girls – their names are Gillian, Jemima and Floella. Maybe, one day, you'll meet them. But I've decided. I'm in. All the way in. It may be Frederick Traube, it may not, but we will find the paedophile filmed abusing Rob and, when we do, Rob will kill him. We will find the paedophile filmed abusing me and, when we do, Lottie will kill him. We will find Travis Hendry, our infamous warden and, when we do, I will kill him."

Oh my. I was not expecting this. And she has not finished.

"I will do all I can to keep those detectives off our backs. I'm by far the most qualified person here to do just that. We will never repeat an MO or any aspect of an MO. Every killing will be unique and fit the crime patterns at the time and the place. Now the identification process. So far it's been Zach and Eileen. Ursula, you may think you're well placed in the Benefits Agency and, Rob, the Serious Fraud Office. My gut feel is that these positions you hold will offer little help but introduce considerable risk. You leave all checks and searches to Eileen and Wade who have more wriggle-room where they work. You must start helping Zach trawl social media. Lottie wanted us to get into the NCA. It didn't work out. And remember, every single check is recorded. Any murder investigation will follow up all searches and checks that have been made on the victim. None of you do a check or a search without discussing it with Eileen and Wade first. To keep ourselves out of prison, we must minimise forensics, both physical and digital. We've done a lot to avoid leaving trails but there's more, much more, we can do."

I have never heard Charlie speak for so long. Wait. She has not finished.

"And always remember, the biggest risk is that we are more than one. Eileen, are you with me on this?"

It is a little while before Eileen speaks. "Yes. Makes perfect sense. It's the sort of discipline we need."

"Wade. Are you with me on this?"

Wade has put his mobile away. "I am." No hesitation but he is as surprised as I am – as we all are. Not just what Charlie said but the feeling behind it.

"Zach?"

"With you, Charlie."

"Rob?"

"Makes sense. You can count on me."

"Ursula?"

Ush is looking down at her feet. Then she stands, places her arms around Charlie's neck and pulls her into the tightest hug. Charlie hugs her back. Ush holds Charlie away and says, "Would you do me a favour, Charlie?"

"Depends," Charlie says.

"I hated my name. You came up with the name Ush. I loved that. Then, when I started calling you Lottie, you reverted to calling me Ursula. We all understand what was going on now. I would so like you to go back to calling me Ush."

"Of course I will."

"It's good to have you back, Charlie."

"It's good to be back, Ush."

* * *

CHARLIE

I've never taken the lead like that. I've always let others like Brady and Cantrell, even Lavender and Kathy, and sniped from the edges. No more. I'm in this for Gillian, Jemima and Floella. I don't know about Sebastian – I don't understand him. I think, most of all, I'm in it for Lottie. I can't imagine what it was like for her, first of all taking the abuse and then having to send the children out there. And Sebastian. He doesn't seem like a real person – like an identity. What was it like for him? What must it have been like enforcing Lottie's selection –

scaring the children so much they would rather face the abuser than say no?

Up until now, I didn't have justification. I had the law and the law says murder is wrong. But these paedophiles have made me a killer. How many others are in a similar position as me? Silently suffering. Scared to come forward. Paedophiles have made me what I am. They can reap the consequences.

Lottie, are you with me on this?

One hundred per cent.

The gang are looking at me. Eileen sitting backwards on a dining chair and resting her chin on her hands. Rob on the sofa next to Zach – they are so alike. Ush has sat back in the armchair, her legs out straight. Wade pulls up another dining room chair, places it next to Eileen and sits – the right way – legs crossed. They are waiting.

"We need to establish rules. Rules for all of us – no exceptions. We need rules about where we meet and how we communicate. Rules about how to use social media and organisational systems and databases. Rules on the setting of alibis."

"What's wrong with our alibi system?" Ush's question is genuine.

Eileen answers for me. "Too precarious. Do you remember the Xavier Viceroy debacle? We made it impossible for Charlie to lay a valid alibi for me. Making her cycle from Ilford to Harrow in less than two hours in the early evening was simply foolhardy. I know we were testing Charlie at that time and we'd compensated, but it was still a stupid thing to do." She extracts a notepad and pencil from a pocket and starts scribbling.

"Thank you, Eileen." Don't need to harp on about that. "We need rules about the approach."

"What's wrong with our approach." Rob's question is answered by Ush.

"What Charlie's saying is that every approach must be different."

"Exactly. But another aspect is that a thumbs-down reaction to the abuse video must be followed up with and corroborated by questioning."

"But we don't have time for that." Zach is wide eyed with disbelief.

Ush answers for me. "We must adjust our approach and make time."

Rob comes in too. "Charlie asked Frank Amos some questions and his responses were just... I don't know... they were..."

"They left no doubt." Eileen has come to Rob's rescue. "I absolutely agree with Charlie. Every approach must be different and every approach must allow for subsequent verification to a thumbs-down."

"The last one I'll mention now is that the method must fit with the current crime patterns. Wade, you're probably best placed to analyse the intel to get that."

Wade nods.

Zach speaks. "Isn't this all getting a bit complicated?"

"I know where you're coming from, Zach. We say it all the time at work, 'If it ain't simple, it won't work.' But there's too much at stake here to take shortcuts. What I'm seeking to do is encourage the resulting murder investigation to place most of its resources on an investigative avenue that turns out to be a blind alley."

"Brilliant." Zach slaps his knees. "I hadn't thought of it like that at all. There's so much finesse going on here, I love it."

"Stop there." I must put an end to Zach's exuberance – this isn't a game. "Zach, in fact, all of you, we'll take every precaution. We'll try and pre-empt any investigation. But be absolutely aware, this is high risk. We are likely to get caught. We are likely to end up in prison. My thoughts on that are that I'm looking forward to the trial. I'm looking forward to seeing how the media and press handle it. I'm looking forward to seeing how the public respond. I don't want to be in that position, but I do think it's a strong possibility. In fact, a probability. I think we're all too far in for any of us to back out. That reminds me. Another rule we must discuss is how we act and what we say if we're arrested."

"Say nothing." Rob said that.

"Sometimes saying nothing is not a good idea. Sure, it's for them to prove the case, but a no-comment interview just gets the detectives' backs up, resulting in them putting more resource into your avenue of investigation. What we want to be doing is encouraging them to select a different investigative avenue. For every approach, we must all be clear on what we will say and what we will do if we're arrested. Again, it's something we must discuss."

"Seems we have quite a lot to discuss." Eileen's waving her notepad. "Meetings and communication, social media and organisational systems, alibis, vary approach MO, corroborative questioning for a thumbs-down, crime patterns and, last but not least, responses when nicked."

Wade starts laughing. "I'm looking forward to that *responses when nicked*. It will be mostly around interview techniques but, rather than asking awkward questions, we'll be focussing on answering awkward questions."

He's right and I'm pleased Wade's lightened the mood.

Can I come in?

"Lottie wants to say something. Hang on."

We switch.

"This is really quite humbling. We have done seven approaches resulting in three thumbs-down and we have not been thinking about half of this. I am so glad Charlie is on board. For Frank Amos, she was a reluctant participant. She was involving herself because she was unsure about me. Let me explain about the *average* Charlie mentioned earlier. For two years, the four of you were abused, on average, once a month. Charlie was abused, on average, once a night. Why Charlie was singled out for that kind of treatment is debatable. Maybe it was the fact that she was tall for an eight-year-old – a little more physically mature – and the paedophiles asked for her. Maybe she really pissed Travis Hendry off. Remember, Charlie *is* an alter. Let us call the original, Charlotte. Charlie formed to take the sustained physical abuse Travis Hendry meted out. Again, why was Charlotte picked on to such an extent that this defence mechanism – this DID – kicked in. This explains why Charlie knows nothing about the sexual abuse because, when things started escalating, I formed. Then, when it got too much for me, Floella formed, quickly followed by Jemima and Gillian. What caused the dissociation is the prolonged, sustained, continuous, unrelenting nature of the abuse. And..."

Lottie. Stop. Far from explaining things to them, you're upsetting them. Allow me.

"...sorry. I have no wish to upset you. Charlie wants to say something."

We switch.

"Gillian calls it *being made to do horrible things*. We've all been there. We've all developed our own responses to it. I learnt about my response following the tanker incident. A few days ago, Lottie showed me the full extent of that response. Now you know about us, we are a team. There must be no more looking sideways at one another. We need to sharpen our act. We're developing a plan for that. We will find and deal with Rob's abuser. If it turns out to be Frederick Taube, result. We will find and deal with my abuser – the one in the video clip we have. But, right now, I want to jump ahead – jump ahead to Travis Hendry. Before we can tackle him we must secure all the videos he took of us being abused. If Travis Hendry's abuse videos surface, then we're horribly exposed. And if Travis Hendry is a murder victim, those videos will surface. I have no idea how to secure those videos. But I think Wade is probably our best bet. We'll get onto that. The thing to remember is that there is no rush. We decide the pace.

"So, let's start. Meetings and communications."

* * *

CHARLIE

At 8pm, I had to leave because I'm on Night Duty, but we'd tackled the subject of meetings and communications. We agreed we would stop meeting in each other's flats – the risk of neighbours noticing was a needless risk to entertain. We'd communicate via burners. I explained how the mobiles were to be used, voice messages, text messages, codes and cyphers, destruction of SIMs and destruction of the mobiles themselves. As far as I could tell, everybody got it. We'd have to set a budget aside for procuring the phones and SIMs but they got the importance of it and how, if we didn't stick to our rules, those phones and SIMs could be damaging for us.

I added to that discussion and talked about anti-surveillance. The equipment we'd need to check that our flats and cars hadn't been penetrated and compromised with covert listening devices and cameras.

"Sweeping?" Ush asked.

"Let's not get technical," Eileen said.

Again, more money.

Wade spoke for a long time on how to use phones, computers and other devices to limit the digital trail. He even got Zach's computer up and running and showed what Ush had been looking at that day.

It was then that I had to leave for work but I was confident they were all starting to realise just how vulnerable they are. Wade was showing them how to limit their exposure to hackers – particularly hackers of the law-enforcement kind.

I was afraid that, on hearing all this, they would get a massive dose of the seconds, but far from it. They wanted to learn. They wanted to know. The team spirit was building and I could feel it.

My mind started drifting to Travis Hendry's abuse videos. If we get our hands on those, what would we do with them?

Would we stop?

Would we want to stop?

CHAPTER EIGHT

LOTTIE

Charlie has said she needs a rest before Night Duty and has disappeared to her *dressing room*. Fair enough, but I hate cycling. Rather than do right turns, I walk the bike across the road. Thank goodness it is still light and the weather is not adverse.

The change in Charlie has surprised me. I knew introducing Charlie to our inner world would give her something to think about but I was not expecting that degree of change.

Just look at how she took charge. When it was me, I was having to persuade, cajole, convince the gang to come along with me and I remember it being an uphill struggle all the way. Charlie had them eating out of her hand. That is leadership. If she had the confidence, she would easily make senior rank. Actually, this is not a confidence thing. She simply does not want to be senior. She enjoys deploying her confidence when tackling criminals – or scrote-bags as she calls them – and the more senior she gets, the more divorced from the... scrote-bags... she would become.

I close my locker, knowing I have forgotten something, when Katherine enters. She walks past me and opens her locker.

I must remember to talk like Charlie. "Hi, Kathy."

Being in half-blues means changing for her takes less than a minute. She slams her locker and says, "See you upstairs," as she leaves the locker room.

Charlie emerges onto the *stage* as I head upstairs.

Katherine is not talking.

I picked up the mood down in my dressing room.

Is this really something to worry about?

Charlie takes the *spot.*

Where's my ASP?

Sorry.

I do not know what ASP stands for but I know she means that telescopic baton she carries.

We head back to the locker room.

Charlie, would it be okay if I stay on the *stage*?

So long as you don't keep badgering me with silly questions.

Ummm. Perhaps now is not the best time to ask Charlie what ASP stands for.

Mary Cantrell starts parade but, within a minute, an urgent call comes over the radio and we are running. A disturbance at a pub. That guy Iffy Ibbotson has been posted as Charlie's operator. Is his first name really Iffy? Goodness, those sirens are loud.

"Have we got any info or intel on this pub?" Charlie talks so calmly as she slides the car sideways out onto the main road.

"If you give me a second, I'll tell you." That was Iffy.

"Front entrance or back." That was Charlie.

"If you drop me off at the front and you go round the back we can meet in the middle."

Those lights are red. Oh no, I cannot shut my eyes. Too scary. *Dressing room* for me. Oh no, wait a second. We are stopping. Iffy gets out and Charlie screeches into the carpark.

We stop, out, running. People are gathered around the garden entrance, all craning to see in. There are crashes and bangs coming from inside the pub. Charlie barges through them while shouting, "Make way. Stand aside." Through the doors, past the toilets, into the bar and o h m y g o o d n e s s.

The first thing I see is a man lying on the floor with blood running from a gash on his head. He seems unconscious. Then a chair flies past and crashes into the fruit machine, knocking it over with a frightful smashing sound. A man in a red shirt jumps on the back of another man in a white shirt and they fall over disappearing behind an upturned table. A large man has three smaller men brandishing chair legs at him but he has a whole chair and is swinging it around himself – like a lion tamer at the circus. I then see Iffy by the main entrance. He is talking into his radio. Of course, I concentrate on Charlie's radio and can hear what Iffy is saying. *"Mike-Sierra, Mike-Sierra from Mike-Three, on scene at the Sleeping Lion, fight in progress, more than ten involved, we need urgent assistance. LAS required. There are…"*

I hear nothing more as two men, who were fighting each other, register Charlie's presence and gang up on her – on me. Oh. The language. So rude.

Charlie pulls out her ASP, swipes it open and holds it up. "Get back," she yells. They come on anyway. Charlie steps towards the nearer one and swings the ASP, making contact with his upper arm. Oh. That must have hurt. But the other guy is on Charlie now. He is too close, she cannot swing her ASP. She jabs him in the face with the handle. And again. Oh. Oh. His nose crunched. Oh. Oh no. So much blood.

Charlie steps back, making space for herself. Others have turned on her. Iffy has appeared by Charlie's side. How did he get over here? Charlie and Iffy stand back to back. The men who were all fighting each other are now all on the same side. Both Iffy and Charlie have their ASPs out but this is not looking good. Where is all that hatred coming from?

I hear a loud bang and then Katherine's voice. "Right you lot. Pack it in."

The aggression fades, but only a little. Katherine's voice is firm and clear. "Drop that glass. Put that chair down. You. Stand still."

The men do as told and stand, looking around themselves. I realise that there must now be more than a dozen police officers in the pub.

Katherine comes over. "Charlie. Iffy. You okay?"

Charlie says, "I'm good."

Iffy says, "If we don't go into detail, I'm fine."

Katherine turns to the group of men. The fight has drained out of them. "Right. Outside the front doors are some police vans. Outside the back doors is the way home." She walks up to the man nearest her, pokes him in the chest and points towards the back doors. "Right. You. Fuck off." She pokes the next guy in the chest. "You. Van." The next guy. "You. Van." The next guy. "You. Fuck off." The next guy. "You. Van." The next guy.

"You. Fuck off." The next guy. "You. Fuck off." The next guy. "You. Van."

This last guy, rather than obediently walking towards the front doors like the others, stops. "What you nicking me for?"

Katherine turns to him. "I beg your pardon?"

"What you nicking me for?"

"Okay then," Katherine says, "let's make this multiple choice. You're being arrested for… a – threatening behaviour, b – affray, c – violent disorder or, d – riot. Now, while you're thinking about that, get in the fucking van."

Paramedics have arrived but no one seems to want their ministrations. Their priority is the man with the head wound.

Sergeant Cantrell is talking to another sergeant I do not recognise. He has LD on his shoulders. Oh, of course. He would be Sergeant Cantrell's equivalent from Brixton. She stops her conversation as Katherine walks past her and puts a hand on Katherine's arm. "Nice work, Kathy," she says.

"Someone had to take charge."

Did Katherine really say that to Sergeant Cantrell?

Sergeant Cantrell holds onto Katherine's arm and makes her stop. "Kathy." Ooooh. She is not happy. "I have my work cut out making what you've just done legal." More than not happy. Angry. "You're going to tell each of those people you've arrested who you are, what station you're from, what offence you have arrested them for, caution them and make a note of their replies.

So, get in the fucking van." Not angry. Furious. I have never heard Sergeant Cantrell swear.

Charlie puts an arm round Katherine's shoulders and says, "Come on, we'll do it together," and guides her away from Sergeant Cantrell.

Charlie. What happened to the bloke whose nose you flattened?

I arrested him, properly, and he's being taken to A&E at KCH. Iffy's going with him.

Why Iffy? Why not you?

He's male. I'm female. It's just easier if Iffy escorts him.

Kathy has finished arresting her four prisoners – properly. Sergeant Cantrell is in the pub talking to the landlord. There are several police vehicles abandoned at odd angles on the road outside the pub, many of their blue lights still flashing.

It will take Charlie the rest of the night to sort this lot out.

Tell you what, Charlie. Leave you to it. I will check on the children.

***Dressing room* patrol?**

Yes, Charlie. That was quite frightening. The children will have picked up on it. I will tell them what happened and reassure them.

Okay, chat later.

The children have gathered together. Even Sebastian has made an appearance. Gillian is crying. Jemima is trying to comfort her. Floella wants to know what happened.

I tell them.

There was a fight and Charlie had to sort it out. It was a bit scary for a few minutes but lots of help arrived and everything was okay.

Can I see what's going on?

Floella is curious.

No.

Sebastian's voice resonates harshly around the blood-red walls.

I must talk with him. But later. Now, I must deal with the children.

Floella. We think it would be a good idea for you all to come and start experiencing what we deal with day to day. But let us take it slowly. I will discuss it with Charlie and Sebastian and we will figure out a plan.

Gillian is calming down.

I leave them and find Sebastian.

Why are you against this?

I don't want the children facing uncertainty.

Strange thing for one who made them so scared they would face a paedophile to appease you.

That was their raison d'être. This is something new. The world that Charlie inhabits is too uncertain. It seems that even Charlie is having difficulty with the uncertainty. You've been with her when she's frozen.

I have but she seems to be managing it. I think the trigger is vehicle accidents, for obvious reasons. The last couple have not made her freeze up.

Even without that, can it be controlled?

The uncertainty increases when Charlie is on duty. It cannot be controlled absolutely but when she is off duty, things are more predictable.

If Charlie is happy with this then I agree.
Charlie suggested it.
We will talk.

Sebastian folds in on himself and I am left in bright blackness and thinking about how things could have turned very nasty back in that pub.

* * *

CHARLIE

"If you lose this guy, I will make life hell for you."

I've given one of the probationers, who wasn't involved at the Sleeping Lion, a lift down to the hospital so he can relieve Iffy who's standing guard on my prisoner with the busted nose. This probationer's quite sharp – Iffy's threat isn't necessary.

Driving back to the Nick, Iffy says, "If you pull over, I'll tell you what I found on this guy."

"Just tell me."

"If you don't pull over, you'll wish you had."

"Oh, for god's sake." I stop. The car behind has to manoeuvre past. He doesn't toot his horn. I turn to Iffy. "What?"

Iffy hands me a property bag.

I recognise what's in it immediately. "Oh my god."

"If he'd got that out we'd now be dealing with something very different."

"The fact you found it on him means we are dealing with something very different. Does it work?"

"One of the best I've seen."

"So I was grappling with a man armed with a flick-knife." This has shaken him up as much as it's shaken me. I get the car going and say, "On the way down to the hospital to pick you up, I was resigned to spending the rest of the night with you and Kathy dealing with four pissed up scrote-bags. On the way back to the Nick, I've found we can hand it over to the CID who will spend the rest of the night dealing with four pissed up scrote-bags, one of whom forgot he had a flick-knife in his pocket. An offensive weapon *per se*. Fancy that. We'll get our notes done and then we'll be back out."

"If the detectives don't say, 'Pub fight, no serious injuries, job for the lids, now fuck off back downstairs and get on with it,' I'd be surprised."

"You don't know Sergeant Cantrell. We'll do our notes and we'll be back out."

CHAPTER NINE

CHARLIE

Up at Borough Market there are pubs licenced to open early morning for the market workers. Sounds weird. So weird that Kathy and I are sat in Samantha's Café with mugs of coffee.

It's been a hectic night. Even after the pub fight, things didn't really let up. Strange for a Wednesday night. I've still got that guy with the flick-knife on my mind. Could things have turned out differently? Definitely. Could I have done anything different? Not really. I push away images of myself in hospital with stab wounds.

One good thing – I've dealt with some vehicle incidents recently and my reaction to them is calmer. Must be a good thing but when I'm assigned to those types of call, I'm filled with dread.

Come on, enough of this. I'm with Kathy and there seems to be a truce drawn up between us. What I mustn't do is push.

Kathy's not in the mood for talking.

I'm finding the silence between us unbearable. I can't imagine what has happened to cause this and I decide to move this impasse along. "I enjoyed meeting Michael last week."

"He enjoyed meeting you. Said you're looking good considering your ordeal with the tanker incident."

She's brought that up. I mustn't bite.

"You going to ditch him or no?"

"I like him. We get on well together. I think, if I'm honest, I don't know what I want. I enjoy being with him but then there are times when I wish he'd bugger off. I don't know, Charlie. Will there ever be a time when I settle down?"

"Only you can tell that."

"You're right. And, Charlie, I've been a bitch recently. And not just to you. To everyone. I don't know why, but I can't help myself."

True – she's been a bitch recently. True – not just to me. She doesn't know why? False. She knows why. She's not saying.

I'm beginning to wish I'd not encouraged her to come for a coffee. I'm dog tired. Yet, here I am, drinking Samantha's coffee and listening to Kathy being disingenuous.

On top of that, I'm having to take on a paradigm shift. It's not just Lottie. There's Gillian, Jemima and Floella and some kind of ghoulish beast called Sebastian.

I'm in no fit state to start quizzing Kathy on what's really upsetting her. I'll get impatient, then I'll lose my temper and I'll be no further forward in figuring out what's up with Kathy. Time to end this. "I'm falling asleep."

"Me too. Oh, Charlie, did you hear what happened to the four guys we nicked at the Sleeping Lion? The landlord doesn't want to know."

"What's it got to do with the landlord? There are substantive offences."

"CID will interview them this morning. We'll find out later, I suppose."

"So Cantrell did get the CID to take it." I knew she would.

"They weren't happy. What do you reckon, threatening behaviour or affray?"

"Whatever. I'm heading home, Kathy."

"Me too. And Charlie…"

I wonder what Kathy's going to say.

"…thanks for supporting me last night. Sargie was really pissed off with me."

Oh. Just that. "Well, I can't say you didn't deserve it. Fucking funny though."

We slap hands in a high five and I refuse Kathy's offer of a lift home.

* * *

CHARLIE
Running home, Lottie comes out on *stage*.

I run faster – I know she hates it.

Any further forward with Katherine?

No. Though I suppose I can say that whatever is wrong is to do with us.

What has she said?

Nothing significant, but she's not being honest with me.

How do you know?

I know when my best mate is lying to me.

Lottie's hanging around. She's never done this before. Dealing with Kathy being stroppy is quite enough. I put on a spurt and halfway up Camberwell Grove, Lottie buggers off.

Wade's already left by the time I get indoors.

I shower and tumble into bed. It won't be long before I'm fast asleep but, as I snuggle down under the duvet, I feel Lottie in the *wings*.

What's the problem?

She comes forward to the *stage*.

I spoke with the children last night. Reaffirmed your suggestion about the children getting real-world experience. Sebastian is against, but willing to talk it through.

Can't this wait till this afternoon?

I just wanted to be able to tell Sebastian that you are comfortable with talking about it.

Tell him I'm happy to talk about it. Good night.

* * *

CHARLIE

I wake up to movement, excitement and Lottie on the *stage*. I'm on a swing. This is the playground on Camberwell Green.

What's going on?

I spoke with Sebastian. He keeled over. So long as the children are supervised, they can take the *spot*. In fact, he even encouraged them.

Lottie is chuffed with herself.

That's great. And the first thing they wanted to do is come to a playground?

While you have been asleep, they have been taking turns on the *spot*. You will not believe this. They did housework. Then they played on your computer. It being a lovely day, Floella persuaded them to come outside. Well, it is a lovely day. Floella does not want to be in the playground but she is happy that Jemima and Gillian are loving it. Jemima likes the roundabout.

Not only chuffed with herself – Lottie's enjoying this.

We're attracting a lot of attention. I take it we're well disguised?

Gillian is having the time of her life and, yes, I made sure we have a good disguise.

I don't know that the other kids think it's fair having a fully grown woman monopolising one of the swings.

Lucky we have such slim hips.

What are you saying?

Nothing.

* * *

CHARLIE

Wade's home by the time we get back to the flat.

"Help me out," says Wade. "What's your name."

"Guess."

"I'd say you're Jemima."

"No."

"Gillian?"

"No." Wade's taking this in his stride.

"You must be Floella."

"How do you know I'm not Charlie?"

"Charlie doesn't giggle that much."

"You're no fun."

"You've obviously had a wonderful day but I'm afraid I have to be the spoilsport. I need to speak with Charlie."

"Oh, not fair."

I take the *spot* as Lottie ushers the children away through the *wings*. "Hi, Wade. This another…"

"It's about Kathy."

He has my full attention. What on earth can he want to be saying about her? "I chatted with her this morning. She opened up a little but she's still being cagey."

"You remember when Inspector Brady asked you to keep an eye out for Kathy. He was directing his comments at me as much as you."

"I remember the guv'nor talking to us – well, Lottie actually."

"I've been invading Kathy's privacy, so to speak."

"What do you mean?"

"I've been looking at what she's been googling."

"In your SO15 capacity?"

Wade waves his hand. "No. In my own capacity."

"Have you left a trail."

"You can't do anything digitally without leaving a trail. The trail I've left… misdirects."

I believe him. I discovered, quite by accident, how he hacked into the security systems at the Elephant & Castle to get CCTV footage. "What have you found out about Kathy?"

"She's researching DID."

CHAPTER TEN

CHARLIE

I'm back on the car. My operator tonight is one of the probationers. Can't remember his name. I like him. The main reason I like him is because he doesn't talk much. I've enough to be thinking about.

When Wade told me what he'd discovered about Kathy, I was stunned. There was silence between us for minutes. Lottie noticed and came back up for a look. Wade explained to her. She was as quiet as me. Neither of us wanted the *spot*.

"What does it mean?" Lottie finally ventured.

Wade and I said nothing. Not because we didn't want to say anything but because we didn't have anything to say.

The Lavender approach is perfect for this circumstance. My probationer deals with the police work and I do the driving. He's good, knows what he's doing, could do with more experience but he's picking things up fast.

He shows massive restraint. It's not until after midnight that he asks. "Charlie. What's wrong? You haven't said a word all night."

"Fair dos. I've got stuff on my mind. I'll snap out of it."

"I was asking about what the CID did with those blokes who were nicked in the Sleeping Lion last night."

"The CID? A pub fight? The CID do not deal with pub fights. They might cause a few but they don't deal with them."

"But I thought…"

"Yes. Cantrell dumped it on the Night Duty CID but when the Early Turn came in, they soon ditched it back to the uniform. They were charged with threatening behaviour – a section four / section five combination."

"Threatening behaviour?"

"The landlord didn't want to know so no criminal damage. The guy who was clouted on the head was okay and didn't want to know."

"What about the flick-knife?"

"He was charged with off weap, pointed article, bladed instrument. Can't remember. Whatever."

"Offensive weapon? He could have killed someone."

"But he didn't." Jonesy has a lot to learn.

"What about the bloke whose nose you splatted?"

"I haven't been charged with assault."

"But what's happened to him?"

"Charged with threatening behaviour."

"I don't believe this."

"Welcome to Walworth." I decide he deserves an explanation. "It was a good night out for the local lads. Meet up. Few beers. Chat up a few of the local girls. Those that succeed bugger off. Those that don't, start a fight. Smash up a load of stuff. Have a ruck with ol' bill. Get nicked. Spend a night in the pokey. Charged. Court date set. Loads to brag about to their mates when they next meet up." I think I'm enjoying his reaction a little too much. "Anyway, that was all last night. What shall we do tonight?"

"Is there any point?"

"Oi. Snap out of it."

He sighs. "Bit of vehicle theft?"

"You want Iffy for that. Latch onto him and you'll learn all about vehicle theft and, as he calls them, the Dodgy Motor Boys."

"Sounds like a band."

"Anyway look, it's Thursday – well, Friday now. What happens Thursday?"

He shakes his head. He knows. He just hasn't cottoned on.

"Dole is paid on Thursdays."

He nods – a self-admonishment. "So all the locals will have money in their pockets."

"And what will they do with it?"

"Buy drugs."

"Who from?"

"Dealers."

"Shall we find ourselves a dealer?"

"In this car?"

Good question. "I'll show you."

I drive to a block of flats on the Aylesbury Estate and send him to the top having told him what to look for. I move away. He calls me a minute or two later and tells me what he can see. I tell him to return to the car. We move onto another block. He gets out.

Kathy comes in on the radio. She's stopped someone and wants the control room to do a check for her.

"Received," she says, on getting the result.

Why is she reading about DID? Not just reading but researching. According to Wade, she's been accessing more than the NHS pages and Doctor Google. She's been reading some serious medical journals. MedScape and Researchgate are a couple Wade mentioned. There are others, the names of which have escaped me. Add that to her dissing me that time outside Morrisons. Add that to her not being friendly – positively aggressive. On top of that, her lying to me. Something's wrong.

We were best mates. No, we are best mates. I need to find out what's bugging her and address it.

What could have sparked her off?

My operator, still can't remember his name, is calling me.

He has nothing. I tell him to return to the car.

We move on. Another block. He gets out.

Why is Kathy reading about DID? What's she seen? What's she heard? What's she been told? Is she doing this on her own or with others?

My operator… Jonesy. Derek Jones. That's his name. …is calling. Nothing. He re-joins me a few minutes later.

"We're not having much luck tonight." Jonesy's voice is soft but clear.

"Be patient. It'll come."

I'm pleased the dealers seem to be taking a night off – I could do with a quiet night. Only *seem to be.* They're out there. We just can't see them. A lot of luck is needed to catch a dealer when in uniform.

"Charlie. Tell me to shut up if you want but can I ask you about the tanker incident?"

"What do you want to know?"

"I've seen that YouTube clip. How did you manage to stay in that car? It must have been agony."

"It was agony."

"But you were in there for twenty-three seconds. What was it like?"

This isn't something I want to be talking about but I like Jonesy. He's not prying. A conversation I had with Lottie comes to mind. I was as curious as Jonesy and I remember what she said. I repeat it for Jonesy. "I must feel pain differently to others."

"I wouldn't have been able to stay in there for that long."

"You'd be surprised what you can do when the adrenalin gets going."

"But I…"

"Jonesy, enough." The memory of that night is more painful to me than the actual night itself.

"I'm sorry, Charlie. I didn't mean to upset you."

"You didn't upset me," and I change the subject. "What did you see when on top of those buildings?"

"Nothing. There was no one about. At one point, though, a couple came by. They seemed in a hurry but they stopped. I think they spoke to someone but I couldn't see who they were speaking to. Then they carried on."

"Oh, Jonesy. It's whoever they spoke to who's of interest."

"I've been wondering about that. How do you circulate the description of a suspect you haven't seen?"

He certainly asks the right questions. He'll go far.

"Difficult one. If I'd been in your position I'd have called in the Team. Gradually sealed off as many exit routes as possible. Then I'd have gone down and confronted him. If he was up to no good, he'd have had it on his toes but, with the Team around me, he'd have been easy to catch."

"What if there's no one there when you arrive?"

"Then you look like a right Charlie."

"I'd have been the laughingstock of the Team." He's right, of course.

"Hey. We've all been there. All I can say is, go with it. It's part and parcel of the job. Take the praise when you get it right. Take the ribbing when you get it wrong. Those who do nothing are unhappy and end up in trouble. Your confidence will grow provided you get stuck in. And try not to worry about getting it wrong. You'll gain respect for having a go."

Jonesy goes quiet. I do like him. He's nineteen. I think about what I was like at nineteen in the first year of my probation with people around me who I felt were ready to rip me apart. But Kathy took me under her wing. Lavender too, to a degree, and some of the others.

I drive us round to Thompson Avenue where Kathy checked out the Toyota a little while back – the one owned by a disqualified driver. "Right, Jonesy. That Toyota belongs to a disqual. How will you find out whether he's driving it?"

"Watch it."

"We don't have that kind of time."

While he's thinking about that, there's something I must think about. It's Kathy, but all this stuff I've just been talking about with Jonesy has put it in a different light. She has loads of confidence but is crap at the intuition thing – or hunch. What has happened to make her start researching DID? It's not a funny feeling because Kathy doesn't have those. So what has she seen? Or what has she heard? Whatever it is, it must have been pretty damned obvious.

* * *

CHARLIE

Wade's leaving for work as I get home. "Veritable ships," he says.

I kiss him and head inside – he's followed me.

"Is Lottie there?"

"Hang on. Yes she's there."

"Gang meeting. This evening. Brockwell Park near the paddling pool. Eighteen-hundred." Wade's being all dramatic.

I'm in no mood for playing along. "Purpose?"

"Approach MO for when we've located Frederick Traube. Also Travis Hendry's videos."

"What? Who? Wade, what do you know?"

"Eighteen-hundred. Brockwell Park near the lido. See you there." He leaves for the railway station.

I hate when he's like this.

Exciting though.

Lottie gives a non-vocalised chuckle. Maybe he and Eileen have made progress.

Who knows? I was ready for a shower and bed and now I'm hyper again.

Just go to your dressing room and relax.

I don't find that easy. Idleness is not me.

Charlie, I will not move until you are asleep.

I don't get how sleep works...

This is something I've been meaning to ask for ages. Now is as good a time as any.

...how can I be rested if you've been up and about. Particularly vice versa.

The brain must sleep. Something to do with a build-up of toxins. Sleep disperses them. We share the sleep so maybe it just seems we get less. When you are asleep, I will have a shower. There are things I want to do.

Lottie always has the answers but I still think she's bullshitting me.

Why won't the shower wake me up?

Maybe those barriers we were talking about.

Would Doctor Slattery know?

Doubt it.

Again, Doctor Slattery dismissed out of hand.

What will you be doing?

After what Wade told us about how to avoid leaving a digital trail, I have been researching. Wade and Eileen will have made better progress than me, but I hope to give them a run for their money.

What have you been researching?

Different MOs.

Well, good luck with that. I'm off to bed.

* * *

LOTTIE

I head for the library on Camberwell Green. I have no idea what needs doing – not even an idea of what I should be doing. I feel surplus to requirements. Is there anything I can contribute? I had a role to play – once – and that role is no longer needed. This is Charlie's world. I thought myself able to convince people black is white. How did I lose that National Crime Agency interview? I could speak to the children and, more often than not, convince them to step forward. Yes, I had Sebastian as a backstop but he was rarely called upon.

Then the gang. I put this project plan together and presented it to them. They were concerned. Murder can never be right. Besides, how would we ever find our abusers? It was the Travis Hendry videos I stole that won them over. Travis Hendry, our warden who facilitated access for a paedophile ring to the children under his care, took secret videos of the abuse. I can only imagine he would use them to protect himself should the paedophiles turn against him.

Yes, I stole five of them. They were brief videos of each of the children being abused by one of the paedophiles. Zachery, Ush, Eileen and Robert – sickening videos of each of them being abused. Nine-year-old Zachery – anal. Eight-year-old Ush – fellatio and… I cannot bear to think about it. And, of course – me.

My abuser and Robert's abuser have not been identified. Frederick Traube might be Robert's – still to be verified.

I was wrong in my approach. Charlie has augmented our identification and verification processes. The thing I overlooked is the MO. If I had been allowed to continue through to the end, the police would have had five identical murder scenes. How could I have missed that?

Charlie instigated a different approach for Frank Amos. Although the Daventry and Pope killings have been linked, the Amos one is still standalone.

So, changing the MO.

Daventry – stab wound under left armpit, paring knife removed from scene, near a children's playground in Primrose Hill, no obvious motive, Wednesday 30th December 2020, evening.

Pope – stab wound under left armpit, paring knife removed from scene, outside his home address, no obvious motive, Wednesday 13th January 2021, evening.

Amos – stab wound under left clavicle, victim's kitchen knife left at scene, home address, made to look like a burglary-disturbed, Friday 5th February 2021, evening.

I look at the computer, following Wade's instruction on how to avoid leaving digital trails. Maybe reading about some real crimes will inspire.

What Charlie did for the Amos killing was show an obvious motive. There was no obvious motive for the Daventry and Pope killings.

So we cannot repeat a burglary-disturbed. A robbery? A drunken brawl? A car crash? No. Wait. We have to be able to do the verification step of the identification process and now more has been added to that in the guise of questions and answers. Add to that the need to avoid leaving forensics. Where to start?

This really is Charlie's scene.

Come on. I can do this. Make it a robbery. It would have to be outdoors. A secluded place like Primrose Hill. Primrose Hill? Secluded? I cannot believe how lucky we were with Peter Daventry. Vincent Pope was better planned and therefore better controlled.

Lottie. It's gone three. How long have you been sitting here?

Charlie has come up.

Not long. I have just returned from the library.

What were you doing there?

Avoiding leaving a digital trail.

How's your research going?

Charlie is genuinely curious.

Not very well. I could not find a manual, governmental or otherwise, on how to commit a murder and not get caught.

Can't think why.

I read some true crime books but quickly came to the conclusion that the reason they have been recorded is because they were caught.

Follows.

Then I looked at some crime fiction.

That's all bollocks.

So I have been reduced to thinking about it in my own little head.

It's not your own little head. I'm in there too – somewhere.

It seems Charlie understands our fractured mind I have been showing her.

I have come to the conclusion that the motive is all important. So Amos was a burglary-disturbed. Maybe the

next could be a robbery. I even thought about luring the victim into somewhere he should not be and then it could be a burglary-disturbed but the other way around.

Lottie. How many crime fiction books did you read?

A few.

In a few hours?

I skim. They are very boring.

Lottie. Thank you for trying. But what's more important is that whatever crime results in our victim's death does not look out of place. That's why we need the crime trend information I mentioned. If the victim is in an area rife with burglaries, we'll make it a burglary gone wrong. If he's in an area where there's loads of drug dealing, we'll make it a drug deal gone wrong. If it's an area where there are loads of vehicle thefts, we'll make it a vehicle theft gone wrong.

You have just made me feel really silly.

Lottie. I don't mean to. You yourself said we have strengths and weaknesses. We must play to our strengths. Leave all the MO and physical forensics stuff to me. Leave all the digital forensics to Wade.

What do I do? I am beginning to feel like I should be put out to grass.

* * *

CHARLIE

I've never heard Lottie sounding so lost.

You have the most important role. You brought the gang together. Your role is to keep the gang together. Ush is contributing little. Eileen is getting distracted by her work. Zach is still on it but I can't imagine how mind-numbingly boring it is trawling social media. Rob is frustrated. There's been a reconciliation, of sorts, between Ush and me. Those close bonds were formed between them and you during the period of the abuse. Not me. You. On top of all the 'holding the gang together', you have your own feelings to deal with. The feelings you have about our abuser. I don't have those experiences. I don't have those feelings. You do. And the rest of the gang know you do.

I suppose.

Don't suppose. Your role is the most crucial. So please, don't go all weird on me.

Okay, Charlie.

And if you want to understand how crime works, crime fiction, I would suggest, is not the best genre. Crime fiction. Jeez. The clue's in the name.

CHAPTER ELEVEN

CHARLIE

Who suggested the paddling pool?

I got us down to Brockwell Park for five (I don't know where Lottie is) so the children could enjoy the playground and, on seeing the paddling pool, Jemima's banging on the *spot*. I move aside and watch myself remove my shoes and socks, roll up my trousers and splash around in the water while other people, both adults and children, watch – bemused. I'm pretty bemused myself. Is this really enjoyable? Jemima thinks so and that's what counts.

My disguise seems to be working.

Eileen arrives, kicks off her shoes and is soon splashing water over me. Jemima screams only to be confronted by Zach who also has his shoes and socks off. He guides Jemima round behind him and kicks water at Eileen. The others arrive.

Ush joins in. "Jemima?"

"Yes. Don't wet me."

Ush does the opposite and the six of us are chasing each other around the pool. Gillian and Floella have come up on stage and are enjoying the fun. Well, Gillian is. Floella's failing to maintain a sulk.

When we find a quiet spot and sit down for our meeting, we're all soaked.

Jemima, you'll find this really boring. Floella, Gillian, you too. Leave it to Lottie and me. When we've finished talking, we'll go on the swings.

They disappear through the *wings* as I take the *spot* and Lottie installs herself on the *stage*.

Charlie, we are soaking wet.

Full of surprises, me.

Wade starts by handing everyone a package. "Use it for sweeping – Ush's technical term for finding surveillance bugs. There are instructions inside. If you find anything, don't interfere with it. Get out and get in touch. We can try and determine who planted it, why it was planted and then consider feeding misinformation back. Right. Frederick Traube."

"Wait a minute." Eileen interrupts. "Where are these from?" She's opened hers and is examining the palm size black box with a detachable arial.

Wade's not surprised by the question. "Amazon."

"Can they be traced back to you?"

"No."

"So you have an untraceable Amazon account."

"Doesn't everyone?"

Eileen starts laughing. "And you, a police officer. Anyway, how much did they cost?"

"A few hundred quid each."

Eileen is flabbergasted. Looks of alarm from the others. "Wade. We can't afford that much."

"If I were to choose between getting into debt and going to prison, I'd probably take the debt option."

"Wade, that's not the point. We've spoken about a budget. We were thinking about a few cheap mobile phones."

"Eileen. Stop. Suffice it to say, I have a rich mummy and daddy."

"So now your parents are involved."

"Alright." Wade is annoyed. I know where this money has come from and I understand why he doesn't want to talk about it but, to satisfy the gang, he must. Wade has paused. He's thinking. He may be a while but I know that when he answers, he will close the conversation dead. "I was an inconvenience to mummy and daddy. To get me out from under their feet they sent me to boarding school. Eton. I have disowned them but I haven't disowned their feelings of guilt. The only conversations we have are brief and to the point. I say, 'Daddy, I need money.' He responds, 'How much?'"

The gang goes quiet.

"Right." Wade, having successfully put that to bed, moves on. "Frederick Traube. We're in luck. He lives in Kingston. He works in Wimbledon. Now for the bit you won't believe."

Wade's doing this drama thing again. I must have a word.

We wait.

"He's a police officer."

We wait a bit longer. Maybe he'll say something else. He doesn't.

Rob, sitting cross-legged, starts shaking.

I move towards him but Ush is already there, her arms around his shoulders, whispering into his ear.

I'm trying to work out the implications of what Wade's just said but I can't. My mind's a blank. A police officer. What does it mean? I know what it means. But what does it mean for us?

"There's more."

Wade has more?

"He's a DCI."

"Detective Chief Inspector," I say for the benefit of the others, though I doubt they need to be told.

"I think we can safely say he doesn't know about that picture of him Zach found."

Eileen comes in. "The picture's a good likeness. Unreliable, I know, but it's a good likeness."

Rob's now resting his head in his hands.

Lottie. Take over. I can't get my head round this.

You think I can?

I need time to think. Take over.

We switch.

"Hey, guys. A DCI. So what. We can start working on the approach. With Charlie and Wade, we will be able to find out more about him than we have for any of our other targets. We will find a way."

"How will we get close to him?" Zach is as fraught as Rob.

"He may be easier to get close to because of his profession and rank."

"You're right Lottie." Wade speaks calmly. "It will be easier to get close to him, but the risk of showing out has increased significantly."

What Lottie and Wade have just said has snapped me out of my brain-freeze. I take the *spot* as Lottie, all too willingly, moves aside. "It's a question of whether we approach him when he's on duty or off duty. On duty will be difficult because DCIs tend to be office bound. Wade and I can engineer meetings with him but then, as Wade says, we show out. Approaching him when he's off duty isn't really any different to the others that have been approached except that, after showing him the video, gauging his reaction and maybe questioning him, if he gets a thumbs-up, he'll report it. He may well see through our disguises. He'll know exactly what to do and he'll do it fast. He could cause us a lot of trouble. Wade and I will chat. We'll work different scenarios and figure out the risk."

The gang are all looking despondent. I don't really know what to say to them. The last thing I want is to fill them with false hope.

Give them something to do.

I get what Lottie's saying but best it comes from her. We switch.

"Surveillance. We did some recently on Katherine's Michael. We must do more. We will get ourselves properly equipped with phones and SIMs. This guy will be…" She clicks her fingers.

Surveillance conscious.

"…surveillance conscious. So we must put in the performance of our lives. I remember Charlie talking about anti-surveillance. We need the detail… and that training starts right now. Charlie."

Jeez. We switch. "Okay. We'll start with comms."

* * *

CHARLIE

We finish before seven and the gang head off on their bikes.

Gillian has appeared and I allow her onto the *spot*. I'm soon swinging high, laughing and giggling.

Wade has sat on one of the benches with other adults. There's that bemused look again. A little boy is patiently waiting his turn. Children's swings. Lucky I'm skinny.

I coax Gillian off the swing and Floella takes a turn on the roundabout.

She's quickly bored and Wade and I prepare our bikes for the ride home. Not far but a steep hill.

As we enter my flat, Wade puts a finger to his lips, extracts his bug finder and moves around the flat, lights flashing. He goes to the consumer unit, cuts the power to the flat and goes round again. Lights flash but he doesn't seem concerned. Something to talk over with Lottie.

Lottie. As you, unlike me, will read the instructions, can I leave all this sweeping shit to you?

You do most of the housework so only fair I suppose.

Wade returns to the consumer unit, switches the power back on and goes round again holding the device up here and pointing it there. "No bugs in here."

It's half-eight. I have to leave for work in an hour. Wade and I have so much to talk about. Lottie's hanging around on the *stage*. She knows there's a heavy conversation in the offing and she doesn't want to miss out. Personally, I want her there.

"Are we being paranoid?" My question's superfluous but I ask it anyway – more for Lottie than me.

"It's only paranoia if you *think* someone's watching you. If you *know* they're watching you, these are sensible precautions." Wade knows why I asked.

"And we must assume that DS John French and DI Steve Reeve are watching us."

"The 'Charlie Quinlan' line of enquiry has taken a back seat and is therefore not being resourced. French and Reeve will have been assigned to other lines of enquiry or other investigations. So a bit belt and braces but, like I said, a sensible precaution."

"Look. It's Friday night. It'll be busy. I need rest. I'll leave you and Lottie to discuss all this. You're off tomorrow, yeah?"

"Yep. I'm now officially an ESSO man. You know, every Sat…"

I hold up my hand. "Wade, save your explanations for Lottie. We'll talk tomorrow."

* * *

CHARLIE

Friday Night Duty came and went. I was paired with Lavender. It wasn't busy but it had its moments. Jonesy got a good arrest. He'd gone to report a burglary near the top of Laird House, a neighbour of Kevan House. Good test of fitness as the lift was broken. On his way back down, he walked into a drug deal. Three blokes. Only two of them ran away as Jonesy had grabbed the third. As luck would have it, the one he'd grabbed turned out to be the dealer. The two punters not only got away, but also got their drugs for free. The dealer was philosophical. "Shit from you is better than shit from my supplier."

That sparked a Lavender story. "I nicked a friggin' dealer once. Searched him, stuck him in the van. Before I closed the back doors, a couple of punters came up asking if he had any gear. I couldn't friggin' believe it."

Nor could I.

I wasn't good company for Lavender. He didn't pry. Maybe he has issues of his own.

All I wanted to do was ask about Frederick Traube, search the directory for him, phone Wimbledon and ask for him. Uh uh. No way.

Attended three vehicle incidents. Dealt with one. No problem.

Wade's asleep when I get home Saturday morning. I slide under the duvet next to him. He's lovely and warm. I cuddle up. He screams and jumps out of bed. "Jesus Charlie!"

"I'm sorry."

He gets back in. "Come here. You're freezing."

"I'm sorry."

"Stop saying you're sorry."

"I'll try, but I do feel like I'm letting you down."

"You're not letting me down. You've given my life meaning. Been thinking about what you said to the gang about how the media might handle our arrest. Imagine saying to the cameras, 'I'm a police officer. When I'm on duty I do police work. When I'm off duty I kill paedophiles. You got a problem with that?'"

How can he go from being sound asleep to wide awake? My hands weren't that cold. It's summer for god's sake. "Everybody will have a problem with that. First, you're always a police officer whether you're on duty or off and second, there's a thing called statute."

"Ah. The rule of law. The thing is, it's open to interpretation and can change. We see it daily. What I'm seeing is that our rule of law falls short of dealing with these circumstances. They need to change. If I end up squatting in a ten-foot cell cogitating over how I contributed to a change in the rule of law that made it easier for circumstances like these to be effectively tried and tested in the courts, then I would feel I'd made a meaningful and worthwhile contribution."

"You could go to college. Study law. Become a lawyer."

"I could and I might."

"Why don't you? More up your street. You're wasted in the police. Leave policing to people like me."

"Had I done that, I wouldn't have escaped mummy and daddy, wouldn't have met you. And no, it's not that I feel sorry for you or that your condition intrigues me. It's the way you're dealing with your condition that I so admire. At least, the discovery of your condition. Like I say, I feel privileged to know you. I know you're having issues with intimacy. Who, in your position, wouldn't? I'm confident you'll resolve these issues and I'll help you if I can. I want you to know I'm here for you".

I cuddle into him, absorbing his warmth. "Wade, those are lovely words, but it could all go so terribly wrong."

"I really believe it's the only way for you. Killing the paedophiles who abused you will bring peace to your fellow alters. I think it's only with that peace that the barriers between you and your alters will be overcome."

"Killing? It goes against all reason that killing can bring peace. I've seen it though. Ush. Zach. Eileen. Not sure about Eileen. Will Gillian, Jemima and Floella feel that same peace?"

"The alternative is exposing the paedophiles. That requires the rule of law. Do we think the rule of law will expose them in these circumstances?" Not only can Wade go from sound asleep to wide awake but also straight into a mind-bending discussion like this.

"No. You mentioned barriers. I've jumped those barriers. I've met them."

"But you don't have their memories, their feelings, their ids."

"Ids?"

"Sorry, posh way of saying identities."

"IDs?"

"More than ID. That's why I say id. Not just who you are. Your essence. Your instinct. Some might say your sub-conscious, maybe your unconscious but I think it's more than that. When you do overcome those barriers, you will all be together as one. No more fighting for time on the *spot*. No more suspicion about the others."

"You're talking integration." I hope Wade's not going to suggest sessions with Doctor Slattery. They're out of the question.

"I suppose so. You will share each other's memories."

"And what happens to me?"

"You'll be you, but joined with Lottie and the children."

"Have you spoken with Lottie about this?"

"Of course not. I'm no psychiatrist."

Now he's mentioned psychiatry. I must put this to bed once and for all. "Well don't. I don't understand it. I don't get it. I'm happy to just let things take their course. If the result is integration, then fine. If the result is that we remain as alters, then fine. But I'm not going to start forcing things in a particular direction when I don't really know where that direction will lead."

"Well said. I'm going to make coffee."

"And I'm going to sleep."

CHAPTER TWELVE

CHARLIE

Wade and I have cycled to Victoria Park in the East End for a gang meeting. It's Ush's neck of the woods. We gather on some grass near the Regents Canal. Everybody says boats look stately. The boats we've seen look a mess.

Our bikes are piled together in an untidy heap. Zach and Rob have brought something to eat and we're sitting on the grass like we're having a picnic.

Lottie has come up onto the *stage* – the hard work of getting here having been done.

The gang's waiting for me.

"I want to talk about establishing surveillance on Frederick Traube. He'll be difficult. All six of us will need to be involved. What we're looking for is a place where we can confront him. Wade, what are the crime trends where he lives?"

"Kingston's a sleepy hollow. They seem to be most concerned about violent crime. But understand, this isn't Walworth or Peckham or Stoke Newington. I think the most interesting thing is that, for the violent crime they have, there are rarely weapons involved. So my recommendation is that a confrontation should be without weapons."

"Without weapons?" Rob's aghast.

I don't want Rob getting freaked out. "Rob, there are weapons and there are weapons. What Wade means is anything that is obviously a weapon."

"What? Like a car?" Zach's thinking laterally.

"Sort of," I turn back to Wade. "Wimbledon similar?"

"Pretty much."

"Right, listen. Knowing the crime trends is not just important for the MO. It's important for us. Keeping tabs on someone in, say, Brixton is completely different to keeping tabs on someone in Kingston. We'll decide the confrontation MO when we've decided the location. Now, for the surveillance, I think we'll need five clear days. Today's Saturday. I'm suggesting five days straight between this coming Wednesday and the following Wednesday. I'm confident I'll be able to get the leave. What about you guys? Wade?"

"Should be okay."

"Ush?"

"Yes. I have my boss in my pocket."

I bet she does. "Rob?"

"This week will be alright. Following week will be difficult."

"Zach?"

"No chance. I'd have to go sick."

"You showed a day sick recently. A Friday. Will your managers wear it?"

"They're going to have to. A weird sort of serendipity, but I've been under the weather recently so it's not like it will be unexpected. The sooner the better."

"Eileen?"

"If we could make it from this Wednesday through to Sunday then great. The following Monday, Tuesday and Wednesday is a non-starter for me."

"Okay. Wednesday through to Sunday. Everybody good with that?"

Nods all round.

"Right. Comms. I have a surprise." I rummage in my bag and produce six radios wrapped in paper. "They're back-to-back. They're not encrypted. I tried them with Wade on the way here – their range isn't even half-a-mile. But that should be enough for us."

"Where did you get them from." Ush is turning one over in her hands.

"Argos. Paid cash. They were only about sixty quid. I disguised myself. No one knows it was me."

"If they're not encrypted, what we say can be intercepted." Zach is unravelling the leads. Rob, Ush and Eileen are connecting theirs up with the earbuds.

"Yes, so we must be disciplined on when we use them and how we talk to one another. I've drawn up radio protocols for us. They're on those sheets the radios were wrapped in. Learn it, memorise it, practise it."

They all seem positive reading the pages I've drafted for them.

"When we're communicating, we use the burners. Remember the rules for using those phones. We'll get more phones and more SIMs. We only use these radios if there isn't the time to use the phones. The thing with these radios is to imagine that DS French and DI Reeve are listening. We must never use our names. I've given you callsigns. Ush, *Sierra*. Zach, *Kilo*. Rob, *Bravo*. Eileen,

Echo. Wade, *Delta.* Lottie, *Tango* and I'll be *Lima.* Don't worry about them too much. We'll rely more on voice recognition. The trick is to make sure that when you say something, you only have to say it once. That's what all this phonetic alphabet and how you say numbers is all about. You don't say fifteen. Sounds too much like fifty. You say one-five. And don't worry about Humpty and Dumpty as Lottie calls them. They won't be listening in but pretend they are."

* * *

CHARLIE

"I've been thinking about what you said this morning." Wade and I are looking after the bikes while the others practise their radio technique – well – chatting. I thought Eileen would be best at this but she's crap. Surprisingly, Ush sounds most natural. Zach sounds stilted and Rob keeps forgetting to release the transmit button. Anyway, they're getting the hang of it.

Wade is waiting for me to continue.

"What I mean is that I like being with you, I want to be with you and I look forward to being with you. When I'm not with you, I'm always thinking about what you would say or what you would think. Then, when we're together, I'm distracted, I'm nervous, I don't know, I'm constantly on edge."

Wade goes to say something but closes his mouth and cocks his head to one side. He's decided that I'm doing my prevarication thing, and he knows the best way to speed things up is to keep quiet. It's that quality of his that infuriated me when I first met him – his way of summing you up – but since the tanker incident, since finding out about Lottie, since we've been closer, it's that quality of his that I love most of all. He knows me better than I know myself.

"When I'm at work, I feel strong. When I'm with you, I feel weak. When I'm on my own, I feel lost. But the thing that's bugging me most is the feeling that I'm letting you down."

Wade raises a finger. It's not him asking permission to speak. It's him telling me to pipe down so he can speak. "May I say, you've just made a significant step forward."

"What do you mean?"

"Lottie was there for your radio briefing. I'd be surprised if she's buggered off and I'd be even more surprised if you're not aware that she's there."

Present but not in need of a tissue – yet.

"You're right. Lottie and I see more eye to eye than we used to – and Lottie is on the *stage*."

"Is this something that's grown since you've been communicating internally – not vocalising."

"Yes. Absolutely. How did you know."

"When I'm with Lottie, I can't tell whether she's communicating with you or not. It's not as obvious as talking to yourself but, when I'm with you, I can tell. It's difficult to describe. It's like you become absent while present and then you resume. I'm wondering if maybe others notice."

"Hang on. I was bleeding my heart out to you. Do you want to talk about others?"

"No. I don't. I'm sorry."

"Stop saying you're sorry."

Wade goes quiet.

I take this opportunity to catch up with Lottie.

To be honest, I'd forgotten you were there.

I gathered.

I haven't embarrassed you, have I?

Not in the slightest.

I was just about to tell Wade to give us more space. To spend more time at his flat and less time at mine.

I have a proposal. The others are coming back. We will talk about it when we are alone.

What proposal?

When we are alone.

Now Lottie's being all dramatic.

A proposal about what?

When we are alone, Charlie.

"Charlie. These radios are great." Ush is all excitement as they rejoin us.

"I find it really weird talking into space." Eileen was getting a lot better.

Rob and Zach are hunched over the user manual.

I stand up. "Okay guys, I'm working tonight. I want to give the children a chance to have a run around. But then I've got to head off. We'll meet six o'clock on Wednesday morning. I'll let you know where."

"Rob and I have been talking about whether the bikes would be useful for the surveillance." Eileen has opened up this subject for general conversation. She'll have her views but she won't push. That's for me.

"Probably as many disadvantages as there are advantages. Main problem will be if you have to leave them in a hurry. With no time to lock them up, they'll be nicked. I'll think about it."

We start gathering our stuff.

"I've thought about it. We'll have three of us on bikes and three of us on foot. I'll go on foot."

"Eileen's a better cyclist than me." Ush looks over to Eileen who shrugs agreement.

"And Rob's better than me," says Zach. Rob's a little more demure than Eileen.

That's divided up nicely. "Okay. Wade, Eileen and Rob. You'll be on your bikes. Be sure to have appropriate changes of clothing. Ush and Zach. You'll be with me on foot."

"What about securing our bikes?"

"Wade and I will scout out Traube's home address. I'll figure that out and let you know."

Ush stands on her pedals. "See you Wednesday," and she's disappearing into the distance.

Soon the others have all gone, leaving just Wade and me – and Lottie – and we head off to the playground.

* * *

CHARLIE

Cantrell authorised my time-off request as Lavender will be available to drive the fast car but, deep joy, she's posted Kathy as my operator tonight.

It being a Saturday night, there shouldn't be much time for sitting around not talking. However, it's quiet.

There wasn't even much left over from Late Turn. I want to talk about why she's researching DID but I can't ask without showing we've been spying on her. All I can do is wait.

Our first call is to a civil dispute in a restaurant. Not something for the fast car but we're nearby, nothing else going on, we take it.

"The food was awful. Greasy. Tasteless. Undercooked."

I've followed Kathy into the restaurant. A man is shouting because he doesn't want to pay. She doesn't need my help to deal with this.

"You ate it though."

"How else would I find out it's inedible?" The man, with nervous wife and two smirking teenage boys, leans into Kathy. "You need to do your job."

The manager seems embarrassed. Other diners watch, wondering how this will play out. Waiters are minimising the disruption.

I approach the manager but the man starts up again.

"This place is a health hazard. Everybody will get food poisoning. My stomach's already churning." He's raised his voice and, although directing his words at Kathy, is addressing the other diners. "So," he looks down at Kathy's shoulder, "officer M S 2 5 5," he continues down to her name badge, "officer Katherine Bond," back up to her eyes, "are you going to do your job?" I don't know what he's expecting from the other diners.

I know what the other diners are expecting – Kathy and me to sort this out. Some of them have recognised me.

I approach the manager, "Do you know who he is?"

"Yes," he says, "from his booking." He hands me the booking form.

I hand it to Kathy.

Kathy looks at it and back at the man. "Got any ID?"

"Bloody typical." He's still shouting. "I pay my taxes. I've come out with my family to enjoy a meal." He stops and looks at me. "Can I expect some help from you, as this officer is clearly incompetent? There's nothing to…"

He's stopped.

"I'm dealing with you." Kathy hasn't noticed the change.

The wife's relaxing. The boys stop their smirking. I step back, freeing my hands. The waiters look our way – one is balancing a tray of dishes at head-height. A diner sets down her glass, a clear chink. A young lad stands, his chair grating.

Kathy's continuing, oblivious to the change in atmosphere. "You're talking to me. Not her. The question for me to consider is when you formed the intention not to pay. If I decide it was before you entered this restaurant, you'll spend the rest of the night slammed in the pokey before being interviewed by detectives in the morning. The question for you to consider is what you will say to your wife and children tomorrow afternoon. Now," she waves the booking form, "got any ID?"

The man smiles. "It's a misunderstanding, officer. You should never have been called. I'm sorry if I've wasted your time." The man pays and, with his family, leaves.

After collating sufficient detail for our report and some polite exchanges with the manager, we return to the car. That man changed – just before Kathy gave him the civil versus criminal lecture.

"You okay, Kathy?" I fire up the engine.

"What an idiot."

Lottie, did you see that?

I caught the end of it.

Did you notice the change?

I would go as far as saying it was a switch.

Yep, Lottie saw it all.

And Kathy didn't notice.

Plenty of people in the restaurant did. Whether they recognised it as a switch is something else entirely.

Talk later.

"He was so close to being nicked." Kathy's still wound up over that incident.

"Funny the way he suddenly changed." I release the handbrake.

"He backed down."

"I thought there was more to it than him just backing down."

"Nah. You changed into a different person, he backed down."

"Pardon?"

"I said you changed into a different person, he backed down."

147

I stop the car. "What do you mean?"

"That time I came round to yours, New Years, you were one person on the 1st and another person on the 2nd. I've been doing some reading. Dissociative Identity Disorder. You should look it up. I'm surprised that brain box of a boyfriend of yours hasn't seen the link."

That explains why she has been reading about DID.

I ignore Lottie.

It may have taken her a while, but Kathy's been joining dots. What else is she putting two and two together about? I must respond and allay her concerns. I have a nagging feeling that there's more to this. Much more. What she just said doesn't seem enough to account for her recent behaviour. But right now I must respond.

"Kathy. Back then I was in a right state. I was recovering from those burns. My salamander tattoo on my wrist lost its tail. I was in agony all day every day. The painkillers I was given weren't even touching it."

"I know, Charlie." She's reached across and put her hand on my arm. "I know you were in a state. Who wouldn't have been? But the change in you was so..."

She's struggling for words. I decide keeping quiet is best.

"...from the 1st to the 2nd you changed so much."

I want to speak but no, leave her to stew in the silence.

"I know you're really good at impersonations but it really was like you were impersonating yourself. It was you but more."

I remember her saying that. Why has it taken her over four months to put all this together? The point is that *all this* is much, much more than my behaviour back on the 1st and 2nd of January.

"I was having good days and bad days. Probably explains it." Doesn't explain it at all. I've got to speak with Lottie. Figure out what happened on those two days.

"Suppose so." Kathy gets on the radio giving the result to the restaurant call.

You seem to have put that one to bed. Lottie's taking advantage of the distraction.

We haven't put it to bed. Nowhere near.

What more is there?

Lottie, we must stop this. Wade says he can tell when I'm communicating with you like this. If he can, others can. And Kathy's looking for it.

Okay. Talk later.

Later.

I release the handbrake and we move off to deal with whatever else this night has to offer.

CHAPTER THIRTEEN

CHARLIE

So Katherine's problem stems from when she met me on New Year's Day. I admit, I was excited about the Daventry killing.

Oh, god. Lottie wants to talk and I'm knackered.

Nothing startling happened for the rest of that Night Duty shift and Lottie had remained on the *stage* to gain some insight into what's bugging Kathy. Lottie thinks it's because Kathy saw such a dramatic change between us – not instantaneous – overnight. I brushed it off with good day, bad day, agony of burns and so on, but Kathy's not satisfied. There's something else and Lottie might have just uncovered it.

You were all excited about the Daventry killing. I remember Kathy saying something like that. That I was grilling her, prising every morsel of information out of her. I had to keep asking her what murder. Eventually she said the Primrose Hill one and that tied in with the newspaper article that had caught my eye.

Oh Charlie. What have I done?

The thing is, Lottie, what's done is done. We can't change it. We must manage it. We'll ask Wade. He's good at seeing through this kind of stuff.

Lottie retreats from the *stage*. First time I've ever seen her embarrassed.

This is serious though. Kathy found our behaviour over New Year weird and, with Lottie's help, has linked it with the Daventry killing. Then came my interview, my arrest and suspension following the Pope killing. Kathy's dissing me outside Morrisons. My reinstatement. Although Lottie ensured we have watertight alibis, the link between the two murders and me, courtesy of Lottie's incriminating calls to Crimestoppers, has been made and two experienced detectives are on our case.

The piece Kathy has that the detectives don't have, is the DID.

Wade's asleep when I get indoors and I let him lie in. I switch on the telly, volume down, and turn these revelations over in my mind.

It all comes down to whether Kathy has spoken to DS French or DI Reeve and, if she hasn't, will she.

Wade starts moving around and visits the bathroom.

By the time he comes through, I have coffee ready for him.

He takes a sip but doesn't say anything. He's picked up that something's wrong.

Lottie emerges onto the *stage*.

"Lottie's here but no need for green and blue towels. I'll do the talking."

Wade takes another sip.

"I was posted with Kathy last night. She's spotted the difference between Lottie and me and that's why she's researching DID."

Wade sets down his coffee. "What's she done about it?"

"Unknown."

"Did you ask her?"

"No."

"What did you say?"

"I put it down to good day, bad day, burns, recovery, that sort of stuff."

"Good. If you'd asked her, it would have cemented in her mind a link between the DID and the Daventry Pope killings. She'd then have had enough to take to DS French. He'd arrest you again. Interview. You won't give them anything. He'll talk to Doctor Slattery. Doctor Slattery won't say anything claiming patient confidentiality. A court order would be sought instructing Doctor Slattery to talk about you. He'd be unlikely to say he thought you had DID as he wrote a favourable report for the CMO who said it would be okay for you to resume."

"We don't know what Doctor Slattery wrote to the CMO."

"We know what he didn't say. He didn't say anything about DID because, had he done so, you wouldn't have been allowed to resume – particularly not to full operational duty."

You hearing this, Lottie.

Yes. I feel like such an idiot. One stupid piece of exuberance and...

Hey. Don't beat yourself up. Leave that to me.

That chat with Wade has settled me enough so I can sleep. Maybe Kathy's information doesn't have quite the evidential value I thought but it would be enough for them to re-open the investigation. Wade is so junior, only just out of his probation and yet he seems able to penetrate these mind-bending problems. Whether he's right or not is a different matter. Whether we've got all the information is a different matter again.

We're also assuming the detectives will play with a straight bat.

Oh, god. I must sleep.

* * *

CHARLIE

I wake up to find myself riding a bike. Well, Lottie's riding the bike.

Thank goodness. Could you take over? Wade is behind. It being a Sunday, why are there so many cars and lorries?

I don't recognise anything.

Where are we?

Kingston. Not far from Frederick Traube's address. I think.

I get it. We need to recce Traube's address and I'm heading into a quick changeover from Sunday Night Duty to Monday Late Turn. Another Late Turn on Tuesday and then I'll be off. Lottie's left me to sleep. Considering how much she hates cycling, I'm impressed. I take the *spot* and Lottie hangs around on the *stage*. It's important she familiarises herself with all this too.

Frederick Traube's home address is a quiet street with trees and would be difficult to watch without showing out but, as luck would have it, there's a pub at the end of the road from which his drive can be seen. Less than a quarter of a mile from the pub, there's a café.

Wade goes to the counter as I take a seat.

Using my cheap phone, I call Rob, Zach, Eileen and Ush, give them the location of the café and tell them to bring their bikes for 7am Wednesday morning.

I encode the number of my next SIM and text it individually to the four of them. I wait till I've received four reciprocal messages from them, replace the old SIM with the new one and put the old one in my pocket. It will be going down the first drain we come across when we leave the café.

Wade comes over with two coffees and sticky buns for us both. "This will be a good place to meet on Wednesday morning. The manageress says they open at seven."

"It says that on the board outside and I've told the others."

"Did you tell them all to bring their bikes. There are secure racks outside where…"

"I've done it."

Wade recovers his fop of hair. He does make me laugh. If something is complicated he'll see a way through it. If something's straight forward, he gets completely lost.

"We'll get here early. About sixish I reckon. If Traube has an early start, we can get onto him and the others can catch up. The chances are that he'll be going to work."

"You've got all this figured out." I'm not joking – I really think he has.

"Full of surprises, me." Cheeky bastard.

After the café, we go into the pub. There are two window seats from which Traube's drive can be seen. While we're there, Wade with his pint, me with my soda and lime, there's movement on Traube's drive. Wade's running, clipping his helmet on as he goes through the doors. A blue Audi reverses out onto the road and drives away from us. Using our walkie-talkies, I pass the description and direction onto Wade as I see him speeding past. Now I'm running, helmet on and out to my bike. Will Wade ever be able to keep up with him? Hopefully, there'll be a lot of traffic.

Wade gives me a couple of street names. They mean nothing to me. I don't know this area well, but Wade's giving a good enough commentary for me to know roughly where he's heading. Then a street name I do recognise.

I push as hard as I can on the pedals while finding the best gear. If I fall too far behind, I'll lose contact. Wade's signals are already weakening. Now there's nothing. I stop. It looked like Traube was heading towards his office at Wimbledon Nick. But I don't know the quickest way.

I put an AtoZ in the backpack. Will that help?
Lottie. You're a life saver.

I find it and work out a route for Wimbledon Nick.

Sure enough, as I get closer to the Nick, Wade comes on the radio. *"Lima from Delta."*

"Go ahead."

"HA to Work. Was in a hurry. I'm at bus stop opposite."

A quick check with the AtoZ and I'm off. There are bike stands near the bus stop. I lock my bike and join Wade.

"I assume he's on call. Hence the sudden flurry of activity." Wade's had a chance to get his breath back.

"Probably." I haven't.

"We could take it in turns to catch buses. We can see the entrance to the Nick's yard but we'll need to concentrate hard on it."

"There's no point. We're trying to work out his routine." Deep breath. "This is not part of it. I've got to get back. Work tonight. We've got his route to the office though."

"That, we have."

"How did you manage to stay with him?" My breathing's calming down.

"Luck. He caught traffic. Won't be a problem during the week."

"Come on. Let's get home."

On the way back to Camberwell, Lottie disappears off the *stage*. Didn't she say she wanted to talk with me? Something about a proposal. Whatever can she mean? And when will I find the time?

* * *

CHARLIE
"You're joking me."

"Afraid not, Charlie. The Late Turn driver crashed the fast car. You're walking tonight."

"What sort of crash? Is everyone alright?"

"Dignity was the only casualty. They're still with the Garage Sergeant."

Parade follows but I'm not really tuned in. I've been posted with Jonesy. He'll be all eager and sticking his nose into anything that moves. Just what I need on the first stint of a quick changeover.

Before we leave the Nick, I tell him to take off his yellow coat. It's a pleasant evening.

He doesn't walk beside me. He walks to my side but slightly behind. No wonder it's called puppy walking. I did it when I was a probby, walking along just to the side and slightly behind Kathy. I'm still not comfortable with her. I feel like most of the problem has been revealed but there's one bit evading me. I reckon the answer lies in Lottie's behaviour back on New Year's Day. Not so much what Lottie would have said to Kathy, more the hidden meanings. Kathy would be the first to admit that she's not good at reading those kinds of signals – the ones that lurk just below the surface. Something upset her though. My arrest and suspension would have helped her put whatever Lottie said into some sort of perspective. I reckon her problem is that she doesn't know what to do with it. I must find out exactly what happened back on New Year's Day. To do that, I must grill Lottie.

"So, what do you think about that?"

Oh, god. Jonesy's been chatting away and I haven't heard a word he's said.

"Sorry Jonesy. Look. We've got the whole night ahead of us. We finish at six and we'll be back on at two for Late Turn. Not good to be out walking all night. We must get indoors. Follow me."

At the top of Coniston House is a view of several other tall blocks. "Right. Jonesy. Climbers. You ever seen one?"

"No."

"You ever reported a burglary which must have been done by a climber?"

"No."

"You'll be amazed." I hand him my binoculars.

"Are these issue?"

"No they're mine. You'd do well to get yourself a pair. You watch all those flats. When you see someone climbing up the side of the building, hopping from balcony to balcony, put it up on the radio. If he disappears in through a window, make sure you can pinpoint which window it is so we're standing outside the correct front door when he comes out. Understand?"

"Okay."

I point at Kevan House. "I'll be at the top of that block looking back at you."

"Okay."

"Laird House is just beyond. That's where you got the dealer the other night. As a result it will go quiet on the drugs front but maybe we'll get something else. Maybe a climber. We'll have to be really lucky for that but keep your eyes peeled. Most important though, Jonesy, is that we're indoors saving energy for the quick changeover."

"Okay."

God. He sounds like Gillian.

There are much better places to do this kind of observation but this place, at least, gives me an excuse.

I leave Jonesy and, at the top of Kevan House, I let myself up onto the roof with the keys I shouldn't have and stand at the spot where Joel launched himself into oblivion. The spot where, just a couple of months ago, I tried to do the same thing.

I sit cross-legged where I sat talking with Joel for over an hour trying to coax him back from the edge.

"Well, Joel. Here I am… again. I'm assuming you've moved on so I'm not going to chat. I'm just going to sit for a while."

I close my eyes and let my arms be heavy.

Frederick Traube. Divisional DCI at Wimbledon. How the hell will we approach him? If it's not him, he'll get a thumbs-up and we'll scarper. He won't let it go. The incident will be reported together with accurate descriptions. When I was talking about varying the approach, I wasn't expecting the degree of variation needed for approaching Frederick Traube. Poor Rob.

No. Wait. There must be a way. What if we…

"Eight-one-six from four-three-seven."

That's Jonesy calling me. "Go ahead."

"Not a climber. Drug deal. Kevan House, fourteenth landing. Six involved."

Drug deal. Weird. "Four-three-seven, Wait. Mike-Sierra, eight-one-six."

"Go ahead."

"We need assistance. Jonesy's watching them from Coniston House. Silent approach from the opposite direction. I'll jam the main door of Kevan House open for the cavalry."

As the control room organises a response from the Team and Jonesy gives detailed descriptions of the suspects who are six floors below me, I call the lift to go down to the ground floor. As I step into the lift I'm thinking this might not be a good idea... Will the radio work? I know the radio will work – been in here enough times. ...when the lift starts slowing and stops – on the fourteenth floor. Shit.

I press the red button on my radio. My microphone is now open and will be for about ten seconds, maybe twenty, can't remember. No one on the talkgroup can transmit and everyone can hear what's going on in this lift. It's called the panic button because it sends the control room into a panic.

The lift door opens.

Two men come in. I step back to make room. They fit Jonesy's descriptions. Not good.

"Evening officer," one of them says.

I nod. I don't know either of them.

They don't smell of drugs. Nor do they seem nervous.

The lift door slides shut.

I hold my finger over the panel of buttons. "Which floor?" I'm surprised my voice is calm and level.

"Ground," one of them says.

At least I've got that I'm in a lift out to the control room courtesy of the open mic. They know which block of flats I'm in.

The lift gets going.

Then I see it. The one who didn't speak adjusts his coat, a coat that's heavy for this time of year. He's moved as if concealing something. The guy who spoke shakes his head, a slight movement, his eyes angry.

Christ. I'm in a lift with two men I don't know who are probably tooled up. Jonesy nicked a dealer on Friday night. One dealer goes down, another takes his place. They'll be carrying a load of gear but what else are they carrying? Find out when we get to the ground floor and meet the reception committee. My radio will be coming back to life before we get there. Both my hands are free and I'm evenly balanced on my feet. The guy in the heavy coat is the threat.

The lift passes the tenth floor.

"I recognise you." That's the other guy.

"Too many people do."

"From when that tanker exploded."

We're passing the eighth floor.

I smile. Hang on. Why the hell did he say that? Why the hell is he even talking to me? I don't want to say anything. Any moment now, my emergency radio activation will cancel and the control room will be calling.

"You shouldn't be on your own." Same guy. He's pushing for me to speak.

We pass the sixth floor.

Wait, there is something that would be worth saying. "My partner's waiting for me downstairs. At least, he better be."

"Eight-one-six from eighty-seven."

My radio's reset itself and Cantrell's calling. Strange. Why isn't it the control room? "Go ahead, sarge."

"I need you back here at the Nick. Where are you?"

"Kevan House."

"Soon as poss. Eighty-seven, out."

Silence. This is very weird. They should be asking me what's wrong. I'm pleased they're not but...

We're passing the fourth floor.

"So he waits in the car leaving you to do all the work."

"Story of my life." Wait. What he just said – too close to home. What Cantrell said – doesn't fit with the circumstances.

We're passing the second floor.

The Team know something I don't.

"Well, good luck, officer."

Ground floor.

The lift door opens.

There's no one there. There's no one there! How can there be no one there? What? I'm left to take these guys out on my own? Two guys who are tooled up? No. Wait. My Team's been warned off. In fact, Cantrell's warned *me* off. Best I get out of here.

"Excuse me," I say and push past the two men. Lavender's in his panda outside. No other cars. I jump in. Jonesy's in the back.

Lavender drives us away from Kevan House and, speaking into his radio, says, "Eight-one-six and four-three-seven are with me. Returning to Mike-Sierra."

"All units from eighty-seven, avoid Kevan House. Do not go to Kevan House." Cantrell starts a rollcall

ensuring everybody on the Team has understood her instruction.

"Christ, Cantrell means business."

Something weird's happening. Lavender's not talking. Jonesy's not talking. Lavender's looking at me. He points to his radio, holds a finger to his lips and drives straight back to the Nick.

Inspector Brady is waiting in the yard. "Charlie. What made you press your red button?"

"I was in the lift, heading down to open the main doors for the troops, when it stopped on the fourteenth floor. I was scared."

Jonesy is standing next to me and Lavender has come over and joined us. He's eyeballing the guv'nor and his body-language says, 'I'm with Charlie – you take her on, you take me on too.' Lavender may be a piss-taking canteen-cowboy but having him on my side is a… I don't know… fills me with… don't know… is a good thing.

"Those two who got in the lift with you. The one doing the talking is an undercover officer. The other one's a Level 2 dealer. The U/C guys have been monitoring our transmissions because they're running an operation. As soon as Jonesy mentioned Kevan House they tuned in. As soon as they realised what he was talking about, they were on the blower. They've infiltrated this dealer's gang with the aim of identifying and getting to the Level 3. Because of what the U/C guys told us, we dispersed the Team. Couldn't tell you though. Must have shitted you out to see the lift doors open and no one there."

"You could say that."

There's just the slightest delay before he carries on. "Anyway, listen, the DI running that op wants to talk to you and Jonesy – do a damage assessment. He'll be here tomorrow afternoon when we start Late Turn."

I'm confused. "What damage? We didn't let on."

"If any of the Team saw the undercover officer, it would have been a fleeting glimpse, so any 'damage' would be considered negligible. The two of you have seen him and would likely recognise him if you see him again. Jonesy was watching him for Christ knows how long through a pair of binoculars and you had a conversation with him in the lift."

I'm not happy, Brady's being coy.

There's a pause – a pregnant one. Brady doesn't seem to know what to say. Or has no more to say. I can't tell if I'm in trouble or not.

Words finally come to me. "Should have just let us nick 'em. There was no need to even tell us it was an undercover op."

"You don't know what the dealer had concealed in his jacket."

I find my voice. "If he'd produced his knife, I'd have taken it off him and…"

Inspector Brady holds up his hand. "Brave words, Charlie. I'm giving you and Jonesy an early-off. Get home. Get some sleep. I want you both bright eyed and bushy tailed for when you meet Brian Gault – the DI running the U/C op."

Lavender doesn't move.

Brady looks at him and turns away – I think he feels he passed the ordeal.

When Brady's disappeared inside, Lavender relaxes. "Come on, Charlie. I'll give you a lift home."

I turn to Jonesy. "You okay? You've got your car here? Yeah?"

He nods. He's clearly bewildered, like me.

I put my hand on his arm. "We'll catch up tomorrow. A DI running a U/C op. It'll be exciting."

He says nothing. Just turns and heads down to the locker rooms.

* * *

CHARLIE

Lavender says nothing as he drives me home.

"What was the *brave words* about?"

Lavender doesn't answer. Something's going on, something weird. Not only is Lavender not swearing, he's not talking either.

It's not until we're stopped outside mine that Lavender speaks. "It wasn't a knife, Charlie. It was a firearm."

CHAPTER FOURTEEN

CHARLIE

I crept in so as not to disturb Wade. Now I'm lying in bed, unable to sleep. A firearm. After a week of Nights, my body clock has adjusted and trying to sleep around midnight isn't going to work. A firearm. It's not just the sleep pattern, that incident with the undercover officer has set me thinking. A firearm. Okay. Okay. Stop thinking about it. Those U/C officers lead a precarious life – they really do need to be able to think on their feet. A firearm. What we're heading into with Frederick Traube, will be similarly demanding on us. A firearm. The difference, of course, is that we don't have any support and the other big difference is that what we're doing is criminal. A firearm.

Lottie's been hovering on the *stage*.

Come on then, Lottie. What's on your mind?

May I ask what happened at Kevan House earlier?

We nearly compromised an undercover operation.

I stop. Should I be talking about this with Lottie? Oh, for god's sake. I carry on.

What made you come up? I didn't notice you.

One thing I won't do is mention the firearm.

When those two guys entered the lift, your emotions went haywire. Maybe not emotions. Maybe adrenalin.

You're right there. When I was going down in the lift and it started slowing for the fourteenth floor, I nearly shat myself.

Oh, Charlie. Please.

I ignore her.

What did you make of it?

What I did get was the sense of jeopardy that undercover officer was feeling. Made me think about our situation. That feeling of not really being in control. A feeling that we could end up in a whole load of trouble through nothing but bad luck.

Sense of jeopardy? We didn't know he was undercover at that point. Whatever.

Has it made you reconsider what we're doing?

Well, with you fully on board, I feel surplus to requirement.

No. Not true. You were great the other day. Pulled everyone back...

No, Charlie. I feel unsure of myself. We cannot afford any self-doubt.

Are you saying that you don't want to play anymore?

Not that. I think I have started to see the risks. We are going up against Frederick Traube, very different to the others. On top of that, we have Katherine Bond behaving out of character and researching our condition.

Lottie sounds very unsure of herself. I must help her regain her confidence.

With Frederick Traube, we must find a way in. I've no idea what that will be, but I'm confident we'll think of something. As far as Kathy's concerned. I think we know

what's sparked her into researching DID. We need to know what she intends doing with what she learns.

Now is the time to grill Lottie about New Year's Day but, with her changing attitude, maybe that should wait. She's coming across as so vulnerable. She's well capable of putting on an act, but I don't believe she is.

As you are aware, on New Year's Day I had the *spot*. Katherine invited herself around. I was not thinking properly. I was not impersonating you. And yes, I was very excited about Peter Daventry's demise.

Lottie's started talking about it on her own. Go with it.

Kathy noticed that. She mentioned it the next day when I was with her. 'So unlike you,' is what she said to me.

And now, with the incriminating calls I made to Crimestoppers to keep you off balance so my access to the *spot* would be easier, your arrest and suspension, she is starting to join the dots.

Lottie's telling me nothing I haven't already figured out. Why?

The way to think about this, Lottie, is what can she do? She can go and see DS French. Another thing she could do is come and speak to me. I do however understand her quandary. These are high stakes and she's trying to balance her sense of duty as a police officer with her friendship for me.

Her sense of duty must win.

Lottie needs to understand there's more to it than a sense of duty.

Yes, but she must be absolutely certain that what she does will get a result – the result being that we are convicted in court. If that result doesn't come, she will not only be treated like a pariah, she will actually be one. That stigma will be with her for the rest of her service and the rest of her life. I'm confident that we can put that New Year's Day behaviour of yours down to the trauma of the tanker incident. If we can convince Kathy of that, we'll be doing her a massive favour and I'm sure she'll revert to the Kathy we all know and love.

* * *

CHARLIE

Wade's getting ready for work. Talking things through with Lottie relaxed me so I did get some sleep – slept for about four hours and woke when Wade stirred.

"What are you doing here?" Wade's alarm has woken him and he's registered I'm beside him.

"Love you too, Wade."

"You know as well as me that we've a long way to go before we can start saying things like that."

He's right. "Strange night. I was given an early-off. I'll tell you about it later."

No sooner has Wade gone, Lottie appears.

Oh, god. I was going to go back to bed.

Not stopping you.

It's true. I want to go back to sleep, but Lottie has changed. She wants to talk. I fire up Wade's coffee machine.

Have you seen the children?

Not since we were in the playground in that park by the canal.

I make a coffee and prop myself up in bed. After drinking this coffee I won't get any more sleep before having to go back to work, but Lottie has something to say and she doesn't know how to approach it. I wait.

I remember you saying you wanted to put more distance between yourself and Wade. How is that going?

She wants to talk about Wade? Wasn't expecting that. Go with it, I suppose – despite the firearm being at the forefront of my mind.

I don't know Lottie. I want to be with him but I'm not sure how things will pan out. I'm not going to plan for a future I don't know.

I thought the idea of planning is to make the future more predictable.

Lottie, I'm really not up for a philosophical discussion. There's something you want to talk about. I thought it was Frederick Traube. But no, it's Wade. Now please, cut to the chase.

Okay. I cannot help but notice that you are having problems with Wade.

What d'you mean?

Intimate problems.

Lottie! This is what you want to talk about?

We have experience that you do not.

Woah! What the hell are you saying?

We can help each other.

Not like that we can't.

Charlie. Hear me out. By no means am I suggesting that I have an intimate relationship with Wade. Certainly not that one of the children should.

Too bloody right...

I'm angry.

Charlie. This is difficult. Please. Hear me out.

What the hell are you suggesting? That you get everything warmed up and invite me in at the end?

No, Charlie. Not at all.

Then what? Jeez. Wade knows the difference between us. D'you really think Wade would be up for it?

Not as we are.

Too bloody right. He wouldn't...

What did Lottie just say? Not as we are? Shit, she's done a Wade on me. She's got this conversation all worked out and there's much more to it than the intimacy issues Wade and I are having. Right. Calm. Breathe. In for four. Out for six.

Lottie. What you're saying clearly goes deep. I won't interrupt.

This must be the proposal she mentioned the other day.

You and I are parts of the same person. There are barriers between us but we're overcoming them. We are able to interact with one another. There are barriers between us and the children. We have started to overcome those too. But there is a way to go.

I can't believe I'm hearing this. Lottie's always been an advocate of the multiple state and scorned the singleton state. Mustn't say anything, let her talk.

Knowing of each other is a start. But the barriers are there for a reason. They are there to keep memories in and protect you from the abuse. But they are not foolproof. Memories of the abuse are not accessible for you, but emotions do leak through. I believe that it is that emotional seepage which is messing with your ability to manage intimacy. Those barriers have served their purpose. They need to come down.

Bloody hell. She's talking integration. Better check.

What happens to us?

I become part of you and you become part of me. That is the easy way of saying it. I think what it really means is that my memories would be available for you and yours would be available for me.

She *is* talking integration.

What happens to the children?

Same. We would be able to access their memories and they would be able to access ours. Remember, our brain formed those barriers to protect you from the trauma of the abuse and, of course, the trauma that comes from the memories of the abuse. Our brain is still protecting you. What I am saying, Charlie, is that our brain is also protecting me. I took the abuse to protect you but I soon found it too much and Floella formed to protect me. It became too much for her and Jemima formed. And again leading to Gillian. I cannot access the children's memories and they cannot access each other's. But I was part of the abuse. I may not have suffered the majority of it but I witnessed it.

IF WE WERE ONE

I've never heard Lottie talking like this. I do believe she's opening up. Mustn't say anything. She has so much more to tell. Say nothing. Breathe. In for four, out for six.

What I have concluded from all my reading and all my research which, I assure you, is far more extensive than Katherine's, is that I need you to help me handle the emotion. Just look at my reaction to this. Kill them all – I have even recruited the gang to make it happen – but is it actually doing any good? Is Ush really better? Zachery and Eileen? What about poor Rob? Is this really the answer for him or am I using them as some form of proxy? I feel that the abusers have won. Whatever they might say, like that sordid Frank Amos, they do not abuse children for physical pleasure. They do it because abusing children is the only means by which they can feel better about themselves. In so doing, they have made a monster. Five of us were fed to the paedophiles. Ush, Zachery, Rob, Eileen and us. They experimented with the five of us. They probably made notes. They probably discussed us. Then they made their choice. Charlie. Every single night. For two years. Every... single... night. They are revelling in the knowledge that they have created this monster.

Wow.

Do you think the paedophile ring is unaware? Unaware that Peter Daventry has been despatched? Vincent Pope? Frank Amos? Not only do they know, they are loving it. It is the only way they can get any excitement into their pathetic, sordid little lives.

Lottie is generalising. Fatal, but at least it's a start.

I noticed how Frank Amos showed fear but quickly moved on to, I don't know, resignation. A sort of,

acceptance. He knew he was going to die. He knew why he was going to die – like it was inevitable.

Absolutely right, Charlie. No pleading. No bargaining. I would not go as far to say that he enjoyed it.

I don't know what to say.

Born that way. Mentally ill. Cycle of abuse. Choice.

Lottie pauses.

Not so sure about choice. Religious persuasion might be another. There are many people who cannot think what to say about the causes of paedophilia. Many of them well qualified.

She does like having a pop at psychiatrists.

Okay, Lottie. Where d'you want this to go?

I always thought that we are stronger as a multiple. Different personalities, different motivations, drives. Different skills. I thought we could take any given circumstance and put forward the alter most suited. Like the National Crime Agency interview. But, with benefit of hindsight, you might have done better at that.

Lottie. Please understand. We were never going to get into the NCA.

I do understand. Lip service to the hero cop. But I do believe, had we both been there, we would have fared better. Thinking about it again though, it could never have worked – one of us on the *spot* with the other on the *stage*. Even with our prowess at quick switching, it would not work. We would end up arguing, the interview board forgotten and how silly would that look?

I'm beginning to feel this change in Lottie is genuine.

Way forward?

What maintains the alters are the barriers. Before we were ten, those barriers were what kept us going. Since the age of ten, those barriers have served to shield you from horrific memories. Now, in our mid-twenties, those barriers have outlived their usefulness. You will be able to manage the children's and my memories.

What about you?

Like Sebastian says, we are one.

Floella? Jemima? Gillian?

They are as much you as you are them. The barriers would be gone. We would all be one.

Our identities?

Our five identities would become one identity.

This is not what I was expecting. I've only just started getting my head round being a multiple. If we do this, what will it be like? Lottie is confident I'll be able to cope with the abuse memories. I'm quite sure I will, but it's not something I'm looking forward to.

Does it mean we need to see Doctor Slattery? Because we can't. That would hand DS French that fragment of evidence he needs.

Integration would be easier with professional help, particularly with the children but, Charlie, can you explain for me? How would evidence of our DID lead to a murder conviction in court.

It won't. Wade has explained this but... he can be difficult to follow sometimes. Currently, the 'Charlie Quinlan' line of enquiry has been closed. If our DID comes to light, the 'Charlie Quinlan' line of enquiry would be reopened and we'd have a team of twenty detectives with unlimited uniform support fired at us. We wouldn't stand a chance.

Oh.

It seems Lottie has finally got it.

If we do end up in front of a psychiatrist we will be doing everything we can to hide our DID. So, as specialised psychiatric help is not available to us, how will we do this... integration?

We will speak to no one other than ourselves.

But we are five individuals. What will it mean for each of us? Without counselling, therapy, whatever, I don't know the words, how will we do it?

We will speak with Sebastian.

CHAPTER FIFTEEN

CHARLIE

"Sarge, can I take today and tomorrow off?"

"But, Charlie. We've got a new car for you."

"I know you've granted my request for leave this coming weekend, but that incident last night with the undercover officer, Lavender told me about the firearm, has shaken me a bit. I really appreciated the early-off last night. We're over minimum strength and Lavender's available to drive the car for today and tomorrow."

"Inspector Brady decided not to tell you about the firearm. I didn't agree but I was outranked and over-ruled. I would have told you anyway but I was caught up in another call. Lavender beat me to it. Anyway, that aside, you surprise me. I wouldn't have thought something like that would have rattled you."

"I don't want to go sick. I have rest days owing."

"Why didn't you call me? We could have done all this over the phone."

"I want to touch base with Jonesy and see that DI from the undercover operation who said he's coming down."

"Understood. Of course you can take today and tomorrow off. With the Early Turn weekend as well, you'll have nine days straight. That DI is already here and chatting with Inspector Brady. After you've seen him, I want to speak to you. Again, that will be with Inspector Brady. Then you can go."

"Thanks sarge."

"No probs."

Cantrell heads off for parade and I head to the Inspectors' Office.

Both Inspector Brady and a bloke I don't know stand as I walk in. Role reversal or what. I go to close the door but Jonesy's coming in behind me.

"This is Detective Inspector Brian Gault," says Inspector Brady. "He wants to talk about what happened last night at Kevan House."

We sit.

There's an ominous mood.

Jonesy's all smiles and enjoying the moment. He won't be in a minute.

DI Gault starts with, "Why were you up on Kevan House?" He's looking at me.

"Keeping observations?"

"What did you expect to observe?"

"Anything suspicious"

"Why Kevan House?"

"I'd put Jonesy in Coniston House. I'd be in a position to act on anything he saw and he'd be able to act on anything I saw."

"Sounds like a wheeze."

I look at Inspector Brady who's looking at me.

Jonesy starts talking. "We were looking for a burglar, a dealer, a car thief…"

I put my hand on Jonesy's arm and he stops. I know what DI Gault means. I also know that Inspector Brady knows what DI Gault means. "We were Nights. I was supposed to be driving the fast car but the Late Turn crashed it so I was walking. I was posted with Jonesy. It was quiet, not too many calls, we had no assignments, we didn't want to be walking all night heading into a quick changeover so I set us up to do observations on some blocks of flats. See what we could see. Maybe a climber. I set him up in Coniston House and I set myself up in Kevan House so we were both looking at one another."

"Why did you choose Coniston and Kevan House?" DI Gault fires this question out with no delay.

"They're not ideal for those kinds of observations but they're on our Beat."

"I understand you were posted to 8 Beat."

"Near our Beat."

"I hope I don't have to ask this question again. Why did you choose Coniston and Kevan House?"

I have no choice. I have to come clean. "Because of Joel."

"Joel?"

"A friend."

"You were visiting a friend?"

"Sort of."

"Tell me about Joel."

Jonesy is looking at me, confused. Inspector Brady doesn't seem perturbed. DI Gault is trying to assess if his undercover officer has been compromised. There's no way I can wriggle out of this – and DI Gault and

Inspector Brady know it. "Joel was a young lad who was on the roof of Kevan House a few years back. I spent an hour trying to talk him down but he threw himself off. I go up there occasionally to remember him, pay my respects."

DI Gault sits back. Is he satisfied? Can't tell. He turns his attention onto Jonesy. "What did you see?"

"I didn't see a climber…"

"I asked what you did see. Not what you didn't see."

Jonesy is flustered. Only a couple of months out of Hendon and he's being subjected to this. Talk about a baptism of fire. Jonesy stumbling over his answers is giving me time to think. Inspector Brady is looking at me – I'm not surprised.

Jonesy has stopped and is taking a moment to compose himself. I'm liking Jonesy more and more. He's really going to be a force to contend with as he gains experience. "Like Charlie said, she set me up on the top landing of Coniston House. She even gave me binoculars. At eleven-fifteen, I saw a group of males come out of a flat and onto the fourteenth-floor landing. They seemed to be arguing. It seemed to me there were two of them against four. Then I decided they weren't arguing, they were just having a laugh. But they weren't all smiling. Through the binoculars, I could see there was tension between them. Then it blew up again. One of them threw something at one of the others. It seemed like a package of some kind. I decided it was a drugs package. Maybe I just wanted it to be drugs. I put it up on the radio. I could see Charlie on the roof six floors above them." He looks at me. "I did wonder what you were doing up there but now you've explained about Joe, it kind of makes sense."

"Joel. And stick to answering the DI's question."

He looks back at the DI. "I saw Charlie run inside and then, down on the fourteenth floor, I saw the two blokes leave the four blokes. I decided it would be worth stopping those two. Charlie took over on the radio and called for assistance. The two headed towards the lift and the four went back into the flat. Then the radios went weird because Charlie had pressed her red button. I started running to get over to Kevan House and help Charlie but it was all over by the time I got there. We were cancelled. I didn't get it. Charlie was still in there and we were being told not to go anywhere near Kevan House. I didn't..."

DI Gault turns back to me. "Why did you press your red button?"

"I was heading down to the ground floor to open the main door so that the assistance, when it arrived, could get in easily. On the way down, the lift started slowing and stopped at the fourteenth floor. I was scared. I used the red button."

"How did you get into Kevan House?"

Ah. Shit. I can't odds this. "I have a key."

"What key?"

"A key to the main door."

"And how did you get up onto the roof?"

I suppose I can now kiss goodbye to my keys. "I have a key for the maintenance door too."

"Why do you have those keys?"

"The incident with Joel. Like I said, we were talking for about an hour before he threw himself off. We'd made some kind of bond. I got the keys from the caretaker but I forgot to give them back to him. With those keys I could get in through the main door without having to call a resident and then up onto the roof."

"How many times have you used those keys?"

Oh, what the hell. This DI Gault needs to know. "I forgot to give the keys back to the caretaker several times."

"Several times?"

"Joel meant a lot to me."

DI Gault stops and looks away. He scratches his nose and holds his hand over his mouth. He looks across at Inspector Brady. "Can you vouch for the Joel incident?"

"Yes. I was on duty that night. Charlie did an excellent job but it just didn't work out."

DI Gault looks back at Jonesy. "Jonesy, for someone so junior, you did a fantastic job." He turns to me. "Charlie, your quick thinking and activation of the red button on your radio, giving the open microphone so we could hear what was going on and the way you handled the conversation in the lift has saved us an undercover operation and substantially reduced the risk to our undercover officer. I will be recommending you for a commendation."

I want to ask about the firearm but I know I won't get anything from this DI. I'll grill Inspector Brady later when I'm with Sergeant Cantrell. I stand up signalling to Jonesy to get up as well. "Thank you, sir."

As we're leaving, DI Gault says, "I'd be surprised and disappointed if Inspector Brady doesn't overlook the irregularity with the keys. I understand you, Charlie, have been granted a day off. If you will allow me, I would like to buy you a drink. I believe your local is called the Half Nelson.

* * *

CHARLIE

Ten minutes later, DI Gault and Jonesy have gone and I'm sat back in the Inspectors' Office with Inspector Brady and Sergeant Cantrell.

Inspector Brady kicks off. "I will overlook the keys. But you give them back to the caretaker. You'll do it when you're on duty and you'll do it with me. Other than that, bloody well done. We're almost expecting this kind of performance from you. Absolutely superb. I hope Brian Gault's commendation recommendation sticks. Bit of a gob-full but thoroughly deserved. Now, Charlie, Sergeant Cantrell tells me she's granted you leave for today and tomorrow. I fully support her decision and with your leave next weekend you'll be away for over a week. I would like to reassure myself that everything's okay with you. You told Sergeant Cantrell you were shaken up by that incident with the undercover officer. Tell me about it from the moment they got in the lift with you."

"Well, I'm assuming the one who did the talking was the undercover officer and the other guy was the dealer. We all heard what was said. But there was a moment when the dealer started adjusting his coat. His coat was too heavy for this weather. If he'd pulled a knife or something, in that confined space, I don't know what would have happened."

It's all bollocks. If he'd pulled a knife, I'd have taken it off him and shoved it up his arse. Neither Brady nor Cantrell respond. Now's the time to ask. "Lavender mentioned a firearm. He wasn't swearing."

Brady looks at Cantrell and then back to me. "Lavender was out of order saying that. Appropriate measures were in place."

"Appropriate measures?"

"You'll be speaking with DI Gault in a minute. He'll have better knowledge of all that than me."

Brady's undoubtedly right there – the issue with the firearm is not what's worked me up – it's something else and DI Gault might be able to help me with that.

After a few minutes more of metaphorical backslapping, I'm out of there and heading for the Half Nelson.

* * *

CHARLIE
And Lottie pops up.

Charlie, something upsetting you?

Nothing. Go back to sleep.

Do not nothing me.

I'm going to meet someone. By all means listen in, but don't distract me.

Brian Gault is sitting at a secluded table. He half stands as I come in. The barman comes across with my usual glass of white wine. "Would you make it a large one?"

Brian Gault smiles and nods. The barman was ready for that and had the bottle to hand.

We sit.

"Brian. What would you like to talk about?" Calling him by his first name feels awkward but calling him 'sir' will earn me a slap.

"The conversation you had in the lift."

"You surprise me. Most people want to talk about the tanker incident."

"I imagine you're sick to death of talking about that."

"Certainly am." There is something on which Brian will be a mine of information, but it would be unwise to raise it directly. I must try and work it in. He wanted to talk to me in this informal setting. All I can do is see where he wants to take it. "Are you comfortable being seen in public with me?"

"Perfectly. I'm not operational. I organise operations."

"Do you miss it?"

"The operational stuff? No. I used to but it really is a game for the youngsters."

Youngsters? Jeez. I'd have placed Brian in his early thirties. I wait. He wants to talk to me. Let's see what he has to say.

"Charlie. This U/C op has been going for over eight months. We've blown all our budgets. That officer you met last night in the lift is totally strung out. That Level 2 dealer is being awkward. It's like he knows. I want to speak with you because you got close to them. We know what you said – because you activated your open mic, we have the whole conversation recorded. I'm talking with you now because it would be helpful to know why you said what you said. It would be helpful to know what you felt. The vibes."

"Oh, god. I think I know what you mean. First of all, Jonesy made a drugs arrest Saturday night – took out a dealer in Laird House. I thought it would all go quiet on the drugs front because of that. I only mentioned climbers to keep Jonesy engaged. You know as well as me, we would never have seen a climber."

"Laird House?"

"Coniston, Kevan and Laird are in a line with Kevan in the middle."

He nods.

"I knew there was something happening on the fourteenth floor. Jonesy had described it as a drugs deal but he wouldn't have been sure. I was pretty sceptical because of what I just said but I ran for the lift."

"Getting in the lift is a bit dodgy. Why didn't you take the stairs?"

"I could just as easily run into them on the stairs. The lift was there on the top floor from when I'd taken it up there. Maybe I was denying them the lift. Maybe I just wanted to get below them. I really don't know. I was flying by the seat of my pants."

"Something you're very good at by all accounts."

I'm no longer embarrassed by this kind of compliment. "Inspector Brady?"

"Him and others. Your superintendent. The Chief Inspector on your NCA board wasn't so complimentary."

Oh, god. Lottie will have heard that.

"You don't have any experience in the Department. I don't really understand why you were given that board. Also why you even applied for the position."

"I think I was just riding a wave after all the drama following the tanker incident. I'd be the first to admit I didn't know whether I was coming or going."

"You've settled back in now."

"I know where I am with emergency response."

"Sorry. You were in the lift."

"Oh, yeah." I laugh. I'd almost forgotten about that. "When I saw the lift was going to stop on the fourteenth floor, I panicked. I'm pretty good at handling myself but I had no idea what was going to come through the lift door."

"When you actually saw the two guys, what did you think? How did you feel?"

"My first impression was that they were not part of the group Jonesy had seen. They matched Jonesy's description, but their behaviour didn't match the circumstances."

Brian waits. He doesn't want to disturb my flow.

"Then I noticed the coat your dealer was wearing was too heavy for this time of year and he twisted it, as if hiding something, you know, pulled one side of it across his front. I thought he was concealing a weapon of some kind – maybe a knife – but your guy did something. Didn't say anything but what he did made the dealer back off. No, not back off. Made the dealer lose interest. I thought at the time that your guy was angry.

Suddenly, I'm uncomfortable.

Lottie, what the fuck am I doing?

Showing off – as is your wont.

Christ. I've got to get away from this guy.

No. Just stop talking about the tells. You are, in effect, talking about our validation process leading to a thumbs-up or a thumbs-down. What you need to do right now is find out whether this Brian Gault is a mate of Humpty.

Lottie's right. The whole thing is too elaborate for such a set up but they may be taking advantage of these developments.

Brian is looking at me. A strange look. Oh, god. I've been non-vocalising with Lottie. Did he notice? Like Wade notices? I must put space between him and me.

I finish my glass of wine. I shouldn't have asked for a large one. "My round. Same again?"

He nods and I go to the bar. How will I find out if DI Brian Gault's been put up to this by DS John French?

I take our two drinks, mine now a small glass of wine, back to our table.

"There you go. They recognised me. The guys in the lift. They knew who I was. Your guy even mentioned it. Anyway, you've heard all that on the recordings. Best I can add is that your bloke had some sort of influence over the dealer. The red button on my radio timed out. I expected a load of shouting but all I got was Sergeant Cantrell, cool as a cucumber, telling me to return to the Nick. At that point I realised something weird was going on and then, to add insult to injury, we got to the ground floor, the doors opened, I was expecting to see half my Team but there was no one. I couldn't stop them. Couldn't search them. I just had to get out of there. Outside, Lavender was waiting in his panda with Jonesy and he drove us straight back to the Nick. Is your guy okay?"

"I tell you what… I think you've answered my question. Sounds like our guy's still on it. Can't tell you how relieved I am."

"There's been talk about a firearm. Your dealer might have been armed with a gun."

Brian doesn't bat an eyelid. "*Might* being the operative word. We'd put in control measures for that risk."

"Control measures?"

"Our guy is surrounded by a surveillance team with firearms capability. One word from him and he'd have firearms support within seconds. Our guy didn't give that word. If he had, you'd have had a reception committee on the ground floor alright and not the one you were organising."

I decide to change the subject.

"Good to hear that your guy's okay."

"The stresses and strains of U/C work. Talking of which, you've been put through the mill recently. Nicked for murder. Suspended."

This is it. Has he been put up to this by DS French? "I don't think Humpty and Dumpty had much choice."

"Humpty and Dumpty?"

"Sorry. I developed a bit of a grudge if I'm honest. The two detectives who were on my case."

"MIT?"

"What's that?"

"Murder Investigation Team."

"Why do the names of these squads keep changing?"

"Call them Homicide if you want."

"I will. And DPS. Maybe you know them. The DPS one hardly said a word, just staring at me through his purple tinted specs."

"Must have been an ordeal for you."

I'm watching him. Does he recognise DI Steve Reeve? I don't think he does. Try him out with DS John French. "I didn't know what to make of the Homicide detective. He would switch from asking invasive questions to just making banal observations and then back again. He was really pissing me off."

"A standard interview technique. Who was he? I might know him."

"John French. A DS."

He shakes his head. "Anyway, that's all behind you now."

I smile. And yes, it is all behind me. And no, I can't tell if DI Brian Gault knows French or Reeve.

"Charlie. There is something I specifically want to talk to you about. There are times when our informants get a bit angsty. I don't have much support but I think, sometimes, seeing a familiar face helps settle them. After hearing you in the lift last night, you're clearly sharp. You were impressive. I'm not suggesting for one minute that you join our department or anything, just that I could call on you if I thought the circumstances were appropriate."

"I'm honoured. Thank you. But may I think about it? I'm only really just regaining some semblance of order in my life."

"You're revelling in emergency response. You love it and good on you, but give it a few years and you may want to move on to something more specialised. What I'm offering you is a taster of sorts. A feel for what it's like in squad land. And, of course, it will be beneficial for me. A win-win."

"Like I say. I need to think about it."

"I understand. Look, here's my card. Talk about it with your mates. See what your inspector thinks. And that sergeant of yours – she seems scary."

"One way of describing Sergeant Cantrell."

"Surprising for someone so small."

I take his card. The detail on it matches up with what I know. This is coming to an end. He seems anxious to get going. He finishes his drink. "I won't call you. The next time we speak will be because you call me. It's been a pleasure meeting you and I've enjoyed our chat. You take care." And he's gone.

I remain at this secluded little table. I quite like it. Maybe I'll make this my spot from now on.

Lottie's there. Waiting. She wants to talk.

Lottie, take the *spot*.

We switch.

Why?

I'm not so good at this non-vocalising as you. I look like I'm talking to myself.

Good point. Well made.

Lottie's almost laughing, cheeky cow.

What d'you think?

Even from the *stage* I was unable to tell if he was being honest or otherwise.

Nor could I, and that worries me.

Why?

If I can't tell whether he was lying, how can we be sure we're reading the signals from our targets correctly? Especially Frederick Traube. DCI Frederick Traube. People like Gault and Traube are well practiced at masking their feelings.

I see your point.

A variation on the MO won't be enough. We need a completely different approach.

CHAPTER SIXTEEN

CHARLIE

Traube is seriously boring.

I came over to Kingston on Tuesday to familiarise myself with the location. I'd have preferred to do it on foot but I used my bike as I could cover more ground more quickly. I now know the area well. I know street names and pub names. I know where they are in relation to one another and I've found short cuts and rat runs and quiet spots and back alleys where we can change our clothing and appearance. Will any of them be any use? Probably not.

The gang turned up on Wednesday morning and we've been able to maintain a constant surveillance on Frederick Traube for the past three days. When he's at home, he's in his house and when he's at work he's in his office. Zach saw him on a rare occasion leave the house and mow the back garden lawn.

His wife – or the person we assume is his wife – goes out. Probably shopping trips, seeing friends, tennis.

Frederick Traube doesn't go anywhere.

Three children, two boys and a girl, all teenagers, live at home and are always off out, going places.

Frederick Traube doesn't go anywhere.

There's a dog that Mrs Traube takes for regular walks.

Frederick Traube doesn't go anywhere.

The gang are sticking to their task admirably. Ush is whingeing a bit but she's on it.

We've had nothing. There hasn't been anything that has made us think we have an opportunity for an approach. Blocking his car to make him get out would be too much like the Vincent Pope approach and burgling his house would be too much like the Frank Amos approach.

All this time, I've been thinking about my two meetings with Gault. The first one, in Inspector Brady's office, where he was being assertive and the second, in the Half Nelson, where he was being friendly.

I asked him whether he knew DS French. He intimated that he didn't. It doesn't matter whether he does or not. The point of it was to see if I could tell whether he was being honest or deceitful. I couldn't and what's worried me most is that it's the accurate reading of this kind of body language that our thumbs-up or thumbs-down relies on. Okay, so the stakes might be different and we've added in a bit of questioning but, with Traube, we're going up against someone who's used to playing these games. He will see through what we're doing instantly.

I said to Lottie we will need a completely different approach. By that I mean a completely different style of approach.

Right, that's it. I call a halt to the surveillance and arrange to meet for a debrief on a piece of green parkland just near the banks of the Thames opposite Strawberry Hill.

"Why there, it's out of our way," Ush complains.

"I like the name and it's a lovely day to sit and watch the river."

* * *

CHARLIE

There's an uncertain mood.

Everybody seems happy to have got the surveillance behind us but they feel bad that no real result was gained despite all our effort.

Since Wednesday morning, they've been at it full on, taking it in turns to rest, taking it in turns to sleep. Not that there was much sleeping. Everyone's dog tired. Lottie and I fared better than the others in that respect – maybe there is a sleep-advantage that comes with being a multiple.

With our bikes stacked against a tree, we settle in a circle. Zach and Rob prop themselves up against their rucksacks. Ush lies back, using her rucksack as a pillow. Wade props himself up on his elbow. Only Eileen sits like me, cross-legged, back straight and comfortable.

"What are we going to do then, Charlie?" That's Ush being provocative.

"I don't know." I'd like to give it up but I'm not sure it's what they want to hear. It's certainly not what Rob wants to hear. Lottie hasn't mentioned the integration conversation we had. I can't tell if she regrets raising the subject and, if I can't read the body language of my own body, what chance do we stand of reading Traube's?

"Surely we just keep going. We've got until tomorrow evening." Eileen's remaining positive. "It's Saturday night. Maybe he'll liven up a bit."

Groans all round.

Eileen pushes on. "We can't keep surveillance on him digitally because of the forensic implications, so I say we carry on. We're due a break."

"Why have we stopped?" That's Rob.

"We may as well carry on until tomorrow night, as planned." Zach's taking the same stance as Eileen.

"Okay, everyone listen up. Traube is not going to be like the other three. He will be more difficult to read. He will not cave in under questioning. He's going to be observant. He's going to know exactly what to do if we give him a thumbs-up. Not just know what to do, he has the authority and clout to mobilise a team of detectives who will be right on our tails." Fortunately I've had a chance to talk with Wade about my meeting with Gault and he's helped me structure this argument so I don't end up prevaricating. The fact that Wade's not chipping in maybe means I'm doing a good job. "We need a radically different approach. We're keeping him under surveillance but without knowing our approach, we don't know what we're looking for."

"I thought we were just looking for a chance to catch him on his own." Rob is pleading.

The others are looking down or away. They're seeing my point.

"Come on guys. Are you backing out on me?" Rob is distraught.

"We're not backing out on you. Everyone here is committed. And I'm including Lottie – and Gillian and Jemima and Floella. All I'm saying is that what we're doing won't work. We need to find a way that will work."

"Sounds to me like you're backing out." Rob is not satisfied. Interestingly, the others aren't trying to mollify him. "Next, you'll be briefing us in what to say when arrested. You said you'd do that a while back. You may as well…"

"Rob, we haven't identified a target for Lottie. We need to locate Travis Hendry. We need to recover all his video clips. We are not backing out. I've taken on the role of keeping us out of prison. I'm not shirking my responsibilities."

"We need to follow him at a distance." Ush said that.

"That would leave a digital forensic trail…"

Wade has sat up. I recognise that look about him. He has an idea. He's formulating it. He won't leap straight in. He'll think it through.

I keep going, just filling the gap before Wade comes in. "…You all know the effort we put in not to leave a trail for police. It's why we ride around on bikes and not in cars. It's why we wear baseball caps and keep our faces turned down. We use digital forensics to our advantage in the setting of alibis. We…"

Wade raises his hand.

I stop.

"Something Ush said," Wade has worked it out. I can tell. It's not the way he's talking, it's his demeanour. "Follow him at a distance."

Eileen goes to speak but I hold up my hand. Eileen sees me and recognises the significance. She realises that Wade is going to come up with something off the wall.

"Right." Wade's formulated his argument. "We send him the video. If he's not the abuser, he will take it to the Child Exploitation mob. The important thing there, is that there isn't a clear image of Rob. To be honest, none of those videos show a clear picture of any of you. The camera has been angled to identify the abuser – not the abused. *We* recognise the abused because *we* know who they are. Anyone else cannot know because there's not enough in those videos for identifying the abused – especially fifteen years on. In addition, there's nothing in those videos that indicate where they were taken."

The others are looking at Wade. They too sense that we might be on the verge of a breakthrough.

Wade continues. "We send him the video and, if he is the abuser, what will he do?"

Oh, god, Wade's being all dramatic again. I've told myself I will have a word with him. I really must do it.

"Destroy it," says Ush.

Wade shakes his head.

"Wank over it," says Eileen.

I wasn't expecting that from her.

Wade shakes his head again.

I've had enough. "Come on, Wade. Spit it out."

"He'll take it to Travis Hendry."

"If Travis Hendry can be found." I know Wade's onto something here but I can't see it.

Wade smiles. "Frederick Traube is a DCI in the Metropolitan Police. He will find Travis Hendry."

We all look at each other in disbelief. There's an awful lot missing here.

Wade continues. "We will have to follow him. Ush suggested, at a distance. With his experience, he'll be expert at anti-surveillance. The chances are, we'll lose him. If following him at a distance, we're even more likely to lose him."

No. No. This won't work. "You want to lump his car?"

"We don't know that he'll take his car."

"What? So we stick a location device on him."

"In effect, he already has one."

"What?" That's everyone.

"I've been doing some hacking. Frederick Traube is financially strapped. That house he has in Kingston is worth over one and a half million. His affluence doesn't come from his job, it comes from his family. But he's massively overstretched himself. He has an outrageous mortgage. This probably explains why he never goes out. He's applied for promotion. Let me tell you, the step-up in pay from the inspecting ranks to the superintendent ranks, better stated as from the federated ranks to the superintending ranks, is substantial. The Superintendents' Association carries a lot more clout than the Federation…"

"Wade. Forget the whys and wherefores. He wants promotion."

"I'd go as far to say, he's desperate for it."

"And so what?"

"If he's sensible, when he goes to see Travis Hendry, he won't take anything with him that would leave a digital trail – for exactly the same reason we don't."

Wade's taking his time but it looks like he's zooming in on Traube's job mobile.

"But he wants that promotion. He has boards in the offing. As a DCI he's permanently on call. Something he cannot allow to happen, is to be out of touch."

"So we have to make something serious happen. Serious enough for a DCI to be called out." Rob hasn't got it. He soon will.

"No. Not at all. The point is, he cannot afford to be without his job telephone. Even if he finds Travis Hendry and goes to see him, he will take his job telephone with him. If or when we lose him, all we have to do, is follow his telephone."

"And you can do that?"

"At risk of flattering myself, yes."

* * *

CHARLIE

"How will it work, Wade?" Ush seems to be more enthusiastic than the others.

"We send him the video."

"How? Exactly."

"Any number of ways – SMS, email, WhatsApp. Personally, I'd put it on a DVD, wrap it in an accompanying note and post it to him."

"If he's half sensible, he won't play it." Zach's engaged.

"If he doesn't, we consider that a thumbs-up. If he does, we consider that as contributary to a thumbs-down. The idea, of course, is to encourage him to play it so we can assess his reaction."

"How? We have no control over what he does or doesn't do." Rob is, once again, seeing his hopes of confronting his abuser spiralling down a drain.

"The accompanying note must come from Travis Hendry."

Now, that has perked Rob up and, not just Rob, all of them.

"Put yourself in his position. What would you do?"

"Does he know who Travis Hendry is?"

"Not known. But, if he does know who and where he is, what will he do?"

"Go see him – confront him even." Rob's nodding his head – a little smile forming.

"And if he knows who he is but doesn't know where he is?"

"He'll use his position to find him."

"And if he doesn't know who Travis Hendry is?"

"He's not my abuser." Rob holds up his hand. Zach leans across and high-fives him. Ush hugs him.

Eileen takes his hand. "I really think Wade has got something here."

Rob is now smiling.

Lottie's pushing and I move aside.

"Rob. This is great news. It is this kind of insight that we needed. Wade and Charlie have brought it to us. Approaching Travis Hendry would confirm Traube's guilt. No ifs. No buts. No need to gauge his reactions. No need to question him."

"But, Lottie. If it's not him, would he hand the video over to Child Exploitation?" Eileen's thinking and assessing. "It's a good likeness. I'd imagine Child Exploitation would have some pretty pertinent questions for him."

"Easy enough to refute and also explains, to a degree, why he was sent the video. Because this video and the note could end up in the hands of Child Exploitation, we cannot name Travis Hendry. We would be horribly exposed if they get his name." It's good to hear Lottie piecing all this together. There's definitely some sort of change come over her. Her talk about integration promptly followed by this. Whatever. Back to the current conversation.

Eileen is speaking. "I suppose we could drop the video through his letterbox at any time but we would have to be ready in case he moves."

"Wade. What are the implications?" Lottie's a natural at involving everyone.

"None as far as I'm concerned. Dropping it through his letter box is an option. Better to post it though, as I think his doorbell has a camera. I'll check that out and come back to you. Good thing is that I can track his job telephone on one of our burners."

"Wouldn't the rest of us want to be able to burst in on Traube and Hendry when they are together?" Rob is now too enthusiastic.

I'll leave it to Lottie to handle this. It's good to see her back and taking the lead.

"We will follow him but as Wade and Charlie are saying, we are likely to lose him. Tracking his phone gives us a backup. A lot of leave has been wasted on this exercise. When will it be feasible to try again with Wade's plan?"

"A month. We can book the leave now to avoid the risk that comes with last minute applications." Wade's enjoying being one step ahead.

"How long would we need?"

"A week."

I don't know what Wade's basing that on.

"Okay. Which week?"

"I'll aim for the middle of June but I'll let you know. The last thing we want is to organise all this only to find he's on leave. We're approaching holiday season."

"That's a good point." Rob sits forward. "As far as I'm concerned, the sooner the better. If I get into trouble at work, then I'll weather that storm when it comes."

"Hang on." Eileen has held up her hand. "That's easy for you to say. When this is all done, you're heading back to paramedic land. I for one have a career to think about."

"Oh, come on, Eileen," Rob's sounding angry. "What's more important? Just because you've done yours. I was there for you and now you're deserting me. Bloody typical…"

"Stop. Stop. Stop." Wow. I've never heard Lottie so forceful. She's been convincing. She's been persuasive. This is real strength. "No one is abandoning you, Rob. Do not even think like that. Everyone is behind you. Our project takes priority but we do have to manage our lives. We must all think about the long-term consequences of what we do. For me, this is something we go for as soon as we can – first opportunity. Charlie must deal with the consequences of that and she will. Ush, what about you?"

"Absolutely." Good to hear Ush so positive.

"Zach?"

"I'm with Rob. Whatever it takes."

"Eileen?"

There's a delay before she answers. "I was out of order. Yes. Rob. I'm right with you. A bit of questionable absence at work is nothing in comparison to our project. I'm sorry I… I'm sorry. I'm with you Rob. One hundred percent. We go at the first opportunity."

There are hugs all round. The mood is good. I leave Lottie on the *spot* to enjoy the moment with the gang.

Ten minutes later, she's left me on the *spot* to enjoy riding the bike back to Camberwell.

CHAPTER SEVENTEEN

LOTTIE

I must try harder. I do not hold the *spot* as much as Charlie because she has to hold down our job. When I do have the *spot*, I enjoy the benefits of a lean and fit body. I was watching the others as we sat on the banks of the Thames. They are also very fit, they do so much cycling, but they move around stiffly. Ush is always complaining about how hard it all is. Zach makes a song and dance about his aching muscles. Rob does not complain but his discomfort is clear. Only Eileen compares with Charlie. Although shorter and squatter, she moves around as easily as Charlie and, when I have the *spot*, as easily as me.

Just watching them stand up – the groans and moans. From sitting cross-legged, I do not even need to use my hands or move my feet. I just stand up.

Wade is fit. He is much bigger than the others but he, too, moves around freely.

I do not know why I spoke with Charlie about integration. Not what I wanted, but now I have no idea what I want. Is it even possible for us to do it ourselves? It just makes sense to me. The reason why the different alters exist is to shield each other from traumatic experiences and memories. Does that mean we are therefore at peace? Of course not. The children are proof. They remember the abuse as if it happened yesterday. To them, it did happen yesterday. Surely Charlie and I can help them with their memories and trauma.

One question keeps coming back. If we integrate, what will happen to us? Whatever the answer is to that question – another question arises. What will we do if one of us resists integration?

I am, of course, assuming that Charlie will be able to cope. What will we do if the children's memories cause Charlie to meltdown? Although her flashbacks are receding, she is not as secure as she makes out. If Charlie has some kind of episode, what will happen to us?

The answers to these questions evade me. Because of Daventry and Pope, we cannot seek help. I know what I have done – taken a bad situation and made it worse. If I had not started this project, we could have sought all the help available. The likes of Doctor Slattery would have guided us through and been there to help us deal with the unveiling of traumatic memories.

Charlie is breathing hard. I wonder where she is. Ah. We are heading up Denmark Hill. Strange route home. I suppose they might have stopped off at Wade's in Streatham for something. Must have missed that. Anyway, nearly home but this is a long steep hill. Another thing about Charlie – she does not make do with second best. Even though she is taking us up this hill as fast as she can, she puts in that little bit more to squeeze out the last ounce of performance – out of the saddle, standing on the pedals, the bike juddering as she changes down a gear, determined to stay with Wade who is ten metres in front.

He does not seem to be putting in anywhere near as much effort.

At last. We have reached the brow, the road is levelling out and we are turning right. Turning right – but this is such a fast and major road. Cars are coming at us from every direction. I cannot watch. Done it and we now weave our way through some back streets before turning onto Camberwell Grove and home. Why does she do that? Scared the living daylights out of me.

* * *

LOTTIE

With bikes locked away, we are indoors on the sofa. Wade has retrieved a bottle of wine from the fridge. Charlie leans into Wade and they share a moment of closeness, Charlie resting her head on his chest, Wade with his arm around her shoulder.

This is for them – like the time I can snatch with Ush – leave them to it…

Lottie, don't go.

I stop.

Charlie gets up and sits, Eileen-style, on a dining chair opposite Wade.

I do hope we will not be indulging in blue-towel-green-towel.

"Lottie's on the *stage*. I think there's something she wants to talk about."

What do I want to talk about? Is this Charlie's way of opening up a conversation about intimacy? Is it her way of starting a discussion on integration?

Charlie has even vacated the *spot*.

Wade is looking at me.

"Having been told there is something I want to talk about, could I be informed what exactly it is I want to talk about?"

"Charlie hasn't confided in me," says Wade.

"What has she not confided in you about?"

"She hasn't confided in me about intimacy. Has she left you to teach me about the birds and the bees?"

Charlie. What have you done? Wade is ahead of us every step of the way.

I haven't done anything. Or said anything.

Right. Well, I will deal with this. Enjoy. I look forward to hearing just how much you enjoyed it.

"Wade. Charlie has intimacy issues because many traumatic intimate moments are hidden from her behind amnesic barriers. Trouble with these barriers is that they are not complete. Feelings and emotions seep through. Every time she gets close to intimacy she is bombarded by those feelings and emotions and they knock her flat."

Wade says nothing.

Charlie, on the *stage*, is not trying to stop me.

Soldier on, I suppose.

"Time will not heal. I think the only way to heal…" Should I move onto integration? May as well. "…is to break down those barriers. Let Charlie confront those traumatic memories. Trouble is, there will be no help.

Our DID cannot become known further afield than our little gang."

Wade sits forward. He drains his glass of wine, refills it and sits back.

"There are various ways we could tackle this. I do not think it appropriate that suggestions come from us. I think they must come from you. I only hope that I have not scared you away."

Wade puts his glass down. "Lottie, is Charlie there?"

"Yes."

"Would you let her take the *spot*?"

"Yes."

"And would you retire to your *dressing room*?"

"Consider me gone."

* * *

LOTTIE

So, I am consigned to my *dressing room*. I could not tell whether Wade was angry, just cross or even cares. His stupid fop of hair did not fall down over his face so this could not have been too much of a surprise for him.

What probably was a surprise was that it was me talking about it – me raising the subject.

Oh. Charlie is upset. With this level of stress I would normally head up to see. But no. I know where she is and who she is with. I also know what they are likely to be talking about.

* * *

CHARLIE

"Charlie, what the hell was that?"

"I'm sorry."

"Stop saying you're sorry."

"I'm sorry, but I thought Lottie might be a bit more subtle."

Wade sits back. In truth, I'm not sorry at all. All I know is, Wade and I need to talk intimacy and I don't have the guts to raise this subject with him. Lottie raised it with me. I figured she could raise it with Wade. I didn't want to plan it with Lottie – it would have come across as contrived and Wade would have seen through that. Now I feel like I've manipulated this whole thing and I feel like shit. Oh, god. What have I done?

Wade has sat back. He's angry. "Right. Charlie. You didn't have the confidence to raise this subject with me – which I find... disconcerting – however, now it has been raised, you can talk about it." Definitely angry.

I've thought about this from every direction I can think of. Truth is, every time I start, I tie myself in knots. All I want, is to talk. How can it have got to this point before I figure out how to approach it? Of course. The piece I'm missing, is Kathy. If Kathy weren't so hostile, I'd be talking it over with her. Not the DID stuff, just my... No point thinking about that. I don't have Kathy. I have Wade. Come on, must do this.

"Wade. You've stood by me. You've put yourself in harm's way for me. You've taken risks for me. You're risking your job, your reputation and... and... I don't have the words."

I'm determined not to say the word *sorry*.

"I think I've said this before, that I feel I'm letting you down, but all I'm getting is, 'it's to be expected, who in your position wouldn't, be patient.' It's not enough. All I know is I need help. I don't know what kind of help. It's undoubtedly the kind of help Doctor Slattery would provide."

I'm getting there. I haven't used the word *sorry*. I feel as if that one word could bring this relationship with Wade crashing down. He's giving no signals as to his thoughts about what I'm saying. Okay. Push on.

"Doctor Slattery is not available to us. With Daventry and Pope, we can't let knowledge of our DID spread beyond the gang and us. Lottie's caused this situation and I believe she's sorr… um… contrite."

Wade has started laughing.

"What can possibly be so funny?" Now I'm angry.

"You're trying so hard not to use the word *sorry*."

And I start laughing.

It's a while… a while before we calm down.

Wade holds up his hand, takes a deep breath and… lets it out. "You've spoken with Lottie about integration. How do you feel about that?"

"Confused. Lottie's introduced me to the children. She talks of barriers. She says if we break down those barriers, I'll be confronted with many traumatic memories. She mentioned Doctor Slattery. She said he would drive a bulldozer through those barriers."

"A bulldozer."

"Her word."

Wade goes quiet. The laughter we just shared has passed. He's thinking. He's analysing. He's working the arguments. He picks up the bottle of wine but, instead of refilling our glasses, he screws on the top. That's not good.

"There is a bulldozer. It's not Doctor Slattery. It's Lottie." He downs the remains of his glass of wine. "I need to get my head around this. To do that, I need time – time on my own. You Late Turn Wednesday?"

I nod.

"I'll see you Tuesday evening, after I've finished work. I'll stay at my flat until then. I'll just gather a few bits." He gets up and moves around the flat dropping things into a sports bag.

I'm losing him.

With his bag zipped up, he sits back down. "My leaving in this way is sending you a message. Please understand. I need space and I need time. Three days. You will feel uncomfortable over those three days, but know this... I want to be with you. Not, I need to be with you. I *want* to be with you. Tuesday evening, we'll talk about a way forward."

He stands. What he has just said was not comforting. I'm fighting back tears.

He's moved over to the front door but stops, his hand on the latch. "And being with you, means being with Lottie and the children as well. You are all part of each other."

CHAPTER EIGHTEEN

CHARLIE

I have three days on my own. *On my own.* That little phrase means something different for me than it does for everyone else I know.

That can't be right. Others have this condition. What I would give to be able to talk with someone who's in the same boat. But Lottie's put paid to that. The only people I have to confide in are Wade, Ush, Eileen, Rob and Zach. They're my friends. They're on my side. They'll be there for me. They hold a greater loyalty to Lottie. Well, not Wade, but there's been a change.

That bulldozer comment. Wade's opened it up for me and it's really got me thinking. The one who's proving herself unreliable here is Lottie. She's been manipulating me all the way. My understanding of this condition we endure really boils down to what Lottie's told me. Wade has done so much reading and research, but what can he offer me? Support? I don't need support, I need resolution.

Eileen's great but she's very matter-of-fact.

Zach and Rob? I don't know. Good friends. But they're with Lottie.

Ush. I nod my head slowly. Ush is changing. It's just a feeling but I feel Ush is moving towards me. What has happened?

I flop onto my sofa, rest my head back and gaze up at the ceiling.

Those days back at the children's home. Ush and I were so close. When, exactly, did she start calling me Lottie? Although, at the time, it hurt, looking back it was just a bit of childish name calling. I remember retaliating and calling her by her full name – the name she hated. But what prompted all that?

I now know. That was when the abuse began.

There's a stain on my ceiling.

I close my eyes. Forget the stain. Lottie's feeling lost. This has coincided with Ush showing greater affection for me. Lottie's capable of misdirecting. She persuaded the gang to embark on a murder spree. Now she's trying to persuade me to join in an integration effort.

I'm developing a feeling that I don't trust Lottie.

She's not on the *stage*. She'll be down in her *dressing room*. The thought comes to me how apt our theatre analogy is. One *spot*. One *stage* with *wings* each side. But several *dressing rooms* – one for each of us. Are there just the five? Are there more? Again, I'm working off what I've been told, what I've been shown. It's Lottie who's been doing all the telling and the showing. Then there's this character called Sebastian. I don't understand him at all.

I've distracted myself. What was she saying? Breaking down barriers – barriers that hold back traumatic memories – barriers that keep those memories away from me. I'm twenty-five years old. Would I collapse under the weight of those memories or would I acknowledge them and move on?

Then she mentioned Sebastian. She mentioned him in a way suggesting he has the answers.

I dig out one of the burners.

"Lottie?"

"Sorry, Ush. It's Charlie."

"Oh. Hi. What makes you want to burn another phone?"

"You free today?"

"Only completely. I did have a prior engagement over in Kingston but that's fallen through." Ush is in a good mood.

"Can I come over?"

"Of course."

"Great. See you in a couple of hours. Where we met by the canal. Remember?"

"Yeah. Yeah. Oh. And Charlie? Will Lottie be coming too?"

"Ha ha."

"And, Charlie?"

"Yes, Ush."

"Do I need to do all that shit with SIMs and text messages?"

"Yes. See you soon."

I spend the next few minutes buggering about with the phone and, as I hit SEND on the text message with the new encoded number, I find I have a little smile on my face. I get the reciprocal text from Ush and the rest of the gang, and replace my SIM. There is a step we're skimping on – the destroying-the-phone step. But I've got to keep the gang on board. We'll destroy phones after three uses – as agreed.

Right. Cycling gear.

* * *

CHARLIE

"Ush. I know it's difficult, but would you be able to tell me all about what happened back at the children's home when the sexual abuse started?"

My question has taken her aback.

This beautiful May day has turned into a beautiful evening. We met about half an hour ago and have enjoyed an ice cream while laughing about Frederick Traube and whether his boringness is evidence supporting a thumbs-up or a thumbs-down.

Now the smiles and laughs have faded.

"Is this really something you want to talk about?"

"Not only do I want to talk about it. I want to talk about it with you."

"I was going to say. Why me? You could talk to Lottie."

"I've spoken with Lottie. It hurts her too."

"Is she there?"

"No."

Ush folds up the wrapper of her finished ice cream and slips it into a pocket of her backpack. "Anything specific?"

"Put it this way. I'm not looking for a detailed description of the abuse. I'm looking for the more general stuff going on around it. Lottie can't help me with that."

"Where do I start?"

Ush seems up for this.

I'm asking myself why I've arranged to meet her to talk about this. All I know, is that it's something I must follow. "Start with Travis Hendry."

Ush arranges her bag as a pillow and lies back. She doesn't look at me but looks up at the blue sky and the few fluffy clouds drifting across. "There was a change in Travis. He would lose his temper at the slightest provocation. And he got very mean. Spiteful, even. I remember thinking at the time that he was behaving like us. There was a lad there called William. Do you remember him?"

I nod. I remember William. "Skinny bloke, cried a lot."

"That's him. I don't think he was on the receiving end of any sexual abuse, but he did come in for a lot of physical abuse. The sort of abuse you got. You know, holding lighted cigarette over your skin, tying you up so your muscles would go into cramp, giving you something heavy to hold for hours on end, making you stand in a cold shower."

"I remember. Dealing with all that is why I'm here."

"I suppose. But I got the feeling that because you'd been moved onto the sexual abuse, he felt he had to find another victim for his own sadistic tendencies. Does that make sense?"

"Yes. I do remember. I just felt so relieved that his spotlight had come off me and gone onto William. I felt bad for William but I felt pleased for myself. I had no idea about the sexual abuse that was coming my way."

"You know what, Charlie. I believe you. I feel really ashamed. All these years, I didn't believe you. I thought you were just deliberately leaving it to Lottie. I think that's why I was spiteful towards you at the home and then, I don't know, the sort of grown-up version of it when we met again a few months back."

I think this is what I've been looking for. Ush has had the answer all the time. Right. The nub of the issue. "The thing that's been puzzling me is that a child suffers abuse and that abuse is so horrible, so traumatic and lasts for a long time – no, not lasts for a long time, keeps happening, incessant, every night, no let-up – the brain forms a barrier to, kind of, package those memories away. That package is called Lottie. That's the dissociation. But I have no memory of the abuse. So what was it that triggered the dissociation that led to Lottie? I don't get it."

"I think, if I'm honest, I didn't get it either. Nor Zach. Nor Rob. Not even Eileen and you know how sharp she is. From what I've read, I think it's called retrograde amnesia – there's an event that causes the amnesia but memories from before the event form part of the amnesia. That's maybe why we turned our backs on you. But I do get it now. I've talked with the others about it and they all agree. I think we all know that you see things others don't. You get a hunch about something and, to all of us, it's a shrug of the shoulders but, to you, it's clear as day. Lottie has even spoken about it. What was the incident she described. A car, the driver had a stolen phone under his seat."

I laugh. "That was when Lottie was trying to defend evidence arising from a funny feeling or a hunch. I can't remember what I said now. It would have been something like we might arrest on suspicion but we don't kill on suspicion."

"Oh, Charlie, you were much more scathing than that. Then came the Frank Amos confrontation. I was laying an alibi for Eileen so I wasn't there but I heard from the others that you took control and you turned that suspicion round into absolute certainty."

"No. Frank Amos turned it round to absolute certainty."

"Whatever. I think it was something Wade said which really moved me, prompted me to rethink everything and made me feel terribly embarrassed about the way I'd been treating you. He used the word 'certainty'. He said you have a certainty about you that he's never seen in anyone else. He said the people who often appear the most confident are those who, um, I can't think of the words he used. Um. Oh yeah. Bluster. He used another word I've never heard before."

"Sophistry."

"That's it. What does that mean?"

"Same as blustering. Sounds like Wade though. Why use one word when there are six available."

We laugh. This is good. I'm so glad I'm getting back on terms with Ush.

"I think," Ush says pushing herself up onto one arm, "whereas we were all suspicious about the oncoming abuse, you were certain of it and maybe that's how you did your dissociation thing before it started. Or it's retrograde amnesia which doesn't make any sense to me. I don't know."

I have no idea whether what Ush is saying makes clinical sense. Or psychiatric sense. Or psychological sense. Retrograde amnesia? What the hell is that? I'm sure Wade would come up with a few more words. But a picture of all this is starting to form for me.

"The thing I don't get," Ush has now eased herself up and is sitting cross-legged – I didn't think she could, "is who you're an alter of. Lottie dissociated from you. Who did you dissociate from?"

And I'm left with my mouth open.

"You see, you got your hunch stroke certainty thing about the sexual abuse and up pops Lottie. Who was having a problem with the physical abuse to the extent that up pops Charlie?"

My mouth's no longer just open. It's wide open.

"Oh, Charlie. I don't mean to upset you. You really need to see someone who can explain all this."

I hold up my hand. Ush goes quiet. I'm thinking. It was Lottie who told me I'm an alter like her. No memories from before I was six years old. Wade confirmed that memories form from around the age of three. What was the word he used? Sustainable? That's it. Most people form sustainable memories from the age of three.

"Ush. How old were you when you joined the children's home?"

"Seven."

"And what about the others."

"The four of you were already there when I joined. I latched onto you and Eileen because we slept near one another. Rob and Zach were on the same landing."

"I remember that. But I don't remember anything from before that."

"Okay. But why is that so important?"

"Sustainable memories start forming around the age of three."

"In everyone or just a majority?"

I stand and walk over to the canal. There's a guy fishing. People are walking by. I'm not happy. I've been hoodwinked. And the person who's deceived me is Lottie.

* * *

CHARLIE

I turn back from the canal.

Ush has brought over our bikes. "Charlie. What we've been talking about is pretty heavy. It's starting to get dark. I know you've got lights and reflective gear and everything but I'm concerned about you riding home. It's a long way for you. And it's Saturday night. I know we have rules about visiting each other's places – neighbours and all that – but I think this must rank as an exception."

I would say no. I am, however heading back to an empty flat. My mind is all over the place. I won't be seeing Wade again until Tuesday evening. Three days on my own. Notwithstanding Lottie.

"You know what, Ush. I think this is an exception. Lead the way."

CHAPTER NINETEEN

CHARLIE

"Make yourself comfortable, Charlie. So, here we are, a beautiful evening and we sit with the windows shut. I know why, we don't want anyone overhearing what we say, but I can't live the rest of my life like this."

I followed Ush back to her flat in Ilford. It was a longer ride than I expected. Our bikes are locked up downstairs and I'm relaxing back into a plush and comfortable armchair. "Do you mind if we talk about something else."

"Let's pick up from where we left off. Memory. What's your earliest memory?"

I shake my head. "I don't know. Does anyone know?"

"I remember things but I don't know when it was. I remember answering a telephone call. It was a desk phone. I picked it up but I didn't speak. Mum was telling me to say something but I didn't and she took the phone off me and I burst into tears. She was all smiles. I remember dad chuckling behind his newspaper. I have no idea how old I was. Maybe four or five. I have other memories that involve them. One I remember was when we were camping and dad couldn't get a peg into the ground without bending it."

"Because your parents were involved, those memories were obviously before you were seven."

"Of course," Ush laughs, "but I don't remember how old I was. I suppose if my mum and dad were still around, they would be able to tell me. So would I be remembering the occasion or would I be remembering what they told me about the occasion? I miss my mum and dad."

"I know you do. I remember when you came to the home. They put you in the bed next to me and you cried all night. I remember trying to comfort you but I think my efforts were pretty much like me comforting prisoners in their cells."

"I hated it. I hated you. I hated everyone. I hated the boy who lost control of his car. I hated the doctors for not saving their lives. That boy killed seven people. No. I really don't want to relive that. Memories are strange. You can place them if you have context. But without any context, I've no idea when they're from."

Ush has told me several times about how her parents, walking home from an evening at the theatre, were wiped up by a motorist, a boy, who lost control of the car he'd nicked and mounted the pavement. She remembers the police officer who came and the reaction of her childminder.

To think – how differently things could have turned out.

My mind drifts back to Lottie. She convinced me I was an alter, like her, on the basis that I have no memories from before I was six. I believed her. Is she right? Dissociation as a result of physical abuse? I remember the abuse – it was painful, it was bad, it was wrong but was it enough to cause a dissociation? I don't know. Those who would know, those who would place this in context for me, those who can help me are no longer available to me.

"How's it going with Wade?"

Oh, god. I'm pleased to move away from the subject of Ush's parents but I'm not so sure about talking intimacy with Ush. Keep it simple. "We're good."

"Come on, Charlie. You can do better than that. I've started dating. Met no one I like. My problem is I don't know what I'm looking for. I don't know how seriously to take it. I don't know what's good or what's bad. I don't even know what's right and what's wrong. Sometimes I feel I'm destined to be on my own."

Ush is probably the most beautiful woman I know. She's not just beautiful in looks, she's beautiful in herself. Boys... Men must be falling over themselves trying to be noticed by her. "I'm struggling with intimacy."

"I know."

"What do you mean? You know. Know what? Has Lottie been talking to you? I know for a fact Wade won't have been."

"Charlie. Nothing like that. You're struggling with intimacy for the same reason I am. For the same reason Rob, Zach and Eileen are. I understand that you didn't suffer the abuse directly – Lottie, Floella, Jemima and Gillian did. But the point is, they are part of you and you are part of them. Those barriers that have sprung up between you don't change that."

I'm fuming. What Ush has just said has shown me up for such a fool. I believed in Lottie. People must work hard to gain my confidence. My trust is hard to earn. And, with what Ush has just said, I'm angry – not with her – with myself. Lottie never earned my trust and, I realise now, she's been taking the piss.

* * *

CHARLIE

I stay the night at Ush's. Lying in her spare bedroom, I can't sleep. I even try my *dressing room* but that doesn't help. I feel I need to be on the *spot*.

Thoughts are flying around my head. Bad thoughts. I can't put them away. Sure, Lottie went behind my back to organise and galvanise the gang into confronting and killing Daventry and Pope. She put me in an impossible position, implicating me in the two murders just to keep me emotionally unstable so she had easier access to the *spot*. Okay, so she made sure I had watertight alibis but she doesn't know how detectives work.

Those two detectives, DS French of Homicide and DI Reeve of DPS are suspicious and they are not going to let go. My case has been put on file for now – but it hasn't been forgotten – not by those two detectives. A single crumb of information is all they need and the case will be reopened, resource will be assigned, the links between Daventry and Pope will be found.

The links with Travis Hendry will be found. Travis Hendry's videos will be found. The link between me and the children's home will be found and DS French's questioning won't be the cat and mouse of banal observations interspersed by incisive questions. It will be nerve-racking observations, one incisive question after another, and they won't stop. They'll be questioning Travis Hendry and I'll be kept in the dark as far as anything he says is concerned. They'll show me the videos. There'll be hundreds. They'll probably include videos of me being abused by Pope and Daventry.

"Interesting how you're abused by Peter Daventry and Vincent Pope and then implicated in their murders by someone who sounds like you and whose voice is a digital match for yours," followed by, "When was the last time you saw Eileen Edison? What did you talk about when you last saw Zachery Novac? Do you keep in touch with Robert Granger? And what about Ursula Keating?" Then, of course, the crippler. "Oh, and here's a video of you being abused by someone called Frank Amos. He too has been killed." Just imagine the questions following that.

Lottie, aided by Eileen, Ush, Rob and Zach, has dropped us all right in the fucking shit. On top of that, Wade is mired in that cess pit too.

I heave myself onto my side and pull the duvet over my head.

Lottie's been talking integration. She's feeling all lost. She doesn't know what her role is anymore. Poor thing. What's her motivation? Why is she telling me I'm an alter? I'm not a bloody alter. I'm the real deal. Lottie is a part of me that has dissociated. Floella, Jemima, Gillian the same. Or are they parts of Lottie? Integration with me means her demise – not mine. I don't even know if what I'm saying makes any sense.

I think the conclusion I'm coming to is that I don't trust Lottie. Not just that I don't trust her – that I can't trust her. I don't know how to address her or how to confront her or how to challenge her. I don't have the knowledge. Doctor Slattery would have that knowledge but Lottie has neatly excluded him. Wade stands a better chance than me but I feel I'd be asking too much of him. No, the confrontation with Lottie must come from me. Wade might help me get my thoughts in order, but I've got to do this myself – with myself.

I pull the duvet down off my face and look up at the ceiling.

There is someone I can talk to. I don't know what he can do for me. I don't know if he will even help me – or take my side – and how do I talk with him without alerting Lottie?

My *dressing room*. That must surely be the gateway. It's weird. Wade would enjoy the puzzle – to gain control, I must relinquish control. I must leave the *spot* vacant. I must evade Lottie.

No point wasting time. Let's go see Sebastian.

* * *

LOTTIE
"Forgive me, Ush. Why did Charlie come over here."

"She called me. Wasted a burner. She wanted to chat. You've told me about a friend of hers called Kathy. I think she was feeling at a bit of a loose end after the

Kingston debacle. I'd have thought she'd have gone to see Kathy. Are they not getting on? We spoke a bit about relationships. You know it's hard for us."

Is Ush being open with me? "Charlie and I have had no opportunity to catch up with each other recently. Not properly. Sounds strange, I know – considering we live inside each other."

Ush is putting some breakfast together. Nothing much – toast, coffee.

I wonder where Charlie is now. Not on the *stage* and not in the *wings* either. I imagine she will be in her *dressing room*. Or gone to see the children. That would be nice but would she know how to? I took her there, showed her the way and she is a quick learner. Yes, I think she would know how to.

Ush is waiting, having poured hot water onto the coffee grounds in the cafetière.

I move a bit closer to her.

She smiles and holds out her arms. I sink into them. She is so warm, so safe, so secure. I hold her. If only it could last. I push her away. I am distraught, but I step back. "I miss you."

"I miss you, too."

I use the sleeve of my dressing gown to wipe away a tear that has started rolling down my cheek. Ush starts plunging the cafetière. I must change the subject. "So what do you think of this plan to provoke Frederick Traube to lead us to Travis Hendry?"

"We haven't been able to find Hendry. It's really quite a cunning plan. We're effectively recruiting one of our abusers to find him for us. I suppose it all depends on whether Wade is good for his promises."

"And the big assumption is that Frederick Traube will take his mobile phone with him. That would be a stupid thing for him to do."

"I'm with you on that, but didn't Wade say it was back-up in case we lose Traube? Hey, Traube's a cop. Wade and Charlie are cops. If anyone knows how Traube's likely to behave, it's those two. If Traube does lead us to Travis Hendry, it's an automatic thumbs-down."

* * *

CHARLIE

I find Sebastian perched on the end of a rickety looking jetty that's poking out into a rippleless lake. He's holding a fishing rod and his white scarf is draped over his shoulder. I walk out onto the jetty but the wooden boards creak and groan. I step back, apprehensive about venturing further.

He turns, his white scarf fluttering in still breeze. He lays down his fishing rod and comes towards me.

Charlie. What brings you here?

I don't really know where *here* is. There are mountains and the sky is red although the sun is bright. A large bird soars in circles. I rein my thoughts back. Sebastian. I must engage with him.

What's Lottie up to?
Straight to the point.
Full of surprises, me.

I know.

He looks around.

Isn't it wonderful, what the human mind can conjure up. Is it a beautiful morning out there?

It is. Would it be different here if it wasn't?

What you're experiencing here is a reflection of what's received through the senses, but more mood-driven.

Whose mood?

You're very good. Think of it like an average.

I'm not keen on averages. I've been on the bitter end of one.

I understand.

He looks out across the lake.

The large bird is turning another graceful circle and a wave washes up and over the jetty. I jump back but the water recedes. Sebastian is not wet but I hear water dripping.

He turns back to me.

You're looking for answers. The only answers I have are ones you already have.

Lottie and I are parts of the same person. Why don't I know her intentions?

Because there are barriers.

So Lottie and I have to communicate like two separate people?

While the barriers are in place, yes.

Take the barriers down.

Not within my gift and, mustn't forget, the barriers are there for a reason.

Another wave rises up around the jetty and the circling bird screeches loud and long.

The barriers were there for a reason. Is that reason still valid?

Yes. They're there for protection.

Whose protection?

Sebastian doesn't answer. It's like he knows the answer but doesn't want to say. The water surges again and rises up my legs but I don't feel it. The bird is joined by another gliding and squawking. They are not friendly to one another. He stoops and runs his hand over the surface of the water like he's stroking it. The water recedes.

We are one.

I don't know what he means.

Here's someone who means a lot to you.

He points past me.

I turn and see a woman falling, her flames rising.

My breath catches.

To your left.

A boy reaching, screaming silently.

And here.

Sebastian moves aside.

On the end of the jetty, a girl in a red coat crying.

I feel myself falling. I'm on my knees. Thunder crushing my ears. Eyes streaming. Oily fingers scratch at my lungs. The stench of burning flesh. The woman, her face bubbling and blistering, pointing with her chin – the slightest of movements.

Please. Make them stop.

Some memories simply won't be locked away.

CHAPTER TWENTY

LOTTIE

Intriguing. I find myself in the Camberwell flat, the *spot* is vacant, Charlie is nowhere to be found and Katherine has turned up. Not sure where we are with Katherine but I do know she has been researching DID. What would have prompted that is the way I behaved when she popped in back at New Year.

I also know that Katherine researching DID is bad. What will she do with the results of her research? What can she do with what she finds?

Charlie and Wade are better placed to figure that out.

A knock on the front door. I deliberately wait a moment before answering. The last thing I want is for Katherine to think I was expecting her. Delaying also gives me a chance to compose. Must talk like Charlie. That was my mistake last time. Not only must I talk like Charlie, I must think like her. Right. Think Charlie, think Charlie, think Charlie. I open the door.

"Kathy! Wow. Wasn't expecting you. Great to see you. Come on in." I stand back and Katherine walks past me into the living room. She seems quite stern. No smile.

I close the door. What would Charlie do? She would not start offering tea or drinks or anything. She would not say, 'To what do I owe this pleasure?' She would wait.

Yes. She would wait. She would stare Katherine out and wait.

I stare at Katherine – and wait.

"Charlie. I've come to apologise. I added two and two and came up with five – probably more than that. I didn't know what to do." She is looking around, maybe not wanting to hold eye-contact.

Whatever, this is a turn up for the books. How should I react? I know. I walk up to her and put my arms on her shoulders. I say nothing and pull her into a hug. I am a few inches taller than her and she clasps her hands around my waist. We both squeeze. The hug goes on. I am feeling uncomfortable but keep squeezing.

Enough. I push her back but hold onto her shoulders. There are tears in her eyes.

"Come on," I say. "Let's see what we can find to drink."

"I'd like that. Where's Wade?"

"He had to go back to his flat. Things to do. Not sure. I expect he'll stay there tonight so we have time to ourselves."

"I'm not intruding, am I?"

"Not at all."

I open the fridge. There is half a bottle of wine in the door and another lying on its side on one of the shelves. No, two lying on their sides. If Wade was involved when they were bought, they are probably quite good.

As I gather a couple of glasses, it dawns on me. I know that what happens right here, right now will be dissected by Charlie and Wade and they will be merciless. I must stay calm and keep my emotions under control. I really do not need Charlie sensing something, coming up to have a look and then heckling from the *stage*.

"So, Kathy, what have you found out from all your research?" Mistake. She is in half-blues, as Charlie calls them, therefore on her way home from work and has popped in on the off-chance. I should have asked her how her Early Turn went. I pour two glasses of wine and see a chance to recover. "You must be on your way home from work. How was your morning?"

"Typical Sunday morning. Nothing happened until midday and then everybody started arguing. We were rushed off our feet for the last two hours."

"I know what you mean." I have no idea what she means.

"I don't know why I was looking at DID. It's so inappropriate. Did you know, it used to be called MPD? Multiple Personality Disorder. Remember that? People in court saying, 'It wasn't me, it was the other me.'"

I laugh because I cannot think of anything else to do.

"Anyway," Katherine has hardly paused for breath, "to dissociate, you know, turn into someone else, you have to have been abused. So it can't be you."

I smile.

"And I'm so embarrassed. I've been so shitty with you. I've behaved like a real bitch. I'm so sorry."

Oh no. Charlie's come out onto the *stage*. How long has she been there? I focus on Katherine. "It wasn't just a bad time for me. It was a bad time for all of us. Lavender pointed out a few hard truths when I resumed. I wasn't myself. I think I'm really only now packing it away in its own little box. I know there'll be times in the future when it will have to be opened but I think maybe we all need our own little boxes."

Katherine is looking at me. What have I said now? She puts her glass down. "You know what, Charlie. I love the way you said that. Its own little box. Not to be forgotten. But it has to be managed. Its own little box. That's how to manage it."

"Wait. Wait. I'm no shrink. The way I look at things seems to be working for me. I don't know whether it'll work for you."

"It's just ideas. You've given me food for thought." She puts her glass down. "Look, I don't really want to stay. And I'm driving so I must be careful what I drink. You know me – if I stay here any longer I won't be able to drive and I'm supposed to be with Michael tonight."

"That's fine. How're you and Michael coming along? You weren't sure about him not so long ago."

"You know what, Charlie. The more I see him, the more I want to see him. That's got to be a good thing, hasn't it?"

"Sounds perfect." I try to make my smile genuine.

"And Charlie, I'm really sorry I treated you so badly."

I put my hand on her arm. "Don't think anything more about it."

She's through the door and gone.

I sit down and release a huge breath. I feel like I've been holding it for all the time Katherine was here.

Charlie is waiting on the *stage*.

That went better than I could have hoped for.

Charlie does not move.

Switching in front of her would have been a bad idea. Especially right in front of her.

Charlie says nothing.

Katherine, I think, has worked out that she is barking up the wrong tree.

Charlie says nothing.

She seems more focussed on her relationship with Michael – which is as it should be.

Charlie says nothing.

Well, come on. What do you think?

I think Kathy came round in an attempt to recreate that New Year thing. So the question is, did you convince someone who has been my best friend for the past seven years that she was talking to me?

I think I did a pretty good job.

But was the job you did, good enough?

What are you saying, Charlie?

She knows that I would have plied her with wine to loosen her tongue and find out what the hell's up with her. What she got was you – and you took everything she said at face value.

I cannot tell if Charlie is cross with me or not.

Do we go after her?

Certainly not. That would help confirm her suspicions.

What do we do?

We try not to feed her anything that will support her suspicions. You see, that's what she's looking for. Her next step is to take her thoughts to DS French. Remember him? The detective you call Humpty? The one who will stew us in our own juices and serve us up on a plate to the Crown Court.

Charlie is cross.

I did nothing that would help confirm her suspicions.

It's not what you did. It's what you didn't do. You didn't try and find out why she suspected DID. You didn't try and find out what her level of knowledge is on DID. You didn't try and find out what her intentions are with what she's found out. You had the opportunity – loads of wine in the fridge, you should have been almost forcing it down her throat. Get her talking. That's what I'd have done. So we can conclude that Kathy now knows that she wasn't talking to me – not by your act but by your omission. 'By act or omission' – something you'll be learning a lot about when we're being grilled by DS French and scrutinised by DI Reeve over a certain pair of murders.

* * *

CHARLIE

I've turned in early. Lottie's buggered off. I don't think she liked the way I spoke to her. So, here I am, lying in bed and all my thoughts are for Wade. If only he were here. He'd be able to help me put all this in proportion. But he's not here and I won't see him for another two days. Won't even be speaking to him for another two days. Depending on what Kathy does, I could be arrested by then.

I suppose the question is whether Lottie and I would be able to hide our dissociation from the likes of Doctor Slattery. Of course we won't be able to. We can't even hide it from the likes of Kathy Bond.

So, what will DS French do with the knowledge of my DID?

Ironic that Kathy spoke of DID being used as evidence for the defence. We'll have DS French trying to use it as evidence for the prosecution. He'll maintain that the DID doesn't just develop on its own – it needs a cause. The cause is sustained and repeated trauma inflicted while a child.

So DS French will be looking for a set of circumstances in my history when I could have been subjected to trauma sufficient to induce DID. He'll find the children's home. He'll find Travis Hendry. Travis Hendry will deny everything. But will DS French find Hendry's videos? Must assume that he will. Daventry, Pope and Amos will be identified. Hendry might even enter into a bit of plea-bargaining. Eileen, Ush, Zach and Rob's names will be given. And, of course, mine. Then the full force of three murder investigations will turn onto the five of us. We'll be held in different police stations. We'll be interviewed and reinterviewed – and re-reinterviewed. Much as I love Ush, she'll be the first to crack. Wade's name will come up. He'll be nicked.

So, two questions… Will Kathy take her DID revelation to DS French? Will Lottie and I be able to hide our DID from the likes of Doctor Slattery?

Even if we can, it's likely that Travis Hendry will be questioned.

I've got to talk this over with Wade. My conclusion is that we've got to go ahead with Traube. If he's the paedophile who abused Rob, he'll find and confront Travis Hendry. We've got to be there. We've got to find

Travis Hendry's stash of videos. When they're recovered, we deal with Traube and Hendry. That will need to look good and direct an investigation away from us.

Doesn't look like I'll be getting much sleep tonight.

CHAPTER TWENTY-ONE

CHARLIE

If I send Wade a message, it has to be an innocuous one. Therefore there's no point in sending him a message. I upset him on Saturday. He went off. He didn't go off in a strop. He went off Wade-style.

So beautiful. Yet again, thoughts of how I treated him when we first met come to mind. I was so impatient, so intolerant. All he has shown me is patience and tolerance. Kathy said something. I'd come up on *stage* just in time to hear it. She said, 'The more I see him, the more I want to see him.' She was talking about Michael.

That's how I'm coming to feel about Wade, but what have I got to offer someone like him? Because of me, he's involved in murder – negative. Because of me, he gained greater standing on the Team – positive. That greater standing probably got him the appropriate write-up allowing his application for SO15 – an application made before he was even out of his probation – possibly a first in the history of the Metropolitan Police. I don't know.

I remember asking him just after his interview, how it went. He evaded all my questions. I remember Lottie's interview for the NCA. With no investigative experience, we stood little chance. Wade's lack of experience meant he stood little chance for SO15. Whereas Lottie just cleverly answered all the questions, I suspect Wade was probably assessing how cleverly they were answering his questions. They must have done quite well as they got the job of being Wade's managers for the next few years.

We are one. That was what Sebastian said. We are one. We are one what? He was stroking the water when he said that and, as he stroked the water, it receded. Did he have control over that? Did he have control over those two birds that were soaring and circling?

Of course, the phrase *we are one* has two meanings. I thought he meant we are like one of the birds. Not at all. He was saying that Floella, Jemima, Gillian, Lottie and I are one. One person. Obviously, his comment includes himself. We are one.

Then he said that some memories can't be locked away. How can he mean that? Lottie has memories that are locked away from me. Same for Floella, Jemima and Gillian.

I have my memories that plague me. Do they plague Lottie and the others? I don't know. I must ask Lottie.

Wait. Wait. Wait. What if we share our memories?

That's it.

Lottie is scared that if we integrate, she'll be lost. She won't at all. She will be incorporated, in exactly the same way as I will be. Floella, Jemima and Gillian too. The barriers will be broken down and we will be one. Our memories will be shared. Sharing the memories will make them manageable.

That's it, that's it, THAT'S IT!

What Sebastian said is that we are one. We ARE one. With these barriers in place, how can we be?

I think I'm getting it. I don't know who Sebastian is. I don't know what he represents but I think I know what he's saying. We are not in a contest. I didn't believe I'm an alter but my thoughts on that are changing. Lottie split off from me to protect me from the trauma of the abuse and its memories. When it got too much for Lottie, Floella formed. Then Jemima. Then Gillian. The four of them are as much a part of me as I am a part of them. They must, all four of them, be holding awful memories.

We are one.

I am an alter like Lottie. But I'm not an alter for the same reason as Lottie. With the sexual abuse came the dissociation resulting in me and Lottie. Lottie was formed as an alter. I was left as an alter. Further abuse, further dissociation. Floella, Jemima and Gillian. I'm thought of as the host because I'm up front on the *spot* most. The hostess with the mostest. That's all.

Because I've occupied the *spot*, I've aged – mentally. Because Lottie found a way and chose to occupy the *stage* so much, she has aged with me. Because the children have been confined, or confined themselves, to their *dressing rooms*, their ageing has stopped. Only by coming up onto the *stage* and *spot* will they encounter the experiences that will enable them to age. Integration will benefit us all. Currently we are one person fractured into five. If we integrate, we all become one person.

I thought of myself as the real deal. There is no real deal. We are five pieces and we need to get back together. We need to be one.

But not yet.

Both Wade and Lottie have lauded the therapeutic effect of killing our abusers. Killing them won't bring us peace. Killing can't ever bring peace. It's integration that will bring us peace. Not just for me. For all of us.

However, the question still stands. What's Lottie up to?

We have a certain project to complete, so not yet, not yet.

* * *

LOTTIE

I think Charlie is smartening up – changing – more patient. Have I made a mistake or misjudged her? I doubt it. By introducing her to our inner world, she has seen what these paedophiles have done to us. She is on board, one hundred per cent. But I remain uncomfortable.

Sebastian selects a ball from the rack. He runs, stoops, swings and the ball rolls down the lane.

Charlie came to see me earlier. Now you, Lottie. Aren't I popular?

What did Charlie want?

The ball slews across the lane and into the gutter.

Suspiciousness is unbecoming.

I am not suspicious. I want answers?

You have those answers.

Those answers are hidden behind barriers.

The ball, pulsing teal and crimson, bobs up onto the rack.

Those barriers are there for your protection.

Those barriers are becoming a threat.

Sebastian takes the pulsing ball.

A threat to who? You?

To all of us.

You're like Charlie. You think like a singleton. You are a multiple. When you start thinking like a multiple, you will be able to make sense of this inner world.

He runs and slings the ball down the lane.

I do understand it.

The best you've managed to learn is how to navigate it. You don't understand it.

How can you say that?

You speak like a singleton. Your motivations are those of a singleton.

The ball crashes into the pins launching fireworks cracking and sparking.

We are one.

Sebastian slaps his thighs. Exploding stars drip from the dark sky. Many people are hurrying and jostling each other. A small dog runs with the crowd. These scenes that Sebastian creates are tiresome. He is not helpful.

He has gone and I am left standing alone in blurred nothingness. I must think like a multiple? That will not do. That will not do at all.

* * *

CHARLIE

Idleness is not me. I've locked the bike up on the stands next to the bus stop opposite Wimbledon Nick. Traube's car is in the yard. I have sufficient disguise – this weather is great, allowing legitimate use of dark glasses – large dark glasses.

It's approaching five on this Monday afternoon. I want to see which way he goes. I want to see if I can keep up with him. A bus pulls up in front of me. I take off my reflective jacket, turn it inside out and put it back on. I was yellow. I'm now orange. As the bus pulls away, I slip a cover over my helmet. It was red. It's now white. And I've swapped my glasses. They were dark monstrous things. They are now yellow safety specs from Wickes.

Quarter-past-five, Traube appears, his car swinging out of the yard. I'm over to my bike and weaving across the road to get in behind him. There are some routes I can take on my bike that are not available to him in his car. I am relying on his predictability and I'm rewarded each time. I have no difficulty keeping up with him and it's easy not showing out – even in all this high-viz.

If I can keep up with him on my own when I know where he's going, six of us with radio communication will be able to keep up with him if we don't know where he's going – so long as he stays in town, so long as he's moving about when there's a lot of traffic. If he goes farther, then we need a contingency. Something to discuss with Wade.

Oh, god. I have a lot to discuss with Wade.

The three Is – Integration. Lottie's intentions. Kathy's interference. Intimacy. Make that four Is.

I've settled myself in the pub and I'm watching Traube's drive from the bay window. I'd like a glass of wine but I still have a long way to ride. A softy it is, which is gone in no time.

Traube's installed for the night. He isn't going anywhere and, if he is, it will be because he's called out. There's no point in staying here.

I head home.

Lottie's intentions. I can't get them out of my mind. On the *we are one* basis, I can't get them out of Lottie's mind either.

There's a barrier holding back Lottie's memories from me. Does that mean that the same barrier is preventing Lottie from accessing my memories?

How do I question Lottie about it? Nearly all my questioning technique depends on reading body language. It's not so much what is said, it's more the way it's said. How do I read the body language of my own body?

I deliberately head up to Vauxhall and turn down towards Camberwell. I'm avoiding the climb up and over Denmark Hill and, if I'm honest, I'm avoiding the temptation of popping in on Wade.

I'm feeling bad about the children. I feel I should be using this time to give them a run out. No. I need to speak to Lottie.

* * *

LOTTIE

Lottie. Get your arse up here. We need to chat.

Charlie sounds upset.

Lottie. Get your arse up here. We need to chat.

Very upset. I cannot hear what she is saying but I am getting the emotion. Come on then, let us find out what she wants. I head up.

Lottie. I said, get your arse up here.

She is standing in front of the mirror in the bathroom. Looks like she has been working out. Punchbag maybe. No, cycling.

Charlie, why are you shouting?

Worked, didn't it?

Chat away.

Who or what is Sebastian?

What a question. I have no idea and non-answers will not cut it with Charlie. Whatever I say must sound good.

He is us.

Which one?

All of us.

I'm in no mood for word salad.

Alright then. She wants it. She can have it.

The first time I was abused... we were abused... he was there. He was not like he is now. He comforted me, made me feel that everything would be alright. In a way, he held my hand for my first ever experience, my first ever memory. There is no need for me to tell you what it was, I am sure your imagination is up to that. I doubt he is an identity or a personality or whatever you want to call us. More like moods, emotions. I think of him as the guardian. He is what keeps the traumatic events and memories away from you so we can go on. He made the barriers. I would even go as far to say he is the barriers. He is us.

I'm sorry, Lottie. That makes no sense. Last I heard, we're a girl. In case you hadn't noticed, he's a man.

Charlie is staring at our reflection. Is she really trying to read me? She has the *spot*. She is looking at herself.

What does Gillian look like to you?

A little girl.

In case you had not noticed, Charlie, we are an adult woman.

Charlie breaks away from the mirror and goes through to the second bedroom where the punchbag hangs from the ceiling instead of a light fitting. I hate this. She is about to punch and kick the living daylights out of this poor helpless punchbag.

She sets the punchbag swinging side to side, adopts a pose, tracks its movement but does not lash out with any kicks or punches. Her swaying is mesmeric.

What do you mean by... so we can go on?

Live.

Do you think Floella, Jemima and Gillian are living?

You are talking about perceptions and perspectives.

So, from their perspective, yesterday they were being sexually abused, today they're playing in a children's playground. I don't call that living.

What else is available to them?

At some point, fifteen years ago, you were like Floella, Jemima and Gillian. How is it they got stuck and you didn't?

I suppose I was more curious than them. I explored.

You didn't think to take them with you?

I did. I...

BANG.

She has just put in a kick. What a noise.

...they were not as inquisitive...

BANG. BANG.

More kicks.

...it is difficult down there. They...

BANG. BANG. BANG. BANG. BANG. BANG. BANG. BANG.

Kicks and punches, one after the other. I hate it. I hate it.

It has gone quiet. Thank goodness. She has returned to her mesmeric swaying. I have half a mind to leave but I know that would be counterproductive. This is a conversation we must have. Maybe if I had forced the conversation, we would now be having it on my terms rather than Charlie's. My terms would not involve quite so much expenditure of energy.

About a week ago, Lottie, you raised the subject of integration. What would you like to happen?

You have spoken with Sebastian.

Don't change the subject.

I am not changing the subject. This is hard. I have hurt us. I have put us in danger. I thought I knew best. I was doing what I thought needed to be done for us to come to terms with our experiences. The world is a baffling and confusing place. I do not understand it and I do not understand the people in it. What I was doing was wrong. Not just wrong as in against the law, but wrong for us. I believe these actions have helped Ush, Zachery and Eileen. I believe they will help Robert. They will help me and the children but we need you to balance out the comeback from the outside world. Even I, with all my reading, cannot do that.

Charlie stops her swaying. I can feel her calming down. She steps forward and settles the punchbag.

* * *

CHARLIE

That's not what I was expecting. If I'm honest, I don't really know what I was expecting. What Lottie just said seemed to come from the heart. I don't know whether my antics with the punchbag made any difference. The most poignant thing was not what she said. It was that she stayed, considering how much she hates all that.

I go through to the kitchen and make coffee, absentmindedly wondering about Wade and how he's coping at his place without his coffee machine.

Not yet time to wind down the pressure.

Let me get this straight. You dissociated from me with the imminent threat of sexual abuse. As a result, I don't have access to any of those memories.

Yes. Then, after dozens of sessions, Floella dissociated from...

Rather than going forward, can we go back? Back to the pots and pans.

Your first memory.

I don't know whether it's my first memory.

At the age of six. Sustainable and retrievable memories generally start around the age of three.

Wade told me that. Who told you?

I read it.

I can't tell if she's lying or perhaps, more kindly, being economic with the truth.

So, I dissociated from whom?

The host.

Lottie's wavering. I didn't hear it. I sensed it. I've got her.

Where's the host now?

Lost.

Lost? Lost where?

Charlie, you have been close to the abyss. That time just after you nearly threw us off the top of Kevan House, you sank down. I came and guided you back.

I remember that, but this still isn't making sense. I'm wondering whether Lottie doesn't know and is pretending she does, or does know and is misleading me. Lot of difference between the two.

The sexual abuse resulted in you. What resulted in me?

The physical abuse.

I want to jump down her throat, but patience. Let her build her web.

Tell me about the physical abuse.

I have no knowledge of that. I was not there.

How did you find out about it?

Sebastian.

I don't believe her. Down there with Sebastian is not a place for idle chatter. Lottie's making this up on the hoof. Patience and time will be enough for her to tie herself in knots.

You spoke about integration. How can we do that without the host?

We do what we can.

But we won't end up with a whole person.

Do you not think that you are a whole person?

And in she comes with her sleazy convincingness – won't work with me.

I feel like a whole person. And, like many other whole persons, I have gaps in my memory. In fact, I'd say like EVERY other whole person.

I want to go for the jugular but now is really not the time. I need to assess what the repercussions will be. Because, of course, going for Lottie's jugular is the same as going for my own.

All memories are stored. Recall is the problem.

And recall is difficult enough for people who don't have barriers like ours.

True.

I need to get out of this. The last thing I want is Lottie thinking I'm onto her.

Lottie, can we pick this up another time? It's grinding me down.

Yes. Sure. I think integration carries with it a lot of unknowns and we all have to be comfortable with it.

I didn't sleep well last night. I'm going for a kip. If you want the *spot*, fill your boots.

CHAPTER TWENTY-TWO

LOTTIE

This is a new experience for me – having the *spot* and not really knowing what to do with it. I feel I should go out and give the children a run about, but Charlie's questions have rattled me. More precisely, her questioning has rattled me. I am as much in the dark regarding the answers to her questions as she is.

To be frank, I am scared. If we integrate, what will become of us? It is all very well, in theory, saying that we will become one or take Sebastian's line that we *are* one. But what will happen to me? What will happen to Floella, Jemima and Gillian?

Integration is definitely the right thing to do. The four of us release our memories to Charlie, she becomes a whole person and we return to... to what? We return to the mother ship? Or do we just die?

I am scared.

Hang on. There is movement outside our front door. A key in the lock. I jump up and find Wade. "I thought you were not going to come back until tomorrow."

"Hi, Lottie. I changed my mind."

"Has something happened?"

"Two things. I'm ready to go with Traube and I'm ready to speak to Charlie."

"Great news." Great about Traube. Not so sure about Charlie. "Do you want to speak with Charlie now?"

"If she's about and, Lottie, I'd like you to listen in."

"Okay but, do you not want to speak to Charlie first." Is he planning to break with Charlie? Surely not. He would not be proceeding with Traube if that were so. What does he need to speak to both of us about? Oh. Charlie has picked up on my anxiety and has come up. Wow. She has never barged me off the *spot* that forcefully.

"Wade. What brings you back so soon?"

"My coffee machine." He comes over and pulls Charlie into the tightest hug. Even Charlie is surprised. I want to leave but he said he wanted to speak to us both. After that hug, I feel a little more secure about Charlie and Wade. I cannot imagine what a nightmare it would be if Wade ditches her.

Coffee made, Wade sits on the sofa. Charlie has sat next to him. I hold station on the *stage*.

"Right. Traube. I have Rob's abuse video ready to be delivered. Zach has physically marked the SD card so we can recognise it again. In addition, I'm set up, ready to track his mobile telephone. We just need to decide when we're going to do it and prepare some contingencies."

In response, Charlie squeezes his hand.

"Now, you. Charlie. Lottie too. Please confirm that she's there."

Charlie nods.

Wade continues. "The wonderful thing about the word *you* is that it is the same in both the singular and the plural.

I've decided you are all aspects of the same person. That, of course, includes the children. In the singleton state, you would be one person with no barriers. In the multiple state, you are one person with barriers. I want to be with you, no matter what state you're in."

Charlie is motionless. She is looking at Wade. Hang on, her eyes are misting. Wow. She has launched herself at Wade. They are hugging and kissing. The sensation I'm feeling is nothing but pleasure.

They separate and Charlie moves along to the far end of the sofa, still holding his hands. I can feel the smile on her face. She wipes away tears.

Wait. What was Wade saying? What he said to Charlie, using the word *you*, was for all of us. He wants to be with all of us because we are all parts of the same person. My god. I am welling up now. I must think about this differently.

It is not her eyes are misting, it is our eyes are misting. It is not she has launched herself at Wade, it is we have launched ourselves at Wade. It is not they are hugging and kissing, it is we are hugging and kissing. The sensation of nothing but pleasure, is our sensation, not just Charlie's. Easy to say but we have to accept this. We all have to accept this.

Wade has thought his way through this further and better than I have.

* * *

CHARLIE
"I actually thought you weren't coming back."

"Never crossed my mind."

Lottie has left and I'm sitting cross-legged facing Wade. He's sitting normally, one leg crossed over the other, looking longingly at his mug of coffee. I laugh and let go of his hands.

He reaches for his coffee and sips it… reverentially. I can't believe how lucky I've been to meet this man and, to think, I hated him. Well, not hated, but just thought of him as a useless tosser. A know-nothing college boy with zero common sense. He wants to be with me and I want to be with him. A bit of work is needed on the words *me* and *I* – and *us* and *we*.

I break the silence. "Have you done much reading on integration?"

"Only everything."

"What did you find out?"

"It takes years, even with professional, skilled clinical help."

"We don't have access to that. As soon as we do, we line ourselves up for an intensive murder investigation – maybe a few intensive murder investigations."

Wade finishes his coffee and sets the mug down on the coffee table. As he sits back, he swings round to face me. We take hold of each other's hands.

"Lottie has left. She's not on the *stage* and, as far as I can tell, not in the *wings*. I recently grilled her on why she thinks I'm an alter like her because I don't think I am. I pulled my punches…"

Wade reacted to that. On the word *alter* – he reacted. He has something. He's figured it out. Must come back to it. Carry on now. Must come back to it. Alter. Alter. Alter.

"…I pulled my punches though. I think she's spinning a yarn but it's difficult to tell. I'm not getting the normal signals."

"Maybe the signals are different."

"You could well be right but, all the same, I still don't know what I'm looking for."

"Tell me, Charlie. Do you know what you're looking for when you've stopped chummy on the street?"

I don't want to be talking about this. I want to talk about alters. Mustn't push. The time will come. "Well, yes. Of course. You know I do. I make the most direct crime arrests… It doesn't matter."

"It does matter. You see, you pick up on signals that chummy's lying. Here's a challenge for you – tell me what those signals are." He hasn't picked up on the signal that I'm completely distracted.

"Well. It's a…"

"Go on."

"Well, you know. When chummy starts, sort of…" I stop. I'm flummoxed.

"You stopped grilling Lottie, not because you couldn't tell whether she was lying, showing dishonesty or being disingenuous. You stopped because she wasn't doing any of those things. Loads of so-called experts have tried identifying and quantifying it all. Rapid eye movements. Sweating. Wavering of the voice. Looking away. Some of those behaviours are even cultural. At the end of the day, I don't pick up on those sorts of signals at all. You, however, are very sensitive to them. You didn't go for Lottie because you concluded she was being honest. She thinks you're an alter like her. She might be wrong but her belief is honestly held."

"Her belief is honestly held? You should be a barrister."

"Not my kind of bar."

"Talking of which, shall we?"

"It's a nice evening. The Fox on the Hill has a garden. We can talk about Traube without worrying about being overheard. Talking of which, have you swept recently?"

"Only every day. At least, Lottie has." ...thinks I'm an alter...might be wrong...belief honestly held...might be wrong...might...might? Wade's definitely figured it out but he's reluctant to say. I'll bide my time. "Come on. Let's get out of here."

* * *

CHARLIE

I tuck my arm in Wade's as we're walking. I can't believe how my feelings have changed towards him. In just two days, I've gone from finding his company enjoyable to wanting to be with him. I realise that we are joined together courtesy of the odd murder but, that aside, I really want to be with him. He steadies me. I used to think of him as weak for being indecisive, but I was so wrong. He's not indecisive, he just needs more information. The result is that when he makes up his mind, he's undoubtedly right.

He's made up his mind about our alter status. I'm nervous about what he'll say but...

It's funny how this thing about him that irritated me so much, him taking so long to make up his mind, I now find attractive – sexy even.

Oh, god. Intimacy. That won't have changed over the past couple of days.

Come on, it's a lovely evening. Let's enjoy it.

We find a table in a part of the pub garden which is secluded. Well, it's a Monday night so not too busy. Wade has his pint of beer and I have my glass of wine.

"I don't think we should let Rob deliver the video." Wade cuts straight to the chase. "I've had a good look and I'm pretty sure his front door has one of those video camera doorbell things. We'll post it."

"Agree." Wade's right. The risk of it not arriving courtesy of Royal Mail is less than the risk of Rob being caught on camera. "I'll leave you to tell them."

"Fine." He slides a piece of paper towards me. "This is the note I think should accompany the video."

You've pissed me off
TH

"To the point."

"I thought you might have a phrase that's memorably his."

"His sadistic bullying was always prewarned with him telling us we'd upset him."

"He'd use that word? Upset?"

"I doubt he'd use it on the paedophiles."

"Doesn't matter. It's shorter. Less forensics." He extracts a pen from an inside pocket of his jacket and rewrites the message.

I'm upset
TH

"That's better. We are of course assuming Traube will know who TH is."

"If he's a thumbs-down, he'll know who TH is." I'm acting out the thumbs-down.

Wade smiles. "You look like Nero deciding the fate of a luckless gladiator."

I fold my thumb away.

"And anyway," Wade continues, "even if he doesn't know the name, he'll figure it out. He may even go to someone else in the paedophile ring."

"I suppose."

Wade folds the piece of paper and places it in his pocket. "I think we'll all need to be there, ready to go."

"Agreed. But this will be the point where it starts getting tricky. We have no idea how he's going to react or how long it will take him to react. What if he doesn't open it?"

"Thought of that. If we've had no noticeable change in behaviour from him within twenty-four hours, we deliver another one. Zach's made copies and marked each one so they can be physically identified."

"Okay. With you on that. If he's a thumbs-up, how will he react?"

"I reckon he'll go to his office, make a phone call, arrange to meet someone from Child Exploitation and then go to that meeting. I think that would all happen the same day. You or I would be able to get close enough to make sure that's who he meets. I think it will be overkill as his behaviour, if he's a thumbs-down, will be somewhat distinct."

My thoughts exactly. I'm looking forward to hearing how Wade describes a *somewhat distinct* behaviour.

"If he's a thumbs-up he'll carry on as usual. If he's a thumbs-down, he'll be running around like Edward II."

What?

Wade notices my incomprehension and explains. "Edward II's assassin explored the royal anus with a red-hot poker."

I'm quite pleased that my stunned silence only lasts a few minutes. "I suppose that would cause a behaviour that is somewhat distinct."

"It's chronicled that his screams could be heard for miles around."

"Wade. Is this what they teach you at Eton?"

"That particular lesson was repeated every morning by the house master doing his rounds in search of boys who weren't getting out of bed as quickly as required."

"Can we get back to the more savoury subject of murdering paedophiles?"

"If a thumbs-down, he'll either go direct to Travis Hendry or he'll approach another member of the paedophile ring. Although I can track his mobile telephone, we will need to be able to move fast if he travels far afield. So we're going to need vehicles."

"What about ANPR?"

"We'll use false plates. How many cars do you think we'll need?"

"You're talking about ringers. There's a guy joined the Team who can spot a ringer as easily as I can spot a lie."

"The cars will only be used for this and then returned to their original identity."

"Wade. How much will that cost."

"Daddy will foot the bill."

"Does *daddy* know what he's footing the bill for?"

"Not at all, though I half suspect that if enlightened, he'd double my request."

Wade's uncomfortable talking about his parents and, anyway, this is bollocks. It won't work. Let him down slowly. "What about documentation for the vehicles, registered owner, keeper, insurance and all that?"

"As usual, you're straight to the weak point."

"It is a weak point. Too weak. You know what it's like trying to keep surveillance on a target without showing out. Actually, you probably don't know. While one of you drives sedately, a safe distance behind – follow, the others have to drive like lunatics to get into position where they can take over – catchup. That's where an incident is likely to happen – stopped by ol' bill, minor collision, serious collision. The likelihood of being caught on ANPR is high. And although the likelihood of being caught up in an incident is low, the consequences of being in an illegal car are massive."

Wade looks crestfallen.

I take hold of his hand. "Why don't we use our own cars? Because of ANPR? If we're caught up in an incident, better to be driving our own cars than illegal ones."

"You're right of course. So I suppose cars are out."

"No, we can't move fast enough or far enough on our bikes. What if he drives up to Leicester or somewhere. How will we ever keep up?"

Wade's looking dispirited. He thought he had this all sorted out and I've just blown his carefully prepared, if unusable, plans apart. There is an answer and I'm sure he can work it out. He just needs a bit of time.

I'll give him a clue. "What won't we be doing when we're driving our cars?"

"Riding our bikes." He's still looking dejected. He's on the right lines though.

Another hint. "And where will our bikes be?"

"On the back of our cars…" He looks up, triumphant. "And we position our bikes so as to cover the rear number plate, thereby defeating most ANPR cameras."

I nod and smile.

He carries on. "If we're stopped by police or involved in an incident, we make up a story for why we're there and we'll get words of advice for the positioning of our bikes."

I lean across the table and give him a hearty slap on the shoulder. "We'll make a policeman of you yet."

* * *

LOTTIE
Charlie has been so distracted I have been able to hold the *stage* without her noticing. It is Wade's comment

about alters 'Lottie might be wrong.' What that implies, of course, is that… 'Lottie might be right.'

CHAPTER TWENTY-THREE

CHARLIE

Lying in bed that evening, Wade is breathing gently post-frigidity. I don't know why he stays with me. I want to be with him. I want to have sex with him, but I can't loosen up. He was so kind, smiling and promising that we would work it out.

I can't sleep. I don't know which is uppermost in my mind. Traube and Hendry, Lottie and me or Wade and me.

Traube and Hendry. I don't have to think too much about them. If Traube is Rob's abuser, then we're on a collision course and Lottie has put us in a position where they can't be left alive to tell their stories – no matter how sordid, no matter how depraved. Just as important – as well as silencing them, we must recover Hendry's videos. Tons and tons of risk associated with all that. If all six of us end up walking away from this, we will have been exceedingly lucky. I think arrest, charge and imprisonment is the more likely outcome.

I roll onto my side and nuzzle Wade. I run my hand over his chest, down over his abdomen and back up to his chest. He stirs but doesn't wake. He's not a hairy guy, thank god. He's well-toned, not an ounce of fat and powerfully built – all things I like. He's a thinker and I like that too. In the pub earlier, he worked his way round to the right conclusion in the end – with a little help. Only a few months ago I'd have been jumping down his throat, deriding him and announcing that, despite being a college boy, he's dimmer than a broken lightbulb. It is funny though, that he can work his way through complex problems but is stumped by simple ones. I kiss his cheek, stroke his chest and roll onto my back.

When it comes to complex problems, roles are reversed. Alters, for example. He could well be thinking of me in the same way as I thought of him.

Lottie. Not only has Lottie set us on a course for imprisonment, but she's also made professional expert psychiatric help unavailable to us. She's now talking integration. Everything I've read tells me this is a process that takes years, even with skilled clinical help. Then combine that with my newfound suspicion of Lottie. The last time we spoke to each other about this, I did feel more at ease but I'm still not confident about her. I might be doing her a great injustice, but I think what she wants is for the integration to go in such a way that she ends up as top dog. I don't see how that can happen. If we'd fractured our leg, the bones would be lined up, they'd knit back together and there'd be no question about whose leg it is. So our brain has been fractured. The parts need lining up and knitting back together. There can't be a question over ownership or identity or whose brain it is. I reckon the answer lies with Sebastian. He seems to have the final say. I remember talking with him about whether the reason for the barriers is still valid and he said they were for protection. I asked whose protection but he didn't answer that. Does he know? Is Sebastian the one who can guide us through the process of integration? I don't even know who or what Sebastian is.

If the purpose of the barrier between Lottie and me is to protect me from traumatic memories, then surely the barrier can be made redundant by Lottie telling me what her memories are.

Let's say she does that. Will I be able to cope?

I think I'd be able to cope. But we're playing with fire. We'd be dabbling in something we don't understand. That would be foolish.

I do, however, think that Sebastian holds the key to solving this puzzle.

And Wade has figured it out…

* * *

CHARLIE

Am I disturbing you?

Lottie's popped up. Wonder what she wants?

Nothing much going on here.

I have been thinking about integration.

Me too.

Are you happy to talk about it?

Why not?

As far as I can tell, Lottie's being genuine. There's a long delay, though, before she starts.

From your perspective, I must seem like someone who keeps changing her mind. You have more time on the *spot* than me so I have to do a lot of reading between the lines. I wanted our project to go ahead and now my enthusiasm

is waning. You wanted to stop the project in its tracks and now you seem to be the main mover and shaker.

This may explain the tortuous dialogue we've been having or, maybe, her sudden loss of confidence. I'm still suspicious though.

The project you started is not one that can be backed out of. Yes, I wanted it to stop, but now I know more about it, it's something that must be continued until we reach a point where it can stop.

Why? What is wrong with just stopping? Forget about Traube. Forget about Hendry.

Because, Lottie, there are two murders on file that are linked. There are two detectives whose suspicions have been roused, they have us in their sights and they won't let go. Now Kathy Bond is starting to piece things together. Your project started when you nicked those five Travis Hendry videos. Your project will end when we've taken possession of them all.

You make it sound so simple.

If it's not simple, it won't work.

Surely, Charlie, you are not suggesting adding Katherine Bond to our project.

No Lottie, I'm not. Let me be quite clear. We are not adding my best friend, Kathy Bond, to this project. I would prefer to do time in prison than harm her. I will kill myself before killing her. Do you understand?

There's something funny going on here. I can't believe Lottie brought Kathy into this in that way. I've made myself clear on that but I need to ram it home and take her to task over it. Lottie hasn't answered. Right, no more pissing about being all nicey nicey.

We haven't approached Frederick Traube yet. We don't have to. But we do have to find Travis Hendry. We have to find him in order to silence him and recover his videos. When Travis Hendry is dead and we have his videos there will be no link between us and the Daventry, Pope and Amos murders. Once we have those videos, we have control so long as, of course, we have all the videos and all copies of them. We'll be relying on Wade to satisfy us about that.

I look over at Wade, he's sleeping soundly.

Now, what the gang really do not need is you getting a touch of the seconds. I don't want to hear anything more about integration; indeed, anything that will rock the boat. Are you with me on that?

Again, there's a long delay. Lottie's emotional.

I carry on.

We'll deal with our condition when we've cleaned up this mess we're in. Do you understand and are you on board with that?

Yes, Charlie. Understood and on board... and sorry.

Stop saying you're sorry. The gang needs you. Your job is to hold them together. I'll do the leg work but there will be times when they start wavering, times when they start questioning what they're doing. That will be your moment. You're the one who can hold them together. You managed to hold them together for Daventry and Pope. You even managed it for Amos when you had me gainsaying you. Your role in this is absolutely vital. And it's your role as there's no one else. Your role. Not my role. Your role.

Lottie's still there, I can feel her.

Thank you, Charlie.

Maybe something to lighten the mood.

Look on the bright side, Lottie. If we get caught for this, and end up with a thirty-year prison sentence, the advantage of being a multiple is that we'll only have to do fifteen years each.

* * *

CHARLIE

I get up, put on my light dressing gown and make myself a cup of tea. I love my little ground floor flat. It's like the communal garden is just mine because my back door opens onto it.

I sit on the back step with my tea and look up at the stars. It's a beautiful night. It's mid-May and this could be August. I don't have to be back at work until Wednesday Late Turn so I have the whole of tomorrow, well today now, to myself, well myself and Wade – and Lottie – and Floella, Jemima and Gillian. And Sebastian – who or whatever he is.

I'm really starting to think that Lottie doesn't have an ulterior motive. She's got herself into something she doesn't understand and she's got herself in too deep. Okay, so she's relying on me to bail her out.

The way she spoke to me was interesting. What she was saying was full of emotion. Not just in the way she said it but I felt it welling up inside. I've never felt that degree of emotion coming from her.

There's movement behind me. It's Wade.

"Thought I might find you here," he says. He's doing up his dressing gown – one I haven't seen before. He must have brought it back with him. "May I have a sip?"

I hand him my cup as he sits next to me on the back step. "I had my doubts about Lottie but I think I wasn't reading the signals right."

"What did she say?"

"Doesn't matter. Suffice it to say she's on board. Changing the subject, I've been thinking about our cars. If we have to follow Traube in our cars, we'll only take four. You in your car and me in mine. We can manage the driving and radio work. The others aren't used to it so we'll double them up. Put Eileen and Zach together in whichever car they use and Ush and Rob together in whichever car they use. That way, one of them can do the driving and the other can be the operator, so to speak. We could drop down to three cars. I don't know what's involved in tracking his mobile. What do you think?"

"I think we should use three cars. I'll have to focus on the readings I'll be getting from Traube's phone. I think you should pair up with Rob. It's important that he's there and, with your driving skills, he's more likely to get there if he's with you."

"Makes sense."

"I'll pair up with Ush."

"Why Ush?"

"Because she's the weakest." Wade doesn't get it – one of the things I'm beginning to find more endearing about him.

Maybe make the point a bit stronger. "Not because she's the most beautiful woman I know, possibly in the whole wide world."

"I thought Ush and Lottie were an item."

My hair, like Wade's, falls down over my face. The light isn't good but Wade picks up on my reaction.

"Oh, Charlie. That was so thoughtless of me. I'm sorry. I'm so sorry."

I resist him as he tries to put his arm around me. I don't know how to handle what he's just said. At the same time I think he's right. No. I know he's right. Ush said she was trying dating. That coincided with Lottie getting all angsty. Other moments come to me. Things Zach and Rob have said. Even Eileen. I've been pushing it away, not wanting to face it. I have to face it now. But... But... HOW THE HELL DO I DEAL WITH THAT?

CHAPTER TWENTY-FOUR

CHARLIE

Any relationship there may or may not be between Lottie and Ush is none of my concern. It's something that needs to be addressed, but it can't be addressed now. We must get Travis Hendry's videos. To get those, we must find Travis Hendry. If Traube doesn't lead us to him, we will have to do the legwork ourselves. Legwork which, up until now, has proved fruitless.

Half of me wants Traube to be a thumbs-down and the other half wants him to be a thumbs-up. If he's a thumbs-up, then what about Rob?

This, of course, leads onto the other big weakness in Lottie's project – the number of people involved. The five of us and now Wade – six of us – not including the complexities of my condition. To reduce the risk of our gang breaking up, we all have to be on an even footing. The even footing changes for Wade and me but the four of them and Lottie need to be in the same place. We need to find and eliminate Rob's abuser. I hope it's Traube, but only because I want all this to end.

Not too far from where Rob lives, is Kelsey Park. This is where we're meeting up. Wade and I have got here early. We'd planned to chat things through but since

Wade's unguarded comment about Lottie and Ush, chatting is off the menu.

Zach is the first to arrive. Then Rob. Then Eileen. Then Ush. I've held onto the *spot* since Wade made that comment. I don't know whether Lottie heard it or not but there hasn't been any contact between Lottie and Ush since then. I'm watching Ush. I'm watching them all, but concentrating on Ush.

I force it out of my mind. Finish the project and then, and only then, will we deal with that.

We're all sitting on the grass around our pile of bikes.

"Okay. If Traube does lead us to Hendry, he will probably do so in his car. And if we're on our bikes, we could end up a very long way behind him – particularly if he drives to another city. We'll use bikes if we can, but we may have to use cars and, if we do, I want us to be ready.

"First of all some tactics. We will use three cars. One car follows, the other two hang back. Come to a junction, the one following turns off and the first of the other two becomes the follow. The one that just turned off is now in catchup and must drive... how shall I say... assertively. Are we all free this coming Saturday morning?"

Nods all round.

"Right, 7am, we'll meet here in our cars and we'll practice."

They all nod.

"By midday Saturday, we'll decide which cars we'll use and who will drive."

They all look shocked. It's Zach who speaks up. "If all six of us are involved, how will we lay alibis."

"Remember, we're using Traube, if he is Rob's abuser, to locate Hendry. Once we've done that, we could deal with them separately with all the necessary planning and contingencies."

They seem relieved but not convinced – and there's a fly in the ointment – worth reiterating. "The purpose of this exercise is to determine two things. Whether Traube is a thumbs-up or a thumbs-down and locate Hendry. When that's done we could step back and plan our next move. The problem is that we need to secure Hendry's videos so we need to be there when and if Traube leads us to him. Is everyone with me on that?"

Nods all round.

Eileen speaks. "We haven't been using our cars for a reason."

"I know. We will not be committing a crime and we can use our bikes to conceal the rear number plate. Not fool proof but it will help reduce the likelihood of being caught by ANPR."

"What about the front number plate?"

"As I say, we can only reduce the likelihood of being caught on ANPR."

"I'm not happy about that." Eileen is a significant voice in this gang. If she starts wavering the others will follow.

"It's our best hope for finding Travis Hendry."

"I get that but we're getting close to our targets in our cars. This is something we said we wouldn't do."

I feel Lottie pushing. "Lottie wants to have a word." I move aside and Lottie takes the *spot*.

"Have any of you had any leads at all on the location of Travis Hendry? I know the answer. The children's home was closed down many years ago. Travis Hendry has moved on. From our complete lack of results, it looks like he has moved on out of childcare altogether. Not sure but I think he was sacked. There has been no result from social media. Frankly, for Travis Hendry, such a result is unlikely. What Wade has come up with is a way for us to break that impasse. The safeguards we have employed have been for when we are making a confrontation. We are not forcing a confrontation and therefore the safeguards and alibis are redundant. I think Eileen is right, we do not want to use our cars. I know Charlie and Wade have discussed using cars with false number plates and concluded that if anything happens, stopped by police, an incident or something, then being in an illegal car would be disastrous.

Charlie has said that obscuring our rear number plates with our bikes is not fool proof – some cameras take pictures from the front for goodness' sake – but it is the best we can do. I suggest that astute positioning of our bikes on the back of our cars so as to obscure or partially obscure the rear number plate reduces any associated risk to an acceptable level."

Lottie has stopped. She is good. The others are looking around at one another. They're nodding. Shrugging. Zach has even started laughing.

Eileen speaks up for them. "Well, if you put it like that…" and they all start laughing.

* * *

CHARLIE

Ush, Zach and Eileen have long rides home. Our ride home isn't long but it's tough. Up and over Crystal Palace and then Denmark Hill. I don't know how Wade does it – he's so powerful. I stay with him, though I'm pretty sure I'm working twice as hard. He makes it seem so easy.

I think of Lavender and how easily he makes driving a car seem. That reminds me – I'm Late Turn tomorrow.

In bed, Wade and I hold each other. We've dispensed with the duvet and are covered by nothing more than a sheet. His hand explores…

"Can we just hold each other?" I realise that's the first I've spoken to him since he made his insensitive comment about Lottie and Ush.

"Whatever you say. We'll go at your pace."

I snuggle into him. For the umpteenth time I think about how many men I know would put up with me.

Not many. No. None. No. One – Wade.

I think again about the chances of us meeting one another. There's no point in thinking about that.

Those thoughts are bugging me and I can't sleep. Wade has dropped off, his breathing slow and rhythmic.

I ease myself out of bed so as not to disturb him. I make myself tea and head out to my back step. The grass, can't call it a lawn, slopes down to the fence which is covered in some sort of climbing plant that is covered in white blousy flowers. The moon is bright and those flowers look eerie. The cat that belongs to a neighbour walks past. I click my fingers and make kissing sounds but I'm ignored. Then I notice – Lottie's there.

Hi Lottie. You feeling lonely?

To be blunt. Yes. You are lucky to have Wade.

I think now might be the time to broach the subject of Ush with Lottie. Actually, I think she wants me to.

You missing Ush?

You know?

Wade spilled the beans. Unlike him to be careless like that.

Do you mind about Ush and me?

Not at all. In fact, I don't understand how I didn't see it.

Thank you for your understanding.

Lottie wants to talk. Best thing is to let her.

Many times, back at the home, I would return to my room after a session of abuse. I could not be on my own.

I can't imagine what that was like for you.

It was what I was there for. More dissociation and I was able to share the load.

Floella?

Yes. Then Jemima. Then Gillian.

There's a question I want to ask about how dissociation works but I don't want to disturb her flow. I prompt her along.

And you decided which one of you would go.

Not really. We took it in turns. We would decide between us but sometimes there was a flare up and Sebastian would step in. I suppose, as I had the longest standing I had more say.

Good god. I'd never thought about the… mechanics of it all.

How do you deal with those memories?

Dealing with those memories is our raison d'être.

And who were you doing this for.

For you, Charlie. I misled you by suggesting you are an alter. It was wrong of me to do that. I have been wrong about a lot of things.

Lottie's been misleading me! She's been lying to me. I should be jumping up and shouting at her. Yelling at the top of my voice. But… But… I don't feel anything like that. All I can think of is the awful life Lottie has led. The children too. All for me. My suspicions about Lottie are fading but I still have questions that need answers. Lottie seems willing to talk so… no time like the present.

What were you hoping to achieve by telling me I'm an alter like you?

Equal status.

Lottie, we're beyond dishonesty and deception. Answer the question truthfully.

Nothing gets past you.

She's not getting away with this.

It's time, Lottie. We must start working together.

After watching you for fifteen years, I had this idea that I could be you. I thought all I had to do was bring you down.

Do I believe her? Lottie's being very open. Too open – and I'm suspicious.

We are one.

You have been talking with Sebastian.

You know I have. I don't know what he is or who he is. When I asked him if he could take down the barriers between us, he said it was not within his gift.

The only ones who can dismantle those barriers are us.

And that can be a lengthy process even with professional help.

Correct.

How does it work?

I do not know.

She sounds genuine.

If all the barriers are doing is keeping memories away from me, what will happen if you tell me all your memories.

In every detail?

Maybe explains why it takes so long. What will happen to you when you've downloaded, or uploaded, your memories?

I'm talking too much. She's come up because she wants to talk and all I'm doing is plying her with questions.

I do not know.

Come on, Lottie. You've read so much. You must have ideas about this.

I fail to be diplomatic before I even start.

I will have no purpose. I will sink into the abyss.

She's starting to make me cross.

No, Lottie. Think about what Sebastian says. We are one. So, another way of looking at it is that you join me and we become one. Just think if we were together. No more wondering what the other's doing. No more looking over your shoulder. No more confusing displacements.

You'd be that part of me that speaks properly, is subtle and commands respect. I'd be that part of you that doesn't trust anyone, is in your face and forces respect.

That would be nice.

Nice? Is that the best she can do?

You've already shown that you can help me with my memories. Maybe I can help you with yours – and the children's. But we can't do it now. We have abuse videos to retrieve and two murders to commit. We'll address integration later when there are less distractions.

Thank you, Charlie. That means a lot to me. I suppose once all this is over, we can seek that professional help.

Yes, if we get away with it. If we don't get away with it, I believe they do a pretty good counselling service in prison.

Prison?

Yes, Lottie. But we're not going to get caught. Now, enough of this.

Something's bugging me. It's something Wade said about alters. 'Lottie might be wrong.' 'Lottie might be right.' Now is not the time to be thinking about this.

You were telling me about your relationship with Ush.

Yes. Oh, yes. Ush. Returning to my room after a session with a paedophile, I could not be on my own. I would find Ush. She always let me into her bed. She held me as I cried. She holds me now – as I cry. At least she did.

She's dating. How do you feel about that?

I feel as though I'm losing her.

She pauses for a long time – over a minute – I don't dare speak – then her non-vocalised words form in my head.

282

What a mess.

You're right. We're living a mess. All we can do is try and clean it up. If we can bring our project to a close, I'm sure we won't be so strung out. I'm sure we'll be more relaxed. If we get it right, the circumstances might enable us to seek help. But let's not get ahead of ourselves.

We push on?

Yes, Lottie. We can't leave those videos out there. If they surface, we'll be exposed.

You have said that before.

I know. Many times. So we get this job done. Then we move on. You were brilliant today. The gang were on the point of rebellion and you pulled them back.

Thank you, Charlie.

Like I say. You really hit the spot. It was a difficult one about cars and how identifiable they are but...

No. Not that. Thank you for your understanding about Ush and me.

CHAPTER TWENTY-FIVE

CHARLIE

I really don't want to be here. One good thing, Lavender's been assigned to the fast car and I've got the van. First job – someone's been nicked up at Tottenham who's wanted here at Walworth. Cantrell's told me to take Jonesy up there to get him.

I suppose it will keep me out of mischief.

Traffic's heavy and we're creeping along.

Fortunately, Jonesy's not in a talkative mood.

Unfortunately, Lottie is.

Charlie, can I ask a favour?

Of course.

On finishing this evening, can we visit Ush?

I want to spend the evening with Wade but, only fair and I'm sure Wade won't mind.

Not a problem.

Charlie?

Don't tell me, you want me to do the cycling and ride us up there.

Less chance of road rash.

Lottie's right there.

But you need the experience.

You can stay at home if you want...

Ha ha.

...but I want you there.

That's interesting.

We're going through the mill at the moment. I understand if you want to spend time with Ush.

Thank you, Charlie.

Believe me, Lottie. I understand the comfort that comes from being close to someone who cares.

Soothing.

More than that. It gives a feeling of completeness. Is that what we're missing? We will only be complete if we're one?

Not sure I'm in the mood for this heavy stuff.

Sebastian says we are one.

Sebastian's wrong. Sebastian's saying we can be one if we behave as though we are one. We can't do that unless we are all on the stage at the same time.

This is that alter thing Wade mentioned. 'Lottie might be right,' implying she might be wrong. Or was it 'Lottie might be wrong,' implying she might be right. Oh god. I'm so confused. I must talk more with Wade about it. Not tonight though.

Do you remember those times when we've been together in the playground?

Yes. I do. It was fun. I want to do that more often.

Me too. Oh shit. Look, Lottie, there's been an accident right in front of us. Jonesy will deal with it but I must concentrate.

As Jonesy slides back his door, Lottie steps back but she's staying on the *stage*.

It's a damage-only but the drivers are out and arguing. One of them has driven into the back of the other. Low speed. She was probably looking at the police van behind her rather than where she was going.

The guy from the car in front is getting stroppy.

I get out. Jonesy's quite capable of dealing with this but, having two of us there does help. I tap the driver from the car behind on her arm and indicate to her to follow me. I lead her round behind the van so she's out of sight of the other driver. My breath is catching but I push it away. In for four out for six.

"What will happen?"

"I don't know. My colleague's dealing with this, he'll decide. He'll probably stick you on for without due care." My breath's calming. I'm okay. I'm reacting to this – how will I cope if it's something serious? Stop this. Must concentrate.

"But that's not fair. He…"

"Come on, it's not the end of the world, give us your details and we'll sort this out and get you on your way."

Although she's upset, she's helpful. By the time Jonesy comes over, I have all her details and I head over to speak with Mr Angry.

But he's no longer angry. He's submissive. I exchange the necessary details and say some words about lucky no one was injured. Then Jonesy's back with me saying he's all done.

I've missed something.

The driver from the car behind is looking smug and the driver from the car in front is subdued.

What's happened?

Jonesy dismisses the drivers and we return to the van.

"The guy in front was funny," Jonesy says as he pulls on his seat belt.

I've definitely missed something.

"Pretending to be angry. I stuck him on for without due care. He'll plead."

Jonesy stuck the driver in front on for without due care? Jeez. I really did miss something.

"He only bought the car yesterday. Hadn't familiarised himself with the controls properly. He stuck it in reverse by mistake and drove backwards into the car behind him."

I missed that. Completely.

"He was angry with himself rather than the other driver. I reckon they'll be dating by the time this is all done and dusted."

I get us going again.

Lottie.

That was funny.

Can we save our little chats for when I'm not on duty. I can't afford to be distracted like that.

Of course. But you have to admit, that was funny. And how can you have missed it. Did you not see his reversing lights come on? I did. You must have done.

* * *

CHARLIE
Come the end of the shift, the Team's come round the Half Nelson to relax.

"Kathy, I've been away for a week. How are things? How are you?"

"Tell you what, Charlie. Michael had a real go at me. Said I was fixating about you. Said I'd probably been affected by the tanker incident as much as you, just without the burns. He's paying for counselling for me."

"That's great. How's it going?"

"I've only had two sessions. It's a lady. She's brilliant. I told her how I'd treated you so badly and how shitty I felt about it and she said that DID generally happens to people who've had a really traumatic childhood – you know, abuse, physical, sexual. I spoke with you about it before but the counsellor has sort of confirmed things for me. I was so out of order, way out of line. Do you forgive me?"

I'm hiding my relief. "Of course I do. It was a tough time for all of us. I got all the attention. If anyone should be asking forgiveness, it's me."

"Tell you what. Let's not talk anymore about it."

I hold out my arms, she pulls me down to her level and I have to work hard to avoid getting lost in her cleavage.

"If you carry on like that," Iffy's joined us, "I'll be selling tickets."

"Back in my day, we'd get a friggin' room."

I won't let Lavender get away with that. "Last I heard, we're not back in your day. We're in today. And tomorrow we'll be in today."

"No it won't. Tomorrow, we'll be in friggin' tomorrow."

"If you make it to tomorrow, it'll be called today." Oh, god. Kathy's joined in now.

"What's the friggin' matter with you all? Today's called today. Tomorrow's called tomorrow."

"And 'back in my day' is called ancient history."

I've got to get out of here. "Guys. Guys. I'd love to stay and see how this scintillating conversation ends. But I've got to go. See you all… tomorrow."

I go back to the Nick and collect my bike. I send Wade a message – nearly used the wrong phone. Got a thumbs-up from Wade and I head north.

Ush's place is seven or eight miles. Shouldn't take long. At least I know the route now. Although it's dark, I'm well lit up and it's a pleasant evening. The ride is easy – no incidents.

As I'm locking up the bike, Lottie appears on the *stage*.

I surrender the *spot*.

Regards to Ush. See you…

No, Charlie, wait. Why not stick around?

I don't know. I don't feel…

Please. Stay.

Okay. But… Oh, I don't know. Yes, of course I'll stay. It will be lovely to spend time with Ush. Time when we're not planning murders.

* * *

CHARLIE

"You rode up here?" Ush is incredulous.

"Charlie did." Lottie is matter of fact.

"Is she there?"

"Yes. We agreed that she would stay."

"Well, this calls for a glass of wine."

Lottie is looking around the living room but I just catch a glimpse of Ush heading out to the kitchen. She returns a moment later with a bottle of white wine and a couple of glasses. The bottle has one of those frozen jackets around it.

Ush pours two glasses, pushes one towards Lottie and sits back.

"Lottie, what's wrong?"

"I feel so useless. You need Charlie now, not me. In fact, she was the one you needed all along. If she had been calling the shots, we would all be in a good place instead of this mess."

Ush has come over and is pulling Lottie into a hug. "Don't talk like that. You were what we had at the time. You talked us through your proposals. We talked them through ourselves. We decided. Not you. All of us."

"I know. But I still feel like such a fraud."

"You're not a fraud. Now come, drink some wine. Let me tell you about what's going on with me. I'm leaving the Benefits Agency. I'm taking a psychoanalysis and counselling course. Regents College. I've missed a couple of lectures recently. Can't think why."

Lottie seems to be cheering up. "Why are you doing that?"

"I think, like you, I'm not really pulling my weight. The Benefits Agency has that facial recognition technology but I don't get anywhere near it. I think we're all a bit strung out. I want to learn about your condition. I want to be able to help."

"You can help, just by being you."

"I could do so much more. I need to understand your condition. I understand professional help isn't available for you. Maybe I'd be able to help. You really need someone who doesn't share your history but that option's not available."

"Our history. What would I have done without you? You made it possible to bear." Lottie is welling up.

"I'll always be here for you, no matter how unbearable it gets."

"I know you will. You mean so much to me."

"Why don't we…"

"I would say yes but Charlie is there. I would hate to push her away."

"Lottie. Come on. Charlie won't mind. It's gone midnight. We need bed. If Charlie's uncomfortable, she has somewhere to go."

Yes. I do have somewhere to go. I'm not going anywhere. I've never seen Lottie so emotional. Ush is being lovely. It wasn't long ago she was hostile towards me. We were so close back at the children's home but things changed. Looking back on it now, things changed with the arrival of Lottie and the abuse. What would Lottie have been telling Ush about me? Whatever it was, it was unlikely to have been complimentary. I ran away, leaving her to face the abuse. Then she ran away leaving it to Floella. And the others? I'm confused. Who is a part of who? And, of course, each identity would think of it as if they'd just been abandoned. It's all very well Sebastian saying *we are one*, but how could that make any sense to poor Gillian popping into existence for what she had to face. I faced some physical abuse at the hands of Travis Hendry. It was nothing I couldn't handle but I wish Ush had been there during that time. She came in at the end and it was so comforting to be able to cuddle up. She'd somehow absorb and disperse all the badness. I'd imagine it was the same for Lottie but far more focussed and concentrated. Lottie's all at sea now. She needs that comfort. I have Wade but that's tainted with frigidity. So, yes, I have somewhere to go but, no, I'm not going anywhere.

The nerves are starting. I can feel them. I can feel myself tensing up. Ush is in bed. She pulls back the duvet as an invitation. She is naked.

Lottie lets her gown slip to the floor. She is naked too – we are naked. I'm nervous. I'm stressed. I don't know what to do. I know what I want to do – I want to escape to my *dressing room*. I stay with it. I feel I must.

Sobbing. Lottie is sobbing. This means so much to her and she wants me to be here. I must stay with it. She slides under the duvet and I feel Ush's warmth and then her skin and Lottie is enveloped by those arms and legs. I feel Ush stroking my hair – our hair. I hear her murmuring into my ear – our ear.

We are one.

Her odour hasn't changed. Memories of the few times we had together are flooding back.

I can feel Lottie's distress and anxiety dropping away as tears of pleasure run off her cheeks and onto Ush's breasts. Ush is cooing and stroking our hair. I feel the warmth of her body, the softness of her flesh, the smoothness of her skin and I feel my tightness and nervousness fading – just like I feel Lottie's distress and anxiety ebbing away.

This is a safe place. This is a warm place. This is a good place.

* * *

CHARLIE

Ush is asleep. I can hear her breathing and feel the softness of her stomach where I'm resting my head watching the rise and fall of her breasts. I'm on the *stage*. It was beautiful. Being there with the two of them as they cuddled and kissed each other. Stroked each other. Spoke soft words.

There was no intimacy although, for a moment, I wanted there to be. Ush and Lottie know what they're about. They know their boundaries.

What are you thinking, Charlie?

Lottie's voice in my head startles me.

What am I thinking? I'm thinking how beautiful this is. I'm thinking how comforting this is. I'm thinking how much I want this. I want more. We didn't do anything. Not really.

We never have. We never will. For Ush and me, this is it. This is our memory — two eight-year-old girls finding solace in a world of anxiety, aggression and pain. You felt it too, if only a few times. For me, this was regular and frequent and it was my release. And, Charlie, it still is. Many of those times when you found you had lost days, I was here with Ush.

But you only lie together.

Yes. We lie next to one another, hold each other and dream.

Do you remember any of those dreams?

Not really, but they were nice dreams, good dreams – not the nightmares that came when I was alone. Very soon we will be back into the horror show that is our life and it is me – it is me who has made it this horror show. For a short while, Charlie, we have respite.

With those words of Lottie's, I realise… My whole life has been a horror show. That short time with Ush was an escape. Not an escape for me – an escape for Lottie. I think of Wade and his escape – his escape from his parents – his escape from a predetermined life. I do believe I'm his escape. And he is mine. I want him. I want to be with him.

Lottie, if we sneak out, will Ush be upset?

Not at all. She will probably be quite relieved if we go. This may be a respite for me, not sure it has quite the same significance for Ush.

It may be a respite for you. It's also a respite for us.

* * *

CHARLIE

This time, I'm happy to do the cycling. To think that it hasn't been long since I considered Lottie the enemy. I would have sympathy for anyone who'd been through what she's been through, yet I had no sympathy for her.

There's another reason why I'm cycling. I want to get home quickly. It was just before five when we left Ush's.

Wade leaves for work around six. I stand up on the pedals.

I'm still trying to make sense of what I experienced last night. I'm wondering why I wasn't sickened by it. All those times with boys on sofas – poking tongues and rough hands under rumpled clothing and me squeezing out saying, 'I'm sorry. I'm sorry.'

I feel like Lottie's given me a download. A file of emotions has landed and I see it. I understand. I push harder on the pedals.

Because it's so early, there's little traffic and I'm able to make my turns easily. I stick to the main drag. Maybe not the straightest route but I can maintain a decent speed. I try and change up but I'm already in top gear.

Camberwell Grove. Bit of a hill but no problem. I'm soon outside my flat.

* * *

LOTTIE

Charlie is eager to get home. I am pleased for her. She has thrown the bike onto the rack and is heading inside. Wade is getting dressed. She marches straight up to him, grabs his head, plants a kiss on his lips while lifting and wrapping her legs round his waist. Wade allows himself to topple back onto the bed, Charlie on top ripping at his clothes.

He flips her over and works his way through the zips of her cycling gear.

She grabs at him but has to let go to free herself from her tight-fitting clothing. No words are spoken. The only sounds are of lust and pleasure.

Time for me to leave.

CHAPTER TWENTY-SIX

CHARLIE

"You're going to be late."

"I'm staying here, with you."

"Wade!"

"Watch me."

Wade takes his job mobile from the collection of phones on his bedside table. "Hi, Sarge. I was vomiting during the night. Hardly got any sleep. Feeling really rough."

There's a voice on the other end of the line but I can't hear what it's saying.

Wade continues, "There's a presentation this morning – Eastern European intelligence systems. If someone could cover it, great, but probably best to postpone."

More talking on the other end but, again, too faint to hear.

"Well, no. I'll be back tomorrow."

More talking.

"That would be good. Thanks, Sarge."

More talking.

"I'll put something together for you. You'll have it by this afternoon."

More talking.

"Brilliant. Thanks again, Sarge."

More talking.

"Okay, Dave. See you Monday. Bye. Yes, bye. Bye, bye, bye. Bye." Wade cuts off the call.

"Is your sergeant called Dave, by any chance?"

"That one is. They say we're to only use first names but I keep forgetting."

"He let you call him Sarge for quite a while before correcting you."

"He's a closet lid."

"I hate that term. It's more demeaning than *wooden-top* or *plod*. I remember once, before you joined us, the then DI had had one too many in the Duke of York, couldn't drive, so phoned the Nick and ordered a lid to drive him home. I was said lid. One too many? He could barely stand up. Instead of taking him home, I drove him back to the Nick and deposited him in Custody. 'Drunk and Incapable,' I announced. 'For fuck's sake,' was all Cantrell said as she got a couple of bigger guys to dump him in his office. I do believe that's the only time I've heard Cantrell swear – until that incident with Kathy in the Sleeping Lion a couple of weeks back."

Wade settles down again, arranging the duvet and pillows so we're snug and cosy.

"Throwing a sicky? You have changed. Don't let it become a habit."

He has that knowing little smile. "You've changed too. What happened last night, at Ush's?"

I think for a while before answering. I don't know how to describe it but, I suppose, if anyone is likely to understand, Wade will. "When Lottie was being abused, her escape from it was in bed with Ush, cuddling, soothing. They've continued that. Last night, they let me stick around on the *stage*."

Wade's eyebrow raises.

"I said I'd go but they seemed to want me to stay. I did and... what's it called when everything comes clear?"

"Epiphany."

"What?"

"You had an epiphany. A damascene moment."

"Well. Everything fell into place."

"Oh, like a game of Tetris."

I punch him and force him over onto his back. "You know what you're going to get for that."

* * *

CHARLIE

After we'd made love again, we prepared breakfast. Then Wade started getting dressed.

"What are you doing?"

"I think we're ready to go with Traube."

"Wait a minute. We can't just stop..." I realise what I'm saying. "Like you, I can just go sick but better to prepare. I'm Late Turn this afternoon. I'll start faking when I'm at work and that will make it easier when I go sick tomorrow."

"Good idea. The others are doing something similar."

"When were you talking with them?"

"Last night. I included you but you must have been distracted."

I find my phones, open them up and start checking them. "Oh, god. The message I sent you last night was from one of my burners. I remember checking. That's a bad mistake. Do we need to do anything about that?"

"One non-descript text message. It'll be alright."

I examine my other phones. The calls and messages from Wade are all there. I missed them. "What about Ush? Did you get responses from her?"

"Yes, this morning, just before you arrived. She must have been as distracted as you. How's Lottie?"

"She's decided to give all this a miss. Oh, Wade. I somehow got my phones mixed up."

"Let me see your phones."

I hand them over. He turns on the ones that are off and starts examining them. A few minutes later, he pronounces everything okay and heads out the front door. Now that I've read the messages, I understand what he's doing. He's posting the envelope with the SD card and note so that it arrives on Traube's doormat tomorrow morning. They're meeting this evening for a briefing. I can't be there for obvious reasons but Wade will run the briefing. It will be about surveillance tactics and forensics.

"I still think we should have delivered it by hand," I say, as he comes back in.

"Doing it this way puts distance between us and the message."

"It may not even get there."

"There are risks associated with both…"

"Don't you start lecturing me on risk."

Wade looks at me, his face stern. "The consequence of the risk associated with mixing up your phones must now be faced."

"What consequences?"

"These," he says, picking me up, carrying me through to the bedroom and throwing me onto the bed.

* * *

CHARLIE

"Unlike you to be late." Cantrell's being all caring.

"I was throwing up in the bogs. I think I'm okay. I'll be alright."

"You ran in."

"I thought I'd be able to run it off. I was wrong."

"Charlie, you can't use morning sickness as an excuse to get off Late Turn."

"You think I'm pregnant?"

"I'm just saying."

"Well, if I'm pregnant, Wade must be too. I caught it off him."

"The way it goes. Look, joking aside, I don't want you here if you can't give it your all and I certainly don't want you here if all you're going to do is give it to everyone else. Lavender will take you home. I don't expect to see you until Monday. Early Turn."

"Yes, sarge," and I'm out of there – before she can change her mind. Once back in my running gear, I find Lavender who's waiting for me in the yard. Iffy's his operator. I jump in the back.

The car takes the three of us out onto the main drag. I still don't know how Lavender does it.

"If you're ill, you shouldn't have come in."

"What do you mean, *if* she's ill. She's friggin' ill. Cantrell said."

"If she's ill," Iffy continues, "she certainly shouldn't be in the back of our car."

"You're right there. Open the friggin' windows."

"It's alright guys. It's the warmest May since time began. I wouldn't want you catching your death of cold."

"What's wrong with you, anyway?"

Time to explain – and feed the gossip. "Cantrell says it's morning sickness."

"If it's morning sickness, we don't need the windows open."

"Morning sickness? I didn't think that Wade friggin' Oliver had it in him."

"It was in him. It's now in me."

Halfway up Camberwell Grove, they get a shout. The car stops. I get out. The car does a neat three-point-turn and carries its two passengers off to whatever load of ol' bollocks the local populace can conjure up for them.

* * *

CHARLIE

What was all that about morning sickness?

Lottie has popped up. Suppose I better brief her.

The package has been posted. It will arrive tomorrow morning. We're meeting the gang this evening up St

James's Park. Full briefing in readiness for whatever happens tomorrow.

I trust you and Wade to have all that in hand. Morning sickness?

It dawns on me. This is not something to be taken lightly. This is not just my body. It's our body.

Lottie. The guys were messing around. Even Cantrell made a joke of it.

Not funny.

I know. It's not their fault. They don't know our situation. It was my fault. I should have been more sensitive. I apologise.

I think I prefer it when you say sorry.

Lottie's sense of humour is back.

I'm on the pill.

Is that all?

What do you mean, all?

You know what I mean.

Now I'm unsure whether Lottie's joking with me.

Okay. I'm sorry, Lottie. I just didn't think. I started taking the pill when Wade and I started sleeping together. It was superfluous, as I think you know.

Yes. I do know. It was difficult being down there with all that frustration raining down on us. This morning, though. What a difference.

I do believe Lottie is genuinely pleased for me.

Fireworks? Explosions? Tremors?

No. No. No. Satisfaction. Contentment. Relief. I was with Sebastian and he commented that some barriers had fallen – his words – not mine."

The barriers between us?

Yes, Charlie. But it is only a start. What do you think about Ush?

I take it you mean about her going into counselling.

Yes. She could...

Lottie. Stop. There's a certain mess we need to extract ourselves from.

Oh, god. How many more times must I say this?

We're no longer doing this for the sake of some therapeutic value. We're doing this to save our skins. We need to silence Travis Hendry and we need to recover his videos. Only then will we be able to start thinking about a future. Briefing, this evening, St James's Park. I think it has a children's playground. We'll get there early and let the children have a run around.

But you have reported sick.

I don't believe for one minute that Cantrell thinks I'm sick. She's just granting me a bit of slack. She wants me performing. She wants me bringing the bodies in.

You mean prisoners, as in thieves and drug dealers.

Oh, yes. Unfortunate turn of phrase. Now, Lottie. I want to spend more time with Wade. I'll give you a shout when we're heading up town.

Okay, Charlie.

CHAPTER TWENTY-SEVEN

CHARLIE

Wade's on his laptop when I get indoors. It's a zoom meeting, or WhatsApp or something. He seems to be talking to just one other person. I hear Wade call him Dave. Must be the sergeant he was speaking to this morning.

"I have company," Wade says. "Can we finish this off when I'm back."

"If you're in tomorrow, great. If not, don't worry. I'll cover it but, I must admit, all I'll be doing is delaying. I don't think there'll be a problem."

"Okay." Wade raises his hand. "Bye. Bye bye bye. Bye."

I really wish he wouldn't do that.

He cuts off the call, puts his computer to one side and gets up. "I wasn't expecting you home this early." He's still in his dressing gown and he pulls me into a hug.

Happy. That's how I feel. Happy. It's the best description I can come up with. I think about what Lottie said earlier about satisfaction, contentment and relief. Does happiness sum all those up?

"So, you convinced Sergeant Cantrell that you were sick. When does she expect you back?"

I find a way into his dressing gown and start stroking his pecs and abs. He has such fine muscle definition. It's not a result of gym work and bodybuilding, it's his lifestyle. Like me, he's always active and, like me, he's fit. I move my hands round to his back. Toned. That describes Wade. Toned. He asked a question. What was it? Oh yes, when am I expected back? "Not until Monday Early Turn. I'll miss out on a quick change over. I don't think she believes me so I don't really understand what's going on."

"She's keeping you sweet. She doesn't want you starting a work-to-rule." His hands move over my back and down around my bum.

This is so lovely. "I would never do that."

"She doesn't know that. And also, you mustn't forget Inspector Brady. She doesn't want to upset him. In a way, she's the most vulnerable. She needs to keep you all working and productive while at the same time managing her supervisor. At least, as a PC, you only cop shit from one direction." He kisses me. A light kiss. Nothing fierce and ferocious. Nice. He's cupping my breast. It feels good. I want to feel his skin against mine.

He lets me go. I feel bereft. I want him and he's moving away from me, over to the windows and pulling the curtains. "I've swept, no bugs, no hidden cameras, no one's filming us."

"Just as well," I say, "as what's about to happen in here would certainly be considered obscene."

* * *

CHARLIE

St James's Park. Wade and I have cycled up here and we're just paying our respects to fallen colleagues at the National Police Memorial before checking my disguise and heading across the park to the children's playground.

Lottie and I sit back and let the children take it in turns. Letting all three of them have an ice cream might have been a mistake. A few strange looks from people nearby but nothing a disarming smile can't manage.

Rob has appeared and joined Wade. Disguises are essential considering the amount of CCTV around here. I think Rob's overdone it a bit, but this is his turn, his moment.

Zach and Eileen arrive at about the same time. Ush turns up a few minutes after. They're smiling as Jemima finishes off her ice cream.

I usher the children away and Lottie spends a moment with Ush.

We find a patch of grass that's secluded… Secluded? There are thousands of people enjoying the park but we've managed to make ourselves a bit of space.

I start.

Surveillance. Nothing too complicated, just how far back to maintain the follow and the other two cars in catchup. Checking that everyone's been able to fit their bike rack so that bikes hang down over the rear number plate. Briefing them on using junctions for switching. "We practised it last weekend. You've got it but remember, it's not just a change of activity, it's a change of mindset. When you're on the follow, you're laid back and casual and when you're in catchup you must switch into urgent. Eileen and I don't have powerful cars, but Ush, don't let your speed creep over a ton." They're all nodding. I think they get it. "It's likely we'll lose him but we have the backup of his work mobile."

Wade nods. "So don't panic if we do lose him. Stay calm. We all have the same maps. We can all communicate with one another."

I look around. They're engaged.

"Moving onto communications. We have our walkie-talkies. Keep your earplugs in as they keep your microphone in place. Keep the handset in your lap. If you have to get out of the car, put it in your pocket and keep your thumb over the transmit button. Most important, release the button when you're not talking. It's called PTT for a reason. Press To Transmit. Some say Press To Talk. If you're not talking, keep your thumb off that button." I look around. They're all nodding. Again, this is something we practised last weekend. I move on. "Remember, their range is not great and that will be reduced in built up areas. We have the backup of our mobiles. I know the procedure for using them as burners is cumbersome but don't be tempted to take shortcuts. We've been using mobiles like this for a while now, so we're well practised."

Next up, forensics.

"Before we move onto forensics, one more thing on comms. Use your callsigns. Don't use names. Maybe a bit belt and braces but, use your callsigns. I'm Lima. Zach?"

"Kilo," says Zach.

"Bravo," says Rob.

"Delta," says Wade.

"Echo," says Eileen.

"Sierra," says Ush.

"Okay…"

"What about Lottie?" says Eileen.

"I'm not switching now."

"Oh, go on," says Ush.

"She's Tango. If she forgets or doesn't use it, I'll kick her where the sun don't shine."

They all laugh. That's good.

Forensics. "Really important. In the event we enter Travis Hendry's address, we must be sealed. We have nitrile gloves?" Nods all round. "We didn't all seal up properly when we were at Amos's place." Eileen's looking embarrassed. I remember her taking her beanie off. "We will have left DNA of some description at that scene. We mustn't leave any more. We tape up. Round the neck, round the cuffs, round the waist and round the ankles. And that reminds me, shoes. Have we all got shoes half a size too small?" Again, nods all round. "I know they're uncomfortable, but remember to change into them if we're going into any likely scene."

Travis Hendry. "In the event of Traube leading us to Hendry, we will have to act. Because of the videos, we can't delay. Top priority is securing those videos. Yes, if Traube's verified, he's to be silenced. Same for Hendry, obviously. I would like, at that point, to step back, take our time, do some planning, organise alibis but we don't have that luxury. We must secure those videos. So we'll be going in. But how we go in – well, we'll have to make it up on the hoof. To outnumber them, we'll probably all need to go in. There are also personal reasons why we'll all be there. We will, however, be providing the investigative team with a forensic fest. Absolutely imperative that we seal up. Use that tape."

"You mentioned alibis. We not bothering with them?" says Eileen. "As soon as we've identified Hendry's address, Ush and I could head off to lay some alibis."

"Happy with that. But this is the culmination of Lottie's project. I think we should all be there. There's also the risk of the alibis being compromised by CCTV." Lottie's pushing. I move aside.

"I think, like Charlie says, we should all be there. It may have started as *kill-them-all* but it has moved on. The recovery of those videos is paramount. Also, if the alibis are done in a rush, they could well become incriminating."

Nods all round. We're in agreement. Lottie is good at bringing the gang along with her. I find myself thinking about what sort of person we'd be as one. Stop thinking about that. Concentrate.

Lottie moves aside. I resume the *spot*. "Sorry, guys. If there is an opportunity to lay alibis, we'll take advantage of it. We've all got each other's identities."

They nod. Eileen even holds up Ush's bank card.

"That's about it. Anyone got any questions or something to say?"

Nothing. Time to bring this to a close.

"Okay. The postman will…"

Eileen talks over me. "You said we would have a story for the police if we're arrested."

Good point. I did say that. I was hoping not to have to say this. "If we're nicked at the scene, doesn't matter what you say, we're fucked. If that happens, the truth is what we say. If we get away from the scene, then we think about stories."

That has made them stop and think... but none of them are coming back at me. Move on – quick.

"Okay. The postman will make his delivery between eight and nine tomorrow morning. We'll be in place at seven."

We're all heading home soon after that.

* * *

CHARLIE

"I'm sorry, I'm sorry."

"You have nothing to be sorry about."

"I have. I don't like to let you down."

"Don't be silly. We've been at it all day."

"I'm nervous about tomorrow. I have absolutely no idea what it will bring. It could go so many different ways and each one will demand life-changing decisions."

Wade and I are in bed, holding and stroking each other. He's embarrassed about his inability to perform. Ever the gentleman. "You're nervous about tomorrow because events will probably demand seat-of-the-pants type decision-making. That's not your thing. Leave that to me."

"What about us? I feel as though we're on the verge of something special."

"Yes, and all we have to do is hold it together for Traube, Hendry and the videos. Now come on, if Traube's a thumbs-down, tomorrow will be a demanding day. If he's a thumb's-up, we're back to square-one with social media."

"You're right."

"Sleep now. I've set the alarm for five. Gives us plenty of time. I really don't want to be rushing around. We'll be in control until the postie delivers the package. Then it will switch to Traube. Sleep now."

He shuffles down a little and pushes his forehead onto my breast. I hold him. Stroking his hair. "When this is all over, we can move forward." But he's asleep.

Because of me, the when in 'when this is all over', could be after a thirty-year prison sentence.

Lottie, please, we must sleep.

I feel so stupid that I failed to include you from the start.

Oh, god. How many more times do we have to go over this?

What's done is done. We now have to manage it. And I mean we. We need to manage it. Us. Not me. Us.

Us. Not me. Us. I like that.

One thing I do need, right now, is sleep.

Night Charlie.

Night Lottie.

CHAPTER TWENTY-EIGHT

CHARLIE

"From Sierra, target's on the move."

Ush sounds very laid back.

I fire up my engine.

Rob bangs the dashboard. "We've got him."

"Not yet, Rob. Not yet. Stay cool."

I'm waiting near the roundabout at the end of Traube's road to see which way he goes.

"From Sierra, he's turning left out of his drive."

So, he's heading away from me. I'm accelerating hard and I just catch a glimpse of him as he passes the pub where Wade and Ush are.

As I pass the pub, I spot Ush and Wade heading towards their car. I can't see them, but Eileen and Zach will be a little way behind me. No. They're there. I can see them.

Junction. Traffic lights. I'm three cars back. Eileen's two back from me. I can't see Ush yet.

The lights turn green and Traube turns left. I carry straight on. Eileen turns left. There'll be two or three cars between her and Traube. Zach's explaining on the radio. I'm using someone's drive to turn around. Shit. The lights have turned red on me. Are these lights ever going to change? I ease forward over the stop line. The lights have gone to the pedestrian phase. Nothing moving. I could jump these lights. No. I breathe. In for four. Our for six.

I see Ush. She's three back heading towards me. The two cars in front of her come past me and she slows, letting me make my right turn. Someone toots.

I accelerate hard and it's not long before I can see Eileen. She's easy to spot because of the bikes on the back.

"He's definitely not heading for the office."

"You're right, Rob. Stay frosty. We still have to figure out his intentions."

More junctions. More switching. The team are doing well – a minimum of radio transmissions.

"From Delta. We have a problem." That, from Wade, is not what I want to hear. He continues. *"His job mobile telephone is back at his house."*

Rob's looking at me. I can sense his alarm.

"It's okay, Rob. Tracking his mobile was only a backup."

Rob's not convinced.

"Rob. We've discussed this – at length. We need to be there when Traube meets Hendry. The mobile phone option was only ever a contingency." Interesting that Traube's not carrying his job mobile. No time to be thinking about that.

I've taken up the follow and I'm five cars back from Traube. He's now heading south on the A3, a motorway-like dual carriageway. Eileen's two cars back from me and Ush is in catchup after relinquishing the follow at the last junction.

On this road, Traube, in his Audi, could open up and sprint into the distance. The only one of us who could stay with him would be Ush in her BMW. Eileen's Yaris and my Fiesta wouldn't stand a chance.

No point thinking about that. Traube's keeping to a steady 70.

We're approaching the junction with the M25. He's moving to the left. He's indicating left. He's coming off. Rob relays this to the others.

Traube's heading up the slip road as I stay on the A3 and floor the accelerator. My little Fiesta's no good for this. I soon find out its top speed is only 95. It's a couple of miles to the next junction. Eileen and Ush will have to manage without me for quite a while.

Zach tells us he's heading clockwise on the M25 towards Heathrow. Ush has taken up the follow and Eileen is now a good distance back from her. They're saying Traube's dropped his speed to 60. Weird. A car like his, driving at the same speed as lorries, looks out of place. Why is he doing it?

Aircraft are rising up into the sky from our right.

Zach's back on the radio. *"From Kilo, looks like he's coming off at the junction with the M4. Yes. He is. Over to you, Delta."*

"Received by Delta. He's leaving the M25. Standby."

I'm still screaming along to catchup with them. Nearly there.

"From Delta, he's westbound on the M4."

"What do you think, Charlie?"

"I don't know. You're thinking too far ahead. We're still in verification. Let's just concentrate on staying with him but not showing out."

"It's okay, Charlie. I'm on it."

But he's not. He was so calm at the Amos confrontation. That, of course was Eileen's.

Traube's speed remains constant at 60mph. At the first junction we come to, Traube carries straight on and Ush slides off, negotiates the roundabout and re-joins. I've taken up the follow. We switch round like this for seven or eight junctions, about twenty miles, and then, "Units from Bravo, he's turning off into the Reading service station."

I follow him in. We'll all be able to take advantage of the loos.

Traube parks at one of the first available parking spaces. We have to drive right past him. We find a space closer to the building's entrance. I find my dark glasses and floppy hat, hop out and head in for the loos. Rob is telling the others exactly where Traube has stopped.

While I'm in the loo, I listen to the others chatting. Eileen and Ush have parked up. Traube has not left his car. As I return to my car, Ush heads in for the loos. Then Eileen. We all go, one at a time maintaining a readiness to follow Traube should he leave.

We're all back in our cars, waiting. Traube hasn't moved. Rob and I can see his car but the way the light's reflecting off his windows means we can't see him. Rob and I hear from the others that Traube has a newspaper out and appears to be reading. They can't see him – he's hidden behind the open newspaper.

I don't like this.

Thirty minutes later, he hasn't moved. He still has the paper open preventing any kind of observation of him.

"What's he doing?" Rob's getting jittery again.

"Anti-surveillance," I say.

The others are asking similar questions and Eileen's explaining. They're talking too much.

I get on the radio. "All units stop the chatter. Echo, Sierra, go and fill up with petrol."

I see them moving off.

Shortly after they've gone, Traube leaves his car and heads inside. Rob follows.

Ush and Eileen finish their fuelling-up.

These are westbound services. On leaving, Traube must travel west. "Echo, Sierra, head off, leave the motorway at the next junction, Junction 12, and wait."

They acknowledge.

Traube comes out and goes to Greggs. He soon emerges from there with a drink and a roll or something. He heads back to his car. Rob jumps in next to me, I start the engine but don't move.

Traube's Audi moves away. I wait till he's out of sight and follow. Rob's telling the others that he's on the move. The others confirm that they're ready to pick him up at the next junction, two miles down the motorway.

I drive round towards the petrol station. Traube's refuelling his car. I stop to fill up as well, pulling up next to a pump as he's finishing. He drives off, Rob lets the others know. I fill my tank – pay at pump.

As I'm re-joining the motorway, the others report that Traube's come off at Junction 12, gone all the way round the roundabout and is re-joining the motorway heading east – back towards London. Rob points him out as he passes us heading in the opposite direction. Ush is about a quarter mile behind him. Eileen is about a quarter mile behind her.

We turn round at Junction 12 and get after them.

* * *

CHARLIE

"From Delta, he's leaving the motorway again, heading into the Reading Services, eastbound, obviously."

This is not good.

"What's he doing?"

I haven't got time for Rob. Radio. "Kilo, don't go into the services. I repeat, don't go into the services. Go to the next junction and wait like you did at the last."

"Received."

Everyone will be jittery like Rob. I must deal with it. "From Lima, what he's doing is standard anti-surveillance. He may have spotted us. He may not have. All we can do is stay cool and stay with him."

"From Delta, he's parking up. Similar to what he did at the westbound services."

"Rob, tell them we're going onto the next junction like Eileen."

He presses his button but doesn't speak. He's lost it. I reach over and put my hand on his knee. "Release the button." He doesn't react. Shit. I can't drive and wrestle the radio from him. "Release the button." He still doesn't react – I have to use his name. "Rob, release the button."

He does, thank god. "Right, Rob, press the button, tell them we're going onto the next junction as well and release the button."

Rob shakes himself. He presses the button. "From Bravo. We're going onto the next junction like Kilo." He releases the button. He presses the button again. "That's Junction 11. I repeat, Junction 11."

Rob's back. I hide my sigh of relief. I know what it's like to freeze – I've been there.

"From Delta. As with the westbound services, he's parked up, newspaper out, can't see him."

He knows we're following him. He's spotted us but there's something weird going on. He's not trying to lose us. It's as if he's helping us. I don't know. I pull up behind Eileen.

The four of us get out and meet on the verge.

Eileen's shaking her head. "Something's very wrong."

"But what can we do about it?" Rob is still a loose cannon.

"Hey, Rob." Zach has spotted Rob's anxiety. "We know who he is. We know where he is. And, if we lose him, we know how to find him. We may not get him today, but we will get him."

Rob looks away. He can't speak.

I ignore him. I don't want to, but I have to.

I turn to Eileen. "What do you think's wrong?"

"He's making it easy for us."

"My thoughts too."

"Are we in danger?"

"I don't think so."

"If he's with the murder detectives, we're showing our hand."

She's right. I don't know what to say.

"Charlie, what's your feeling about this?"

"I say we push on." In truth, I don't know what to do.

* * *

CHARLIE

It's dark by the time Traube's taken us on a tour of southwest and northwest London and stopped outside a semidetached house in Neasden. He's not moving. He's just sitting in his car.

I've found a spot to park at the end of the road he's stopped on. Rob and I can see his car. We're watching him from his rear offside. He hasn't parked by the kerb. He's parked across the end of the short drive. We can't see him but we will be able to see if he gets out of his car. There's a car parked on the drive and he's blocked it in. After twenty minutes and no movement, I decide this is where his game, whatever it is, will play out.

"Delta from Lima."

"Go ahead."

"Link up with Kilo and cover the back on foot. You may have to do a bit of scrabbling around in back gardens. Remember to tape up. Be careful. We don't want local ol' bill being called out to a suspects-on-premises."

"Received."

"Sierra, Echo, stay in your cars."

"Received."

"Received."

Rob and I sit still, listening to the chatter between Wade and Zach as they search for a way through to the back of the house Traube's parked outside.

There's movement.

Traube's out of his car. He doesn't lock it. Interesting. He walks up to the front door of the house and knocks.

"Delta from Lima. He's just knocked on the door of the house he's parked outside."

"Received."

The door opens.

I can't see the person who opens the door but Traube barges inside.

I turn to Rob, "Did you see who opened the door?"

"Yes. Hendry."

I raise my hand. Rob gives me a high five and opens his door.

"Wait, Rob. This could be a trap. I need to think. I need to know what the others think."

Rob pulls his door shut.

"From Lima. When target got out of his car, he didn't lock it – at least, I don't think he did. He approached the front door. Knocked. Our warden answered. Target barged his way in. Door now shut. Before Rob and I go in, give me your thoughts."

"From Sierra. There's two of them and two of you. Not good."

"From Echo. Target barged his way in. They're not together. There may even be more."

"Received. Thanks. Delta, Kilo, you round back?"

"From Delta. Yes. No movement."

"From Kilo. This could be a trap."

"From Sierra. I'm with Kilo. You could meet anything on the other side of that door."

"From Echo. We don't have enough intel."

"From Kilo. The risk is too great."

"All Units, standby."

"I think we should go."

"Rob. We've got time. Just wait."

I've not really heard anything from Wade. He'll be thinking this through. God, I need him to talk to me.

Charlie. This is no time to hesitate.

Instead of Wade, I've got Lottie talking to me.

Why do you say that?

How else will we find out what Traube's game is?

We wait. We know Traube's a thumbs-down. We've located Hendry. We can deal with them in our own time on our own terms.

Top priority is the recovery of those videos.

Lottie's now telling me what I've been telling her – time and time again.

I know, but going now, we really don't know what we're going into.

Unlike you to have a touch of the seconds but this is very much your show.

Lottie. It's not my show. Now is the time for you to do your bit and fill the gang with confidence. Christ. Fill me with confidence.

I really am not sure about...

Lottie's now wavering.

Lottie. Take the *spot*. Remember, it's those videos that are key.

Let us wait to hear what Wade thinks.

No. Now.

Alright.

I move aside.

From the *stage*, I watch as Lottie presses to talk, says nothing and releases the button. I can feel her composing herself. She's taking a moment. She's closed her eyes. Jeez. I could really do with being able to see at the moment. It's okay. It's okay. Rob will shout soon enough if anything changes.

Lottie opens her eyes and presses to talk.

"Hi everyone. I think you know who this is. The priority is those videos. We have worked so hard to get to this point. This is an opportunity. I believe the target, for whatever reason, has presented us with this opportunity. I think we must take it. There is risk, but there has been risk all along. We have never been afraid of the risk. We have wrapped it up, dealt with it and come out the other side. We can deal with this risk."

Lottie's transmission is met with silence.

I wait.

Nothing.

Then Lottie in my head.

What do you think?

I don't know.

If only Wade would talk to me.

Then he does. *"From Delta. I'm with Tango. Target's behaviour today has been an invitation. He's been driving slowly making it easy for us to stay with him. He's led us to the warden. He's also left his car unlocked. Definitely an invitation. We go. Question is, how."*

I'm with Wade but must wait... wait for the others. In for four, out for six... and they come back.

"From Echo. Accept that priority is the videos. It's a go."

"From Kilo. Agree. It's a go."

"From Sierra. I agree it's a go but I'm not happy with just Lima and Bravo going through that front door."

"From Echo, I assume you will go up to the door and knock like the target did. What will you do if there's no answer?"

"From Lima. All understood. Delta. How secure is the back door?"

"Not secure. One kick and we're in."

"From Lima. It's a go go go."

Rob and I put on our beanies, tight shoes and help each other tape up. We're out of the car and marching towards the front door of the semidetached house in Neasden.

CHAPTER TWENTY-NINE

CHARLIE

Frederick Traube answers the door. He doesn't seem surprised. "Come in, leave the door on the latch and tell your friends to join us."

I follow Traube down a short hallway and left into a living room. Rob's right behind me.

On the radio, I say to the gang, "Situation controlled. Sierra, Echo, join us. Gloves, shoes, beanies and tape."

Traube nods. "You're well organised. You have a plan. You're even well dressed. Nitrile gloves, tape... Impressed."

"Thank you." I can't think of anything else to say.

He can. "What's my fate?"

"Death."

Traube sighs. "Saves me having to do it."

I point at one of the armchairs. "Bravo, check that armchair. Make sure there's nothing concealed in it."

Rob lifts the cushions. Nothing there. He tips the whole chair back. Nothing underneath. He sets the armchair back upright.

"Sit," I say to Traube. He complies. "Where's Hendry?"

"Dining room. Look. Don't go in. This house will become a murder scene. Minimise forensics. You seem prepared for that."

Ush and Eileen come in – eyes wide.

My focus is on Traube. "Bravo. Check the dining room. Don't go in. Echo, Sierra, check the rest of the house. Make sure there's no one else here."

I don't understand how Traube can be so calm. He's in control and I must take that control from him. I hold my stance. If he moves, he'll receive a barrage of kicks and punches.

Rob returns from the dining room. "Report," I say.

Rob doesn't speak.

Keeping my eyes on Traube, I say again, "Bravo. Report."

Something's wrong. When Rob finally speaks, his voice is weak. "Travis Hendry's in there. Couldn't see him properly. Unconscious, possibly dead. Head injury. Kitchen's a mess. Looks like there's been a fight."

"I inflicted that injury." Traube sounds casual.

Ush and Eileen return. Eileen says, "No one else in the house. We've checked every room. Under beds. In wardrobes. Couldn't check the loft but it doesn't look as though it's hatch has been opened – ever."

It's the best we can do.

Back to Traube. "Hendry's videos?"

He points. "In that first aid box."

I saw the white plastic box on the coffee table as I came in. A foot square, nine inches deep, green cross on the lid. I don't take my eyes off Traube. "Check it out."

While Rob, Ush and Eileen are rummaging and sorting, Traube speaks. "You can dispense with the callsigns. Your name's Charlie Quinlan. He's Rob Granger. She's Ursula Keating. She's Eileen Edison. Outside is Zach Novac and Wade Oliver."

Rob speaks. "How does he know our names?"

"Because he's good at his job. What's in that first aid box."

After more sorting. It's Eileen who speaks. "Over five-hundred memory sticks and SD cards. Mostly SD cards."

"Labelled?"

"No."

"Sorted? Categorised?"

"No. Just piled in."

"Put them back in the box."

I haven't turned away from Traube but I focus back on him. "Explain how you know our names."

Traube waves his hand, giving a wry smile. "You said I'm good at my job. I consider that a compliment, thank you. John French and Steve Reeve are good but they don't know the link between Daventry, Pope and Amos and how they are linked to you and your colleagues. I do. You've covered your tracks well. The only people who can solve those murders are people with a lot to lose if those murders are solved. People like me. The arrival of that video was a game-changer. I'd like to know how you identified me."

"I'm sure you would. How did you know we were following you?"

"So, you won't tell me. Suggests you haven't decided on my fate." He waves a hand. "There's loads of cyclists in London but there was a sudden increase earlier this week. Then I saw you standing at the bus stop opposite Wimbledon Nick. Your disguises were good but not good enough. You don't realise how well known you are from that tanker incident. Then, today, every time I stop, there are cars nearby with bikes on the back, neatly obscuring the rear number plate. I recommend you don't choose surveillance as a career path. You're crap at it."

The person we're about to kill has just called me an idiot.

Traube continues. "Your inexperience did, however, complicate my countersurveillance. I had to drive so bloody slowly."

"Countersurveillance?"

"Keeping you with me."

A double idiot.

"Get some plates made up, correct letters and numbers but invert two of them. That will circumvent ANPR and it's easy to explain if you're stopped by police. And change your car every couple of years. Not fool-proof but even John French would have to be going some to penetrate all that."

My mind flicks back to DI Brian Gault and his description of the team of about twenty that would have been on that undercover officer. I didn't notice a thing.

There's noise from the dining room.

"That'll be Hendry. After what I said before clouting him with a cast-iron saucepan, he'll be surprised he's woken up. Remember what I said about forensics." Traube's enjoying himself and I'm missing something. I feel like he's calling the shots. Maybe I should tell him how we identified him. Seems pointless but I need to take the control from him.

Rob clips down the top of the first aid box and heads for the dining room. I speak into the radio. "Kilo, Delta, come in. Front door's on the latch. Beanies on and taped up."

Hendry's looking groggy as Rob assists him into the living room and into an armchair like the one Traube's in.

We're joined by Wade and Zach.

I feel better now we have them properly outnumbered, but Traube's way too relaxed – he still seems to have the upper hand. Rob is checking out Hendry but everybody's waiting – waiting for me.

"Wade, search them both."

Traube stands and places his hands on his head. Wade pats him down and empties his pockets. Out come keys. A plain envelope. An SD card. Tissues. Wallet. Three mobile phones. Seven SIMs. Loose change. Wade lays them down by the first aid box. I motion Traube to sit. He does.

Hendry doesn't move. Rob has one arm, Zach takes the other and they stand him up. Wade searches him. Nothing found. Makes sense – he's at home.

"Rob, what's Hendry's condition?"

"Stable, no concussion, coordinated and coherent." Rob knows his stuff but he's still rattled.

I keep my eyes on Traube. "Travis. Do you know who we are?"

"Freddy told me." His voice is slurred but, like Rob said, he's alert.

"Wade. Watch Traube." Wade takes my place and I move over and stand in front of Hendry who's looking around, his eyes darting. He hasn't changed much. Skinnier with a bit of grey showing above his ears. His eyes are droopy but that's probably due to his head injury. "Talk to me about what's in the first aid box."

"Find out yourself."

Left foot. Round kick. BANG.

He screams and grabs his right upper arm.

"First aid box – what's in it?"

"You're a fucking nutter."

Left foot. Heel kick. BANG.

He screams again.

I think I might have broken his left arm. "Don't scream."

Now nursing his left arm, he says, "What d'you want from me?" His voice is almost a sob and he's pulled his knees up to his chest.

"I want you to tell me what's in that first aid box."

"Video clips."

"Of what?"

"You, mainly."

"Who else?"

He looks past me at the others. "Them, but not so many."

"Who else?"

"Perverts."

"What are they doing?"

"You know what they're doing."

His belligerence is returning. Standing on my left leg, I lift my right and tap his cheek with my toe. "I asked you a question."

"Fucking your mouth. Fucking your arse. Fucking your..."

Right foot. Side kick. BANG.

His jaw is left hanging. His scream comes out as a pathetic squawk.

"Travis," I say, "that was for the times you held a lighted cigarette over my skin."

Right foot. Side kick. BANG.

His left leg now has two knees.

"Travis," I say, "that was for the times you ironed my clothes when I was wearing them."

Left foot. Front kick. BANG.

I felt the ribs on the lower right side of his chest splinter and crack.

"Rob," I say, "What's the proper name for a punctured lung?"

"Pneumothorax and you mean a collapsed lung."

"Will it kill him?"

"Could do."

"Travis," I say, "that was for the times you switched me from a boiling hot bath to a freezing cold bath and back – several times."

Right foot. Round kick. BANG.

Teeth fly from his mouth.

"Travis," I say, "that was for the times you slotted silver foil between my teeth."

Right foot. Front kick. BANG.

There wasn't much noise coming from him before that kick. Now, with a crushed larynx, there's no noise coming from him at all.

"Travis," I say, "that was for facilitating a paedophile ring's access to the children's home."

"You." I point at Traube. "How much did you pay him?"

"Don't know. He was remunerated by the ring." Traube's serenity is still confusing me.

"You've mentioned their names but I need you to confirm. Daventry? Was he a member of the ring?"

"Yes."

"Pope?"

"Yes."

"Amos?"

"Yes." He pauses, then says, "I have a request. Like a... last request."

"Go on."

"Make it look like Hendry killed me and he died later of the injuries I inflicted on him. Make sure he dies before anyone speaks to him. I've spoken with him about those videos before you came in. Take those videos and watch them so you know who you're looking for. Then destroy them as they will incriminate you. There are some in which the abuser can be identified and the child cannot. Keep one for each abuser. You'll have fourteen. Then visit each of them. You do not need to change the MOs. Making Daventry and Pope's demise virtually the same was foolish but only while those videos were out there as it's those videos, together with Travis Hendry, that join the dots for the likes of John French. Once you've silenced Travis Hendry and destroyed the videos in which you can be identified, there will be no link between you and the murders you're committing. But leave a message. A message for the world. 'This is the fate of paedophiles'."

"Why are you…" My voice cracks. I can't finish what I'm saying. Lottie's pushing. I move aside.

"Why are you telling us this?"

Traube's eyes open wide. "Dissociative Identity Disorder."

"Yes. Charlie's way of coping with the likes of you. Now, answer the question, why are you telling us this?" Lottie's sounding very forceful. Not the convincingness she can put on – this is anger.

"A vain attempt to do the right thing. I realise I'm taking the coward's way out. I suppose that's what I am. A coward."

"In that video we sent you, you were abusing Rob. This is Rob."

Lottie steps back and Rob steps forward.

"Wait." Wade puts a hand on Rob's shoulder. "This needs to be managed." He turns to Traube. "That SD card I took out of your pocket. Was it the one we sent you?"

Traube smirks. "Yes."

Oh my god. The way he said that. Something's changed. What? What's happened?

"Zach, is that the card?" I wish Wade wouldn't turn away from Traube.

Lottie too!

He hasn't moved. It's okay.

Lottie is watching Zach as he leans over and takes a picture of it with his mobile. He examines the picture, zooming in. He looks up. "Yes. That's it."

I can't leave Lottie on the spot. This position's too precarious.

Watch Traube! Watch Traube!

Lottie turns back to him.

Traube hasn't moved, thank god. Something's so terribly wrong. It's like he's changed but he hasn't.

Wade turns back to Traube. "Convince me that you haven't made a copy."

"I couldn't have made a copy because it hasn't been copied."

Wade crouches down, looking at Traube, their eyes at the same level. "Convince me you've watched the video."

"Rob's pleasuring me because I'm pleasuring him."

Rob is simmering, both Eileen and Ush put their arms round Rob, Wade's put himself in a vulnerable position, Lottie's looking at everything other than Traube and I'm doing my nut. Everything's wrong. Traube's emotions are wrong. Traube's behaviour is wrong. What Traube's saying doesn't make any sense and is inconsistent. I'm screaming at Lottie but she's not picking up.

Wade's carrying on. "What you're filmed doing is wrong."

"It's sex. Not wrong. Rob was enjoying it because sex is enjoyable."

This is sick.

I can see by Wade's demeanour, he's thinking hard. "Circular arguments." And with those two words, I relax.

I don't know what they mean or what they even refer to but it's clear that Wade does. "The premise supports the conclusion. The conclusion supports the premise. You talk in logical fallacies."

Wade's in control. He's achieved what I couldn't. He has control of Traube. I don't know how but he has control. He continues. "Frederick Traube would not be able to attain the rank and position of DCI in the MPS, let alone hold onto it, if his thought processes operated that way. Who are you?"

"You're good."

There's that change again! Is it DID, like us?

"Identities?" Wade's on the same wavelength but how he's still thinking through all this beats me.

"No. Moods. I've just given you a taste of *manic me*."

"Bipolar?"

"Yes."

"Mood stabilisers?"

"Don't work."

"You mean they don't work for you."

Traube hesitates.

Wade shakes his head, slowly. I recognise it. Wade's got it all figured out. I haven't a clue but Wade's sussed it. "You're addicted to your mania."

"You don't know what it's like to have rocket fuel for blood."

"Downside?"

"Depression is hard."

Wade goes to ask another question but stops, mouth open. He's figured out the problem but he doesn't know where to take it. Lottie's as stumped as Wade. I push. He needs help. I think I've seen a way in. I push harder and Lottie relinquishes the *spot*.

I crouch down next to Wade, my eyes level with Traube's. "Earlier, before the others came in, you asked your fate and I said death and you said it would save you having to do it. Sounds like a kind of escape."

Wade looks at me. I wish he'd keep his eyes on Traube.

Traube nods. "*Escape* is a good word. However, *release* seems more appropriate."

"You seem to want death. Have you considered suicide?"

"Many times."

"Why haven't you done it?"

"Not brave enough."

I don't know what to make of what he's saying. It's as if he's trying his hardest to help us kill him. I check around, breaking my own discipline of focussing on Traube. Rob seems to have calmed down though Ush and Eileen still have their arms around him. Hendry's breathing is laboured. Not sure whether he's conscious. His lips are blue.

Wade moves back.

I stand and resume my stance in front of Traube. "You're being very helpful. Why?"

"I want to know how you identified me."

"What difference does it make. You're going to die anyway."

He pushes his legs out straight, purses his lips and blows out.

Actually. There's a lot we can learn from him. Keep him sweet. This is beyond weird. "We found a picture of you on social media. You'd been tagged. Had you not seen the tag?"

He gives a faint little smile, a little shake of the head and looks down. "An omission? Deliberate? No, but hard to say. I want it to end."

"What? What do you want to end?"

"This life."

"What life? Your life?"

"It doesn't feel like my life. As manic me, I feel invincible. I feel justified. It's absolutely right. Afterwards comes the shame." He shakes his head. "Shame's not an adequate word. Loathing. Disgust. Horror. None of those words quite capture how I feel. Pity. I pity myself. I want it to end. I want to be released."

I can feel Lottie's emotions soaring. Again, I allow myself to look away from Traube. Ush sits, no, falls back onto the settee, curls up and buries her face. Eileen drops to her knees, her anguish evident, no effort to try and hide it. Zach leaves the room saying, "I'm sorry. I'm sorry. I'm sorry." Rob, unlike the others, gets angry but Eileen and Ush are no longer holding him. I can see it welling up inside him. I can't see his face because of his beanie but it's clear he won't be able to hold on. He doesn't. "This is bullshit," he yells. "Bullshit. I'm not letting you blame your bloody perversions on some… on some…"

Lottie's pushing. I move aside. Lottie takes the *spot*.

"Rob. Rob. Come here. Come here." Lottie pulls Rob in, enveloping him. "Let him speak. Let him say what he has to say. He knows he will die tonight. We may not like what he says but we can at least listen. Let him speak."

Rob relaxes.

Lottie turns back to Traube. "There are some serious emotions here. Bear that in mind. Show us that consideration and we will reciprocate in how cleanly you die."

"I understand."

I'm still suspicious. He's way too calm and I feel like he's maintaining the upper hand. Considering what's happening here, how can he do that?

"How well do you know the other members of the paedophile ring?" This is a side of Lottie I haven't met before.

"Fairly well. We're not close but I've had dealings with them."

"If they were to talk as openly and calmly as you, would they say the same thing?"

"Doubt it." He sits forward. I want to move but Lottie has the *spot*. Traube continues. "In fact, no. I don't believe they would. There's what they'd say if they think they could get away from you. There's what they'd say if they think you might waver. You'll be dealing with dishonest people. You'll be dealing with sick people. You'll be dealing with people whose worldview is so different… distorted. You've killed three. What did you make of them?"

Wade steps in. "Don't answer that." Wade looks down at Traube. "Did you abuse all of them?"

"Yes. All five."

"I feel like I should be grilling you for all the information you've got on the other members of your paedophile ring but I'm not sure I've got the stomach for it."

"I understand."

"Not much of a detective, am I?"

"With experience, you'll be fine."

"You're a detective with plenty of experience. You have got the stomach for this. You know what we need to know. Don't make us ask the questions. Give us the information we need."

Traube nods. "That envelope you found when you searched me. Open it."

Wade does so, removes a sheet of paper and scans it. "A list of fourteen names and addresses."

"Yes." Traube looks towards the first aid box on the table. "Images of them as well."

Wade looks up from the sheet of paper. "Thank you."

"I hope you feel that's worth some reciprocity."

"Not my call."

Lottie's at a loss for something to say. I resume the *spot*. "When did you learn about these video clips?"

"On receiving your package."

"Explain how you pieced it all together."

"I heard about the deaths of Daventry and Pope. I was considering approaching French and Reeve. But there was something I was missing – the answer to the question of how they'd been identified. Without that knowledge, I couldn't move. I started a dialogue with the other members of the paedophile ring. We decided Travis Hendry would be a good port of call. We started the necessary enquiries to find him. Then Amos died. We intensified our efforts. There are some influential people in this ring – as you will discover. We found out Hendry's location at about the same time as you guys appeared in my neighbourhood – with your bikes and high viz. Like I said, the arrival of your package was the game changer."

"How many of the other fourteen know about these videos?"

"None. I've told no one but they're jittery, understandably, because they don't know what direction you'll be coming from. I'm bequeathing you that advantage. Please, make good use of it."

Hendry's breathing is very shallow, a rasping noise grinding from his throat. Rob moves over to him and does some checks. "He doesn't have long."

Traube's no longer a concern but the gang is. Ush is crumpled on the settee. Eileen's a sobbing wreck on the floor. Zach has buggered off. They need something, something to do. "Zach, get back in here."

Zach reappears. He's distraught but holding it together.

"Right. Wade, Rob and I are staying. Zach, Eileen and Ush, get going. You have our credit and debit cards. We need alibis, good ones. We'll hold on for as long as we can but that depends on Travis. Rob says he doesn't have long."

As Zach, Eileen and Ush leave, Wade takes over. He's had that bit of time he needs to get his head around the problem. He addresses Traube. "You spoke earlier of a message for the world. How do we show that the victims are linked with paedophilia?"

"I said earlier to keep the videos of the abusers where the five of you are unidentifiable. Once you've killed one, insert the relevant video in his mouth – it will be found in the *post-mortem*." He looks around at each of us. "As for the manner of death... This is where my request for reciprocity comes in. I ask that you make my death clean. If you decide not to, I will understand and respect your decision." He stops again. "Right," he says, "As for the manner of death – have you ever read about the demise of Edward II? Be careful though. His screams were heard for miles around."

CHAPTER THIRTY

CHARLIE

"Charlie, you need to see this."

Oh god. Is a little peace and quiet too much to ask? I leave my punch bag swinging and find Wade watching the telly in the living room – unusual for him. I soon cotton on to what's attracted his attention.

A news channel.

On screen is a semi-detached house. I don't so much recognise the house but the car parked outside is Traube's Audi. Blocked in on the drive is another car – Hendry's. People in whites are milling around the cars – forensics.

I sit next to Wade and take his hand. He seems relaxed. I'm far from relaxed.

There's the voice of a female news anchor talking over the pictures.

"...bodies of two men. Our crime reporter, Burke Devlin, is at the scene. What can you tell us, Burke?'

The picture shifts to a figure in a black leather jacket holding a microphone.

"Morning Cat. Police are being tight-lipped about their investigation so far. What we know is that police were called to the scene earlier today by neighbours concerned about this car behind me." The camera focusses on Traube's Audi. "This vehicle, abandoned and unlocked, has been here for several days. Police officers examined the car and then entered this semi-detached house," the camera moves to the house as the reporter continues, "and the house was soon taped off. Police have been examining the scene for several hours and, just recently, two bodies were removed on stretchers with sheets covering their faces."

At this point I see DS John French emerging from the front door of the house.

The reporter hustles towards him, leading with his microphone.

"Detective, can you confirm that you're treating this as a murder scene?"

French is irritated but quickly regains his composure. "Yes, but there is very little I can say at this time. Forensic officers are examining the property and we are conducting door to door inquiries."

French tries to continue walking, but the reporter skilfully blocks his way while throwing questions.

"Are you linking the deaths of these two men with other so far unsolved murders? I'm thinking specifically of the tragic death of Vincent Pope earlier this year. His car was abandoned in a similar way to the cars here."

"Anything I say at this stage would be conjecture."

"Can you confirm one of the victims is a fellow Met Police officer?"

French breathes in deeply before responding. "I'm afraid I'm going to have to ask you to direct any further questions through the press office."

He pushes past the reporter and joins a group of his colleagues.

The interview is over and the picture switches back to the news anchor.

"Thank you, Burke. Our crime reporter, Burke Devlin, at the scene of a double murder in north-west London. We'll bring you more on that story as soon as we have it. In other news…"

Wade turns the telly off. "Charlie? You okay?"

I'm holding his hand so tightly, I've concerned him.

Even Lottie has emerged onto the *stage*.

Is something wrong, Charlie?

I shake my head.

I heard the last few exchanges. Their body language suggests confusion.

I shake my head, more deliberately.

Wade is talking, unaware that Lottie's there. "I think we've presented them with an unfathomable conundrum."

I shake my head, again. Why does Wade use such bloody silly words.

Charlie, whatever is wrong?

"Charlie. You're clearly not happy. What's attracted your attention?"

I run my fingers through my hair. It's blindingly obvious but I suppose Wade and Lottie need it pointing out. I take a deep breath. "What I would have expected John French to say was that they're always looking for similarities between crime scenes. But he didn't."

"So what?"

So what?

"Means they've already found them."

THE END